ROCK OF AGES

ADVANCE UNCORRECTED GALLEY

238 pp   ISBN: 1-57962-128-7

Pub. Date: May 2006 $26 hardcover

Also by Howard Owen

ROCK OF AGES

Howard Owen

ADVANCE UNCORRECTED GALLEY

000 pp   ISBN: 1-57962-128-7

Pub. Date: May 2006 $26 hardcover

THE PERMANENT PRESS
Sag Harbor, New York 11968

Copyright © 2006 by Howard Owen.

ISBN 1-57962-128-7

Library of Congress Cataloging-in-Publication Data.

Printed in The United States of America.

To Karen, my lover, editor and best friend.

December 18

My parents delivered me from evil.

They made sure I hung out with the "right" crowd, gave me an overload of adult supervision, knew every teacher I ever had.

Our idea of evil was skipping one day of school our senior year or showing some boy the good parts of *Candy*. We teased evil with a very long stick.

My friends and I professed to like the Rolling Stones and the Doors. Anything with a whiff of sulfur. We didn't really want to be bad. We just wanted to slip the surly bonds of out hometown, soar briefly above the somnolence before drifting back into the Jovian gravity of East Geddie.

Evil was exciting, an exotic land that you always threatened to visit but never did. It was the college boy you flirted with at the dance when you were 14. Maybe you let him cop a feel, but you never went out to the car with him.

There's no easy way to say it: I am being raped as these thoughts ramble unbidden through my brain. If it's my life I'm watching here, looking down on my pitiful, battered, middle-aged body bent over a picnic table in this ghost world devoid of mercy, I guess that's not a good thing.

The rape itself isn't as horrible as you might expect, at least physically. I'm just kind of numb. If only I could breathe. I'm pinned down and can't seem to get enough air.

What I'm dreading is what comes next. This is obviously a prelude to the main event. The pain in my head is almost enough to knock me out, but not quite. Things are definitely broken.

You think about dying, but you're always sure it'll be next year, next decade, some other time than right now. You'll find a way to make it not hurt. And part of you thinks you'll live forever, anyhow.

But I'm afraid this is Right Now.

The thing I mind most is being the public victim, evil's plaything, somehow painted with the same brush as the monster on top of me. *East Geddie woman/ raped, murdered. Recently moved/back to Scots County.* (Everyone's thought balloon: *What was she doing out there, anyhow?*)

What would you do, my out-of-body mind sings to me, mocking the old country song as I fade to black. *What would you do, if evil came to spend some time with you?*

CHAPTER ONE

October 17

When the phone rang, she had been in the process of wrapping up and refrigerating the three-quarters of her famous vegetarian lasagna that the homecoming crowd chose not to eat.

Was she kin to "a Jenny McLaurin, white female, age about 80"? Georgia said yes, Jenny was her cousin.

"Well," said the deputy, "she's drowned."

Georgia thought to ask the location. She went back to the stairs and called up to where Justin and Leeza were doing God knows what, surely not *that*, with her this far along.

"Justin," she said. "We've got a . . . a little emergency. You remember Cousin Jenny, don't you?" (Why the hell would he?)

A noncommittal answer was followed in half a minute by a head of uncombed hair leaning over the railing.

"What's wrong?"

As if he hoped it would be something that could be fixed without his active participation.

"What's wrong, Mom?"

Georgia could think of no other way to say it.

"She's drowned."

It took Justin five minutes to get reasonably close to fully dressed—flannel shirt and Levi's, shoes but no socks. Leeza insisted on coming, too. Justin helped her down the steep, dark stairs a step at a time, the girl's swelling belly bulging under the light blue smock, the rest of her so thin still that Georgia knew she would lose every damn ounce once the baby was born.

9

Justin insisted on driving. Leeza, after only minimal insistence on Georgia's part, rode up front. In the back seat, Georgia looked out at Kenny's harvested fields, corn and tobacco stalks waiting for the burning and plowing under, fodder for another season. She rolled the back window down, then back up again as the stench from the hogs reached her.

The lane was smooth clay and dirt now, no more ruts to loosen your fillings. At the end, where it met the paved road into East Geddie, was a little green street sign in the middle of working farms and fallow fields full of mobile homes. The state had decreed that everything bigger than a driveway had to have a name, so the rescue squad could find you in case you had a stroke or your house was on fire.

Georgia wondered if Cousin Jenny's house had a street sign in front of it.

Kenny or the Geddies could have named the dirt road anything they wanted, but the green sign, not much different from one you might see in Washington or New York, read "Littlejohn McCain Road" in letters shrunk enough to squeeze them all into one line.

"That's the only proper name for it," Kenny had told her when she thanked him for the cost-free but generous gesture. "Annabelle and Blue and I were in total agreement on that, at least."

He told her about two families half a mile farther from town who had shared the same small sand road peacefully for three generations and then fell out so badly over which of their names to put on their new sign that they wound up going to court. Rather than abide by the judge's Solomonic decision to call it BunceJacobs Road, they named it Copperhead Lane.

Now, though, the street sign seemed like just one more rebuke to Georgia as they turned right, a piece of green metal silently asking *Where were you? Aren't you ashamed of yourself?*

At the flashing red light in East Geddie, they turned right again, on Old Geddie Road, with Georgia giving what she did not think were too many directions and Justin saying "I know, I know" to each of them.

The old store where she once walked to buy grape Nehis and meet the bookmobile now sold farm supplies. The fields across the way, surrounded by the circular road that served a majority of the town's residents, had sprouted houses of their own, mostly modular and temporary-looking, connected to the half-moon lane by more dirt lanes with more green street signs.

Half a mile farther, they passed under the interstate that now linked Raleigh and beyond with Newport and the Atlantic beaches. The highway still seemed strange to Georgia, even though it was five years old. Not far from the road they were on, it cut through a lush edge of the farm. Now, ocean-bound traffic rushed above some of the best land, where the strawberries had grown and no tobacco was ever planted. It was Blue's land now.

Everyone had known that they would build the interstate eventually, but Georgia doubted her father gave it much thought when he rewrote his will. Still, she agreed that it was a shame. A good 10 acres were taken by the right-of-way, and another 10 or so were ruined, cut off from any road, flooded when the big highway changed the drainage patterns.

Old Geddie Road was now paved all the way to Route 47, and when they reached the state highway, they turned left and soon came to Jenny McLaurin's home, upon which half the county seemed to have descended.

There were at least 20 cars parked in the yard and along the path that ran past the house and the pond behind it. Three sheriff's cars were there, along with an ambulance and a fire truck, although Jenny's body already had been taken away.

They walked through a curious and sympathetic crowd that parted for them, and soon they were standing on a little raised bank, staring down into a murky expanse of water measuring perhaps 50 yards by 30 yards.

"It just goes straight down," the sheriff said, his words only slightly garbled by a golf ball of tobacco in his cheek. "I don't reckon she could swim. She was drug out right over there."

Georgia remembered the pond. As a child, when they would visit here, her mother and especially her father would warn her about playing around it. Even if you *can* swim, they told her, there's no way to climb out.

11

It was true, then and now. She had enjoyed tempting fate by slipping away back then and standing atop the bank, getting a thrill when either her parents or Harold or Jenny would come running as if she were really getting ready to do a swan dive into the nasty water, home to bream, spot and bullfrogs, plus the occasional moccasin from the swamp that stretched behind it.

No one said anything for a few minutes. Justin stood beside her with his hands in his pockets. He had not seen Jenny, Georgia knew, in 10 years at least, since the summer he turned 16. Leeza, who had never been in Scots County in her life until two months before and probably had never even heard Jenny's name mentioned until this bright fall afternoon, was crying softly. Georgia stifled the urge to tell her to shut up.

Justin reached over and squeezed his mother's shoulder.

"So," he said, "she was your cousin, right?"

"And yours. Second, or first once removed. I can't ever remember how that goes. They didn't have any children, and she didn't have much family. . ." Any family, Georgia thought, that ever gave a tinker's damn about her. *But I did. I did. I just didn't know.* She knew she was going to start crying, her tears falling into Harold McLaurin's worthless snake pond, if she didn't take some kind of head-clearing action.

She turned away at last from the water to face a crowd that had grown still larger, hanging back as if torn between manners and curiosity. She recognized two members of the church among them, younger men whom she didn't really know, babies when she had left for college. She walked past their mumbled "anything I can do's" in a daze, looking for the sheriff, who had drifted off at some point. Still in her Sunday clothes, she almost tripped over the tangled thickness of the centipede grass in her high heels. Supporting arms caught hers, and she supposed everyone thought she was overcome with shock and grief.

She caught up with Wade Hairr standing by his brown-and-gold patrol car adorned with a cartoon star on each side.

"Sheriff," she said, tapping him on the shoulder. She felt foolish calling him that, Wade Hairr who finished Geddie High School two years behind her, a short, thin, acne-scarred boy with an irritating laugh who played no sports, made average grades and drove a school bus. The ones who stayed were sometimes rewarded for their diligence, moved to the head of the class past the beauty queens and football stars, past the college-bound, all the deserters who left and never came back. And when they did come back, if only temporarily, Georgia supposed that it was only fair that they should know it was not their world anymore, that it belonged to the faithful, to the Wade Hairrs.

He turned from the young deputy whom he had just told to "get these people out of here. This idn't a picnic."

"Sheriff," Georgia started again, and he told her to call him Wade. "Who identified her? I mean, didn't somebody have to do that?"

"Oh, Miss Forsythia Crumpler did that. You know she lives right next door."

"Right. I'd forgotten."

She had been Georgia's seventh-grade teacher. Older brothers and sisters would tell their siblings about her corporal punishment administered with a Fly-Back paddle, her zero tolerance for chewing gum, lost homework and ignorance.

Georgia, a teacher's kid, a straight-A student who wanted a challenge and a chance to shine, had adored her. Forsythia Crumpler made her feel she was special. One day, she asked Georgia to stay for a minute as the rest of the class went to lunch, and she gave her a copy of *Rebecca*, the first real novel Georgia McCain would read. Others followed, and the teacher would always ask Georgia what she thought of certain characters and scenes, usually just nodding but sometimes pointing out nuances lost to the seventh-grade mind.

In some ways, she had steered Georgia more than her own mother did. Sara McCain would teach Georgia in both the ninth and 12th grades at Geddie High, but she and her daughter were too much alike for knowledge to change hands easily. "The quickest way to make Georgia go east," Sara told Littlejohn once, "is for me to tell her to go west."

Forsythia Crumpler was a lifelong member of Geddie Presbyterian Church, and Georgia would see her on a more or less regular basis until she finished college and moved away permanently. For years, she and her old teacher would exchange gifts long-distance at Christmas—always a paperback version of some book one was sure the other would particularly like. Georgia did not remember when or why they stopped.

In the 11 years since her father's death, Georgia had only been to East Geddie five times, visiting Jenny each time but only crossing over the tall hedge that bordered the McLaurins' yard on two occasions to say hello to her favorite teacher. The last time had been three years ago.

Georgia looked around but did not see her old teacher anywhere in the thinning crowd.

"I think she went back home," Wade Hairr said. "She identified the, ah, deceased, and then she left."

Georgia started to walk across the yard, in search of Forsythia Crumpler, then stopped.

"Why was she out there by the pond in the first place? I know she couldn't swim at all."

The sheriff looked away, as if pondering life's mysteries.

"Well, you know how old people are," he said. "You can't tell what they're liable to do. Maybe she was just going out to feed the fish or something."

"But she definitely drowned, right?"

"Right."

Georgia found a gap in the photinia hedge between Jenny's wooden two-storey house and Forsythia Crumpler's brick rancher. She walked along the edge of the thick grass until she found the flagstone walk, Justin and Leeza following in her steps.

She rang the bell, noticing as she did that everything that could be painted apparently had been in the last few months.

A few seconds later, the door opened a couple of feet.

"Mrs. Crumpler? It's me. Georgia. Georgia McCain. I just wanted to thank you . . ."

Forsythia Crumpler was no more than 5 feet tall, and Georgia supposed she must be 80 years old herself, but she still had a presence. Maybe it was the ice-blue eyes that still burned brightly, or

14

the way she carried herself, chin still jutting forward. Even bifocals didn't do much to soften her.

"I know who you are," she said to Georgia and the pair standing behind her on the lowest step.

"I just wanted to thank you . . ."

"Let me ask you something." Forsythia Crumpler stepped out on her front porch, barely leaving room for her guest. "When was the last time you saw Jenny McLaurin? When was the last anybody came to see her, other than me and her circle-meeting group, or maybe those sorry Blackwells now and then? You know she would cry sometimes, talking about how she didn't have any family any more, how lonesome she got."

Georgia moved back as far as she could, the hollies that surrounded the porch pricking her rear and legs.

Forsythia Crumpler seemed to be just getting started. It looked as if she might have been crying.

"I didn't know . . ." Georgia began, trying to gain some conversational traction.

"You didn't even send her a Christmas card last year," the older woman exclaimed. "She was so hurt that she told me about it."

"Why didn't somebody tell me?"

"Tell you to send her a Christmas card?"

Georgia hadn't sent any Christmas cards, something she didn't think was worth introducing as an ameliorating factor.

"Why didn't someone tell me she was so lonely? I could have come to see her."

Forsythia Crumpler shook her head in disgust.

"I wish I had. But you know Jenny. Or I suppose you do . . . did. She was proud. She specifically told me not to write you, every time I threatened to. I wish to God I had anyhow, though. We tried to look out for each other, two old ladies without any family to speak of." She nearly spit the last part out.

Georgia could feel the stares of Justin and Leeza behind her.

"I sent her money," she said, regretting it even as she said it.

"Money. Fifty dollars a month. Not enough to keep her from canceling her subscription to the paper. I let her borrow mine."

15

"She canceled her subscription to the paper?" Jenny would read the newspaper front to back. Even Georgia remembered that.

"I'll bet you don't even know about the Blackwells, do you?"

Georgia shook her head. "The Blackwells?"

"This is how lonesome and scared she was. She was so lonely, so worried that nobody would look after her, that she might die alone, that she gave up her house."

"What do you mean, gave up her house? She was living here, wasn't she?"

The older woman stopped to catch her breath.

"Well," she said after a few seconds, "you'll find out about it pretty soon, I suppose. I'm not the one who ought to be telling you.

"I'll tell you this, though, Georgia McCain. I am purely ashamed of you. How long have you been back down here, a week?"

Georgia could only nod.

"And you hadn't come by here once. Not once. She knew you were here, too. I taught you better than that, girl, and your momma and daddy taught you better. Jenny McLaurin was family. Your family."

"We didn't know she was this bad off," Justin said, the first time he'd spoken.

Forsythia Crumpler gave him the same laser glare she had used to pin smart-ass seventh-grade boys to the wall for 40 years. Georgia saw him take a half-step backward.

"Son," the older woman said, looking down at him, "nobody ever knows anything they don't want to know."

Georgia could feel the tears welling up. Her eyes burned.

Her old teacher turned again to her.

"Georgia McCain," she said, in a voice appropriate for a star student caught cheating on a final exam, "I thought I would always be proud of you."

And then she turned and walked, stiff with pride and arthritis, back into her brick rancher, shutting the door quietly but firmly.

CHAPTER TWO

October 18

Even before Georgia took her sabbatical, before she packed what she could in a hurry and drove south, the monkey was on her.

She used to be a world-class sleeper.

If thunder or snoring awakened her in the middle of the night, no matter. Five minutes later, she would be out again, sometimes stepping back into the same dream as if picking up a novel she had just put down. It was a pleasure to look at the bedside clock and see that she had two more hours, or even just one, before the alarm rang.

"If they ever make sleeping an Olympic sport," Phil would say, "Georgia's got the gold wrapped up."

Recently, though, a strange noise or a full bladder has meant she might as well get up and write a letter or grade some papers. Even on nights when she felt she never wanted to rise again, she could not get back to sleep.

In her father's time, the monkey would "get" tobacco croppers on a hot and muggy Carolina day. The phrase stuck with Georgia and has evolved perfectly into the beast that sits on her runaway heart and whispers all the worries of the world into her nocturnal ear.

She writes some of it off to the onset of menopause, some to the losses and worries that seem harder to shake every year.

Something like Jenny's death just makes the monkey weigh a little more and jabber a little more insistently.

She looks over at the bedside clock. She's been awake for at least an hour, and it's only 4:30. The little gadget that approximates the sound of rain on the roof roars away, but it only makes her want to get up and go to the bathroom.

Why am I here? Why did I come at all? I could be worthless as shit up in Montclair, without the bother of packing and moving.

When it came to her late father's house, Georgia never really had a plan.

It was built in the 1890s. Its kitchen and bathrooms were last modernized 30 years ago.

It is a fine example of a North Carolina farm dwelling belonging to a family that was able to replace what needed replacing and careful or lucky enough not to burn it down. Vinyl siding covers the old pine boards, and the red tin roof is only 12 years old. The windows are modern and double-paned; Georgia had them replaced only seven years ago, after consecutive tenants had complained about water leaking in and warm air leaking out. There is central air conditioning and gas heat.

It has two stories, five usable bedrooms, a living room, dining room and kitchen, plus two baths. The back porch is screened; the front is not. It sits on as good a hill as East Geddie has to offer.

Georgia started renting it to strangers because Kenny Locklear said he knew someone who wanted to move out to the country and would pay a relatively good price. She always balked at selling, even if it was the last place on Earth that she would ever want to live.

But the renters started staying for shorter and shorter periods, opting for a mobile home or an apartment in town, and the gaps between them seemed to widen.

Twice, despite Kenny's best efforts, thieves broke in while the house was unoccupied.

The first time, they got some of the old furniture stored in one of the downstairs bedrooms, things Georgia didn't want to sell or move, and the dining room chandelier.

The second time, they took copper pipe from underneath the house and an old bureau that had been in the family at least since her father was a boy. They also stole, apparently for meanness, old annuals and other books that had been in the plunder room for

18

decades. That time, just three months ago, the intruders evidently had been so put out by the lack of theft possibilities that one of them had defecated in the middle of the living room floor.

"I'm sorry," Kenny had told her when he called her that time. "If I could catch the bastards, I'd shoot 'em."

That was in August. Georgia saw it as a sign. She had told Justin, who was as much at liberty as she was, that she planned to sell the farm, or as much of it as they still owned. He surprised her by offering to go down and get it ready to show. He had become quite handy in the Peace Corps, and there were many things that needed attention.

And Leeza, already five months pregnant then, seemed eager to go with him. Perhaps they welcomed the chance to be somewhere by themselves, Georgia thought, under some roof that could at least temporarily be theirs alone.

The open house came and went with no serious interest, and the farm has been on the market for a month and a half now. Justin has repaired doors and windows, painted the inside and had the siding power-washed. He has kept the grass mowed and the bushes trimmed. He has overseen the repairs to the plumbing and has even put a fresh coat of paint on the carhouse—a fool's errand, Georgia thinks, the way old wood drinks paint, but it will look good for long enough, until some other fool buys the house, the outbuildings and the few dozen acres around it.

She hadn't meant to come herself, other than for a necessary weekend or two. But, as she told Cathy Rayner while she packed up the smallest U-Haul trailer she could rent from the Amoco station two blocks away from her brick rancher, you never know.

"Never know what?" Cathy said. She had been trying for days to talk Georgia out of doing "anything rash." She had warned her of decisions made in grief and haste.

"Anything," Georgia had told her. "You never know anything."

The SUV to which the trailer was hitched was a high-riding monster whose driver and passengers were so far off the ground that it made Georgia feel mildly dizzy sometimes. She had never liked it and should have sold it already, but it was Phil's when she first met him. He had loved it, even if the roughest obstacle it had to muscle over was the speed bump in the grocery-store parking lot.

Georgia backed out onto the cul-de-sac, waved once to Cathy, who was shaking her head as she waved back, and she was gone.

What the hell, she wondered before she came to the first stop sign, am I doing?

* * *

The first Thursday in October, she had awakened at 5:15 from a dream so real that it would rub against her all day. She tried to go back to sleep, but after half an hour, she knew it was hopeless.

She had gone back to sleeping in the king-size bed they had shared, and now she thrashed around on it, lost in alien territory, sometimes opening her eyes to find she had drifted 90 degrees or more from where she began the night before.

The dream was about Phil and her. She was trying to save him, somehow, jumping from the telephone to his prone body to the phone again. He was saying something, but she couldn't remember the words later. Finally, she was running, trying to scream for help. But her legs were like lead and her mouth was silent, and she woke up tired and hopelessly tangled up in the bottom sheet, crying and saying, over and over, "I'm sorry. I'm sorry."

The dream would stay there on the periphery of her consciousness all day, a ghost always just out of reach.

After she gave up on sleep, she showered and dressed, then made herself some coffee, ate her cereal and took her vitamins. She was supposed to be working on a book (the official reason for her break from teaching), something on the early, uncollected short stories of J.D. Salinger. By 8 o'clock, though, she knew she could not face a day at the keyboard.

She lay on the living room couch, switching channels 20 times, picking up and putting down three magazines and two books, dozing off twice and taking a desultory lunch of uncooked wieners and half a large bag of corn chips with chive dip.

She still kept a little marijuana around, a habit as dated as psychedelic album covers and bell-bottoms, she knew, but it made her feel good from time to time. She rolled a sloppy, out-of-practice joint and smoked it all. After that, she spent the rest of the afternoon watching one live-audience television show after another. She ate a dozen of the small chocolate candies that she had bought in anticipation of Halloween.

When she started to come down, just in time for the 5:30 news, she got the blues. She put on a George Winston CD that reminded her of Phil and cold weather, and she burrowed farther into the couch. She felt she could not have moved if the house had been on fire.

By 8:00, she had managed to rouse herself enough to entertain the thought of doing at least one positive thing before the day was lost forever. So she went to the bedroom and started looking for her exercise clothes, thinking about the Stairmaster down at the YMCA, or maybe a swim.

But by the time she had packed her gym bag, it was 8:30, and she couldn't remember whether the Y closed at 9 o'clock or 10, and she was feeling a little light-headed, so she said to herself, screw it.

But then, half dressed, she thought of something she had done years ago, during her first marriage. One Halloween, she had surprised Jeff Bowman by slipping out of her clothes and into a raincoat, then going out the back door and around the house to ring the front doorbell. When he had answered, she flung open the raincoat and said "Trick or treat, mister." They made love three times that night.

Maybe it was the memory, or maybe it was just a wild hair. Georgia took off the gym shorts, panties, tee-shirt and sports bra and walked over to the window. She peeked out through the closed blinds. It was dark, and Georgia was known, among her friends, to get a wild hair now and then.

She put her running shoes back on, no socks, and picked up the house key off the dining room table, just in case she locked herself out. Just one lap around the house, she told herself, for old times' sake. To prove I'm still alive.

She went out the back door and almost turned around, but she'd had enough false starts. She ran across the yard, wearing only the shoes, then turned and sprinted through the area between her home and the Wyndhams' next door, ducking under a dogwood limb, dodging the rose bushes, the cool early fall breeze tickling her bare skin, her heart thumping. She could hear a television and the drone of porch voices. She made the turn into the front yard.

She didn't even think about the motion detector until it came on. She froze like a deer in some car's headlights for an instant, and then she heard the voices stop.

The light, bright as the sun, stayed on, would not go out. She had just recovered enough to start running again, with her hand shielding her eyes, when she heard Sally Wyndham call across the side yard, timidly, "Georgia? Are you all right?" Bob had to be out there, too, sitting and rocking on their front porch, a country quirk in a neighborhood where everyone else retreated to the back.

"Fine," she called over her shoulder as she sprinted away from them. "I'm fine. Really." She reached the darkness on the far side of the house and finally, mercifully, the door from which she left. So much, she thought to herself, for spontaneity. There was a time when she would have evoked a little excitement among the neighborhood husbands if she had been caught naked in her front yard, a naughty scamp who might do anything, who wasn't afraid of anything. Who, though, wanted to see a 51-year-old English professor's tits and ass? She could imagine the whispering, the head-shaking, the pity. Poor Georgia. She ought to get some help.

She didn't think her body was that bad, although she could hardly bear to look at what gravity and age had done to it when she was safely inside again, and she didn't really think she was having a breakdown, no matter what anybody said. But people would *think* she was a pathetic, addled, menopausal hag, and that threw her.

She sat up late, listening to some old rock 'n' roll now, dipping into the bourbon, not answering the phone. She was still there at half past midnight when she finally figured that she had to go, that she could not let every bit of the past leave her without some kind of illogical, nostalgic gesture.

Do something, as Phil would have said, even if it's wrong.

Part of it, she thought later, was the realization that nothing, not one damn thing really, kept her in Montclair except ennui and

22

fear. She had a little money, she was relatively fit (though not young enough, she conceded, to live on raw hot dogs, corn chips, chive dip, marijuana, bourbon and Almond Joys, certainly not young enough to be caught buck naked in her yard). She could travel to Nepal, or join the Peace Corps like Justin, or take off and see America, the whole country, take months. Hell, she could live in the back of Phil's suburban assault vehicle.

She could do all of that. Maybe East Geddie would be a start at least.

She did worry a little about herself. Justin, before he left, could not get her out of the house except for a handful of safe, familiar places, all in Montclair itself.

Today, a trip around the house buck naked, she thought. Tomorrow, a drive down to North Carolina. The next day, who knows? Before losing Phil, she had long enjoyed describing herself as counterphobic. She had always tried to attack, to embrace, that which scared her.

That night, she thought that maybe what scared her was the world itself.

It took her two days to get everything more or less in order, and on the third day she left. Cathy Rayner was still waving, a little sadly she thought, as she turned a corner.

*　*　*

Now, eight days later, Georgia lies defeated on her marsh-mallow mattress.

She is thinking about Jenny, about Justin and Leeza, about how anyone could possibly want to buy this old house, about yard sales and the strange noise the gas heater is making and Forsythia Crumpler and then back to Jenny.

She finally gets up in the dark and turns off the artificial rain-fall. She sits in a chair and reads by the bedside lamp for another hour, listening to the old house's arthritic creaking, then rises to shower and make her breakfast.

She is in the refurbished kitchen, which will always be too small, but at least it has bright counter tops and late 20th-century

23

appliances, even a dishwasher. By the time Justin comes in, she has made some coffee and is slicing a grocery-store bagel.

He mumbles a good morning and leans against the counter. He is a handsome boy, except Georgia has to stop thinking of him as a boy. He's 27 years old, has lived in what she thinks of as the wild for two years. But with his hair uncombed and the sleep still on him, he might be the fifth-grader she always had to call at least twice before he would rise for school. He has her eyes, bright and full of life, her cheekbones, and her tan, aided by the Guatemalan sun. His hair, unfashionably long, flips up at its ends the way hers does.

"Still can't sleep?" he asks her.

"Not always. Sometimes I do, sometimes I don't. I can nap."

"What that old lady said . . ." he begins.

Georgia pours her son a cup of coffee. "She was right. Hell, I should have done more. I should have nagged you to go see her. I just didn't know how bad off she was."

She looks out the kitchen window. It's barely dawn now, and individual trees cast long shadows in the golden light. It's as lovely as East Geddie gets. A rabbit hops—safe for now from Kenny's beagles—across the back yard. It disappears in the tall grass behind the old shed where clothes once were washed with lye soap.

"What was she like?" Justin asks. "I don't really remember her very well."

"Cousin Jenny? Well, she was quiet, kind of country-seeming, I guess. Her husband Harold was kind of a mean redneck, although I don't think he ever hit her or anything. I just remember him using the N-word a lot and being kind of a bully."

Actually, Georgia admits to herself, she never really cared that much for Jenny, despite (or maybe because of) all that Jenny did for her over the years. She was her first cousin, but she was 27 years older, more like an aunt. She sent Georgia birthday money, no more than five dollars ever, until she was well into her 20s, and Georgia would feel obligated to write her a thank-you note.

Once, Jenny asked her to please not mention the birthday money to Harold, who was known to be close with a dollar.

What it came down to, Georgia knows, is that Jenny reminded her of everything she always wanted to leave behind. Jenny had looked after her mother after her father died, forcing the tight-fisted Harold to build a room for her on the back of their house, connected by a walkway. When Century died, Jenny was at her bedside *not driving away from East Geddie as fast as she could, damn glad to be out of there.*

On Georgia's visits to East Geddie before her own father's death, old neighbors and friends would come by to visit, or—on rarer occasions—Georgia would visit them. Jenny was one of their few common points of reference.

That Jenny McLaurin, everyone agreed, was a good woman.

Georgia would nod her head, knowing that the very things that made Jenny good made *her* bad. Jenny stayed. Georgia left. Jenny looked after her parents. Georgia deserted hers to move Up North (Virginia being for all intents and purposes Yankee country from the East Geddie perspective). Jenny endured with a quiet smile, never saying more than was absolutely necessary. Georgia found, especially on visits back home, that she couldn't shut up, that she always somehow hoped she could give old acquaintances enough amazing detail about her life to make them understand why she didn't stay.

Nobody ever asked her why she couldn't be like Jenny. They didn't have to.

Jenny, she wanted to tell them, didn't have a chance to do what I did. If she'd had the chance, she might have done the same things, might have loved it, like I did, might've never wanted to come back and spend the rest of her life among bedpans and Wednesday night prayer meetings and neighbors who know every time you go out for groceries.

Now, watching the rabbit reappear and continue its rounds, stopping dead still suddenly at the sound of some perceived, far-away danger, Georgia shakes her head.

"You know, Justin, you have to live with some guilt sometimes, or it will drive you nuts. You can't do everything. You can't sacrifice your life for other people's happiness all the time, or it'll just make you crazy."

Justin laughs, and she turns sharply toward him.

"What?"

"Well," he says, "that sounds like what I said when I told you Leeza and I weren't going to get married just yet and you got so upset."

"I wasn't upset." *Liar.* "I just thought it would be better, you know, for the baby and all. I just didn't want my grandchild to be illegitimate."

"Mom, I don't think they even use that word any more."

She lets it drop. She knows she is talking to someone who has spent two years living with the poorest people of a poor country, for not much more than room and board. He's a good person, she tells herself. Get over it.

Besides, she thinks, I can live with a little guilt. I've done it this long. Hit me with your best shot, Forsythia Crumpler.

She stands there with her son, trying to digest the bagel, saying nothing else, watching the day come in.

CHAPTER THREE

October 19

The funeral is well-attended, although the only blood relatives present are Georgia and Justin. A handful of cousins from the Atlanta suburbs send their condolences and regrets.

Georgia isn't really sure what comes next.

She has no real interest in dealing with another sad old home no one seems likely to want; she doesn't think she has the energy.

Her own father's property is proving to be a hard enough sell. No real estate agents are calling to ask if the house's residents can disappear for an hour so prospective buyers can have an undisturbed look at what the multiple-listings book calls "a real charmer, a testament to country living. Be the master of your own estate less than 10 minutes from downtown offices."

As if, Georgia thinks, there were many offices left in downtown Port Campbell—only the police and fire departments and social services, which were not allowed to follow the stores to the suburbs.

Jenny's house might bring someone some money, but Georgia doesn't really need money. She isn't rich, but what her father unexpectedly left her, plus her own savings, invested well, should be enough. Plus, she inherited a respectable sum and a nearly-paid-for house from Phil. And she has a good pension. She can see herself living a life, 20 years in the future, that includes a tidy, low-maintenance condominium near the campus, a good meal in a good restaurant once or twice a week and a trip to Europe every year. She won't be rich, but who would be fool enough to expect that, after a life teaching English literature?

The congregation of Geddie Presbyterian Church has grown older and smaller. In Georgia's youth, the church boasted more than 250 members. Now, there are 61, most of them far beyond retirement age.

"The Presbyterians just don't seem like they want to go out and recruit," Jenny herself had told Georgia once, years ago.

Most of them seem to be present at Jenny's funeral, along with many from Shady Green Baptist Church on the Ammon Road, where much of the rest of East Geddie's white population worships. A handful of mourners come from the AME Zion congregation, including Blue Geddie, his wife Sherita and his mother, Annabelle.

Georgia noticed that everyone at the homecoming two days before was white. The churches around East Geddie are as segregated as they ever were.

Georgia was amazed at how short a space it took to chronicle Jenny McLaurin's life in the paid obituary the Port Campbell Post ran Monday and Tuesday mornings. Lifelong member of Geddie Presbyterian. Sunday School teacher. Church historian for 35 years. Preceded by loving husband, Harold, and son, Wallace. No other mention of the little boy who, with his friends, liked to see how close he could get to the Campbell and Cool Spring freight train that came through twice a day, whose closed-casket funeral in 1958 Georgia was allowed to forgo.

Georgia, on the front row, thinks her own funeral probably will draw a larger crowd—the rare past student whom she actually helped, her peers making what for many will be an obligatory appearance, neighbors and a handful of real friends, maybe a couple of ex-husbands.

She wonders, though, if there will be the sense of loss, the true mourning, that she feels and sees here.

It isn't that people throw themselves on Jenny's casket in loud, inconsolable grief. They are too country Presbyterian for that, too much of a world where effusiveness is a suspicious trait, a hint that there is something insubstantial in one's very being. Georgia has been to funerals, usually Catholic and urban, where people stood up and told funny stories, often with the deceased as the butt of an affectionate joke, where the parishioners laughed and cried, and she has wished at times she had grown up in such a church.

Here, there is a sense of quiet despair, the loneliness of seeing a lifelong friend depart forever. Women who have gone to grade school with Jenny sit stoically, dabbing wet eyes. Many of them have known her so long as Jenny Bunce that they still called her that even after she was married, for the rest of her life. They sit patiently, enduring and accepting loss as they have been trained to, while the minister, a man with no chin and a red face, leads them through familiar hymns and prayers, noting how this "good and faithful servant" has gone on to a better world. Reverend Weeks has been in East Geddie only 18 months, and he keeps referring to his notes.

Most of the mourners follow the family to the memorial park in Port Campbell, eight miles from the church. Georgia notices that no one seems anymore to observe the old country tradition of pulling off the highway when meeting a funeral procession. There is much honking of horns and at least one near-collision as older drivers try to get through red lights and stay with the line of cars in front of them.

At the gravesite, the little tent with two rows of folding chairs has room only for the minister, Georgia, Justin and 10 or so of the oldest, closest friends. Under the tent and among those huddled outside in the gloom, Georgia sees the sagging shoulders, the trembling lips of old women bearing up.

After a short prayer by Rev. Weeks, it is suddenly over. The crowd slowly disperses, stepping carefully around the ground-level grave markers, some drifting away to visit departed family members. Men and women whom Georgia knew well in her first 18 years come up to shake her hand and say whatever they can think to say. Some just nod.

"She was a good woman. She was so sweet and so patient," one of the women in Jenny's circle-meeting group tells Georgia, dabbing her eyes with a tissue.

"She made the best watermelon pickles," another offers, shyly.

"We tried to look after each other," a third says, forcing a smile, and Georgia can only smile back. "We tried to see her when we could."

Georgia is looking around for Justin. She sees him, at the edge of the crowd, introducing Leeza (*as what? My common-law wife? My concubine?*), very pregnant and clinging a little uneasily to his arm. The first few drops of what promises to be an all-night rain begin to fall.

Forsythia Crumpler is standing to their left, farther back. She is looking in her purse.

Another friend of Jenny's stops, and they talk for a few seconds. Forsythia pats her hand, and the other woman totters off to her car.

For an instant, Georgia's eyes meet those of her favorite teacher. She wondered whether Forsythia would decide to skip the funeral, but even after all these years away, Georgia knows that no one in East Geddie misses a funeral of anyone even vaguely known. It would be the ultimate disrespect.

Georgia starts walking toward her, thinking that one more bit of unpleasantness can't possibly make her day any worse, and she wants to take a chance on making it better. Just then, though, another woman calls to Forsythia, who turns and walks toward her, the chance gone as quickly as that.

Georgia promises herself that she will, by God, patch things up with Forsythia Crumpler. She has always been able to make others like and respect her. She will not be pummeled by the flinty eye and sharp tongue of this self-appointed conscience. Isn't she doing a good enough job without any help?

Justin and Leeza are walking toward her, and the raindrops are falling more insistently when Georgia feels a tap on her shoulder.

"I bet you don't even remember me, do you?"

Georgia does have to think for a moment. It has been a long time.

She has seen William Blackwell perhaps twice in the last 25 years, at the only class reunion she attended and in a chance encounter when Georgia was visiting Jenny.

He had retained then, and does now, his one great talent.

William Blackwell scared people.

The Blackwells live approximately half a mile east of Jenny's house on Route 47. William, Georgia knows second-hand, has done well. He is now the patriarch of a family that lives in various dwellings over several acres, all within eyesight of each other. They own several hundred acres of farmland and lease much more than that, occasionally selling some off to real-estate developers, then buying more farther back in the country.

In high school, William Blackwell had not played any sports to speak of, and he had been a sullen, indifferent student.

Nobody, though, trifled with him. That was understood. He had not been a Bill or a Billy, even in grammar school. The lifelong "William" seemed to imply some sense of raw country hardness that did not truck with little-boy names.

William Blackwell had been the best fighter in Geddie High School. Not even the best athletes—and Geddie had gone all the way to the state football championship game Georgia's junior year—wanted any part of him. She could still remember seeing him beat one of the stars of the basketball team senseless. The other boy had taken offense because William had been caught down by the railroad tracks after midnight one evening with the basketball player's steady girl, a friend of Georgia's who thought she liked danger.

What Georgia remembers of the fight is how William never lost the little smile, how he never said a word as he beat the basketball player, who was half a foot taller, from one side of the Soda Shoppe parking lot to the other, the other boy trying to engage him in conversation, trying to talk his way out of the worst beating he would ever take while still saving face.

When it was over, William Blackwell was not even winded. He just picked up his London Fog jacket and walked off with it over his shoulder. The basketball player lost two teeth and missed three games with a broken nose.

He had intimidated the teachers, most of whom chose to look the other way when William decided to slow-walk into class late, or leave early, or smoke a cigarette in the boys' bathroom.

He was famous for his cheating, blatantly copying other, smarter boys' work, getting them to hunch a shoulder down, or just making them pass their test papers to his calm, scarred hand.

Georgia's senior year, there was a new math teacher. Mr. Jackson was a thin, pale 22-year-old with glasses, acne-scarred and fresh out of East Carolina. He noticed after one mid-semester test that William Blackwell not only had the same exact score as Harold Willey, who sat directly in front of him, but also had missed the same three questions. William and Harold denied cheating, but Mr. Jackson gave them both zeroes on the test and made it clear that he would not tolerate dishonesty.

Four nights later, as Mr. Jackson was getting out of his Volkswagen Beetle at the little house he rented in Port Campbell, he was set upon by three assailants, whom he said he couldn't identify. He spent a week in the hospital. When he was released, he took the rest of the term off, then got a teaching job in another county.

Georgia had known, as had half the senior class, who the attackers were. Dwayne Sheets and Robert Packer usually rode around with William. Georgia had heard Robert Packer's bragging account of what happened that night. William Blackwell had told the teacher, at about the same time he was breaking his ribs with his steel-toed boots, that he had better develop a case of amnesia, that if anybody went to jail over this, somebody was going to die.

Thirty-four years later, the smile is still there, although not nearly as menacing, and his hands are the same. William Blackwell never had his hands in his pockets, or crossed, never carried any books in them. His hands always seemed to be hanging loose, a fraction of a second away from the side of someone's head.

He had been a handsome boy, in a somewhat frightening way, with deep gray-green eyes that never seemed to blink. He was hard and thin; he never seemed skinny, only spare, as if the weight-room muscles of the athletes were too childish for his consideration. He had light brown, brilliantine hair that was always parted in a straight, severe line, cut every week by a country barber. Even as others succumbed to Beatle bangs, William Blackwell's forehead shone high and proud. He could pass for 21 when Georgia and her friends were trying to get their first driver's licenses.

Once, when Georgia was breathlessly relating the latest William Blackwell atrocity to her father, he had sighed and said, "Well, he came by it honest."

Whenever some questionable transaction had been effected by intimidation or stealth among the farmers and store-owners in the flat bottomland east of them, her father or mother would refer to it as a "Blackwell operation." They always managed to get elected to such offices as their education enabled them to handle, a commissioner's post or a school-board seat sometimes passing from father to son. They have flourished, as much as is possible without leaving eastern Scots County or getting a college degree, pouncing on large and small scraps of patronage.

Georgia has heard stories over the years, from her father and mother and then from Jenny and in the occasional letter from old friends who never moved away. There was a fight with a Hittite man from down near the Marsay Pond, when William was 22. The man died of stab wounds, and it was ruled, finally, self-defense. There was a neighbor whose house burned after the neighbor sued, claiming he was cheated by William on a property transaction. The transaction had resulted in William owning land where the cloverleaf connecting the interstate to Route 47 was to be built. No one was ever charged.

"William Blackwell," Georgia says, extending her hand. "You haven't changed a bit."

He has gained some weight. Anyone eating the deep-fried cuisine of Scots County would, and Georgia knows that what is considered hog-fat in her university town is no more than pleasingly plump in the land of her birth.

The young man standing next to him, though, is fat even by Geddie standards.

"This is my son, Pooh."

"Pooh?" Georgia can't help smiling.

"It's William Junior, but that's what they call him."

The man towering over William is a couple of inches over 6 feet tall and weighs well in excess of 300 pounds. His face, instead of the chiseled lines his father still possesses, is round and red, his thick red lips encircled by a Fu Manchu mustache, his eyes a pair of squinched-up slits.

Pooh, looking into the distance, seems uneasy in his ill-fitting jacket and clip-on tie.

"Hello, uh, Pooh," Georgia says, and the younger man grunts a greeting. He meets her hand with what can only be called a paw, red like his face, hairy and freckled.

By now, Justin and Leeza are at Georgia's side, and she introduces them to her old classmate and his son.

"Georgia," William says, lowering his voice, "this idn't a good time to talk, I know, but there's something we need to discuss, about Cousin Jenny, bless her heart. She was a fine woman."

Georgia agrees that, indeed, Jenny was a fine woman.

"You know, we'd been taking care of things up there, mowing the yard and checking in on her and all."

Georgia thanks him.

"Well, she said she wanted to show her appreciation to us somehow, and that's what we need to talk about."

Georgia suddenly remembers what Forsythia Crumpler said two days before. And she knows.

The house. She gave them the goddamn house.

"Yes, William," Georgia said, "I guess we do need to talk. Do you think I need to get a lawyer?"

The small smile. "Oh, Lord no. I mean, I can get David Sheets—you remember Dwayne, don't you? Well, he goes by David now, has for years—I'll just get him to come on over, to make it official and all. Can you picture ol' Dwayne a lawyer?"

Georgia can't. She heard that he had come back from Vietnam and somehow gotten through McDonald College in five years, then was admitted into the first, easiest class at a new law school nobody seemed to need or want. She's even heard about how he's made everyone start calling him David because he thought Dwayne sounded too red-neck.

Georgia suddenly feels a headache coming on, the kind she's gotten occasionally over the past seven months, the kind she used to get from eating ice cream too fast.

"Here," she says, taking out a pen and a scrap of paper and writing out her phone number. "Call me. I've got to go."

34

And she leaves William Blackwell and Pooh standing next to Jenny McLaurin's burial tent.

William calls that night and invites all three of them to come for dinner the next Sunday; he says they can talk business afterward, "maybe have ol' David over, too." Georgia already has planned to visit an old college friend in Greensboro on Saturday night, though, and tells him she won't be back until late Sunday. They finally settle on a 2 o'clock meeting the following Tuesday afternoon at David Sheets' office.

* * *

The day of the meeting, Justin comes with Georgia. The office is on the 12th and top floor of Port Campbell's tallest building, on the old market square. It is one of the few addresses listed on the information board mounted by the lobby elevator doors. Ghosts of letters long-removed sandwich "Warren and Sheets" top and bottom.

David Sheets and William Blackwell are already there, although Georgia made sure she arrived at least 10 minutes before 2. They look as if they have just shared a dirty joke.

Georgia calls the lawyer "Dwayne" out of habit and is politely corrected. They talk for a few minutes about school days, when they had as little or less in common than they do now.

Their business is over in 45 minutes. The building in which they sit is on the last substantial hill between Port Campbell and the coast, and David Sheets' office looks out to the east. Georgia, staring out the window, can identify the rusted-out water tower in Geddie itself, and she imagines she could see Littlejohn McCain's old farmhouse from here if she had a pair of binoculars.

She adds little to the conversation—Justin actually has more questions than she does. The entire experience reminds her too much of the day they read her father's will in this same building, and of the frantic drive back from Virginia that preceded it.

She is appalled at what has happened, but she feels she has no right to carp if Jenny wanted to give her house and the small piece of land around it to people who are only distantly related to her husband. At least they did something, came around and checked up on her, kept her from dying of loneliness.

"The deal, in plain English, is this," the lawyer says. "Jenny Bunce McLaurin agreed in writing that, in exchange for certain considerations by William Blackwell Sr., William Blackwell Jr. and other family members, William Sr. and William Jr. would have all property owned by her and her late husband Harold, upon her death."

The "considerations" seem somewhat amorphous to Georgia and Justin—assurance that her bills would be paid should she run out of money, that she would be cared for in her home and not have to go to a rest home, that she would be visited on a regular basis and have groceries brought to her, that she would be taken to the doctor's office when necessary.

"Her health had failed right much in the past few years," William says, seeming to assume that Georgia didn't know about Jenny's failing heart and crippling arthritis.

"But she just signed everything over to you?" Justin asks.

"Well," David Sheets says, "no. As I said, she left certain items, family heirlooms I guess, to your mother."

There is a dresser taken by Jenny's mother from the home where Georgia is staying now. A portrait of Jenny and Harold that hangs over the mantelpiece. Photo albums and old letters. Jenny's old cedar jewelry box and the contents thereof.

"You can pick that stuff up whenever you want," William says. "Any time you want to come by, just give us a call."

Georgia gets up and stands next to the glass, looking east. She is not surprised, now that she has had a week to think about it. She is sure that Jenny never even really read the words that the lawyer and William Blackwell put in front of her. The way it would have worked, William would have promised her solemnly that he and his family would look after her "from here on out," that she would never have to go to a rest home, and she would have told him that the house was his when she died. The will—getting it down on paper—would have been William's idea.

"Did she have any savings at all when she died?"

Georgia hears the lawyer clear his throat.

"Almost nothing. It appears that she was living mostly on her Social Security, and you know that won't get you far these days. Plus what you sent, of course."

"We wrote the checks for her bills the last six months," William adds, and Georgia thanks him again.

The meeting is soon over. They shake hands, promise to get together soon, and Georgia and Justin leave.

"You're just going to let them take her house?" Justin asks her on the elevator down.

"Who are we to say otherwise? Were we here when she needed somebody, needed family?"

"No, Mom. We weren't here. But it still doesn't seem right."

Georgia says nothing. She agrees with Justin, but she also feels that she has no standing in her old community, especially when it comes to Jenny McLaurin.

"I don't know," she says as she gets into his car. "I don't know how it came to this."

"Well, we need to do something."

"What for? It won't do Jenny any good now, and God knows I don't deserve anything from her except a kick in the butt."

Mother and son are quiet for the first minute of the drive home.

"I don't know," Georgia says at last, "maybe I'll ask Kenny."

CHAPTER FOUR

October 29

Kenny Locklear always seems to be on the move.

His brick rancher, not much different from the one Georgia fled in Montclair, is within eyesight of the old house, but she has seen him only twice in the three weeks she's been here.

Georgia used to resentfully pick butterbeans and field peas where his home stands now. The pole-hung grapevine where she plucked and ate fat, reddish-purple scuppernongs is behind it, restored to productivity.

Kenny Locklear has watched over the McCain home since the day, 11 years ago, when he learned he would inherit 160 acres of Littlejohn McCain's property, an unexpected godsend for a landless farmer.

The poetry of it occasionally thrills him even now, with the farm struggling and Teresa and Tommy living with her parents, receiving alimony and child support.

When they were married, the farm was always a point of friction. Lying in bed, he would tell her she knew she was marrying a farmer. I thought you might get it out of your system, she would respond. You've got a college education. You're a teacher.

An agriculture teacher, he'd remind her. Those that don't have land, teach ag.

You just want to see that damn rock every morning when you get up, she'd say, playing her trump card. They would chew over the same argument, never resolving it before they went to sleep, having it cold for breakfast.

From his screened porch on the northeast corner of the rancher, he can, indeed, see the Rock of Ages.

It sits on the edge of his full-acre back yard. (Teresa didn't like that part of it, either. Why, she asked over and over, do you have to spend three hours every two weeks mowing that damn field? Don't you work hard enough, between school and this so-called farm?)

It is larger by far than any other rock nearby. It was rolled there, Kenny and other Lumbee children were told, long ago from far away, perhaps after a famous victory. (Hell, Kenny thinks, that narrows it a little. How many victories have we had? He sometimes scoffs at the old stories, but the more he hears and lives, the more he believes in oral history. It has become a kind of late-blooming faith.)

When Kenny inherited the land, he, Blue and Annabelle worked it out so Kenny had a small parcel near the rock, across the farm road from the rest of his inheritance. Within a year, the footings were dug next to the trailer where he was living in the interim. By the time the house was ready, he and Teresa already were engaged.

Many small pieces of the rock have been chipped off in the last decade. Anyone claiming to be a Lumbee is welcome to come and see it, have someone take his picture next to it, or bring a chisel and take home a small chunk. (Please take only a small piece, the hand-painted sign asks, and most comply.) For all the chipping, the rock seems no smaller.

He answers the doorbell at 4 this Friday afternoon.

"Hi, Kenny," Georgia says. "I brought you some lasagna. It's vegetarian. I hope that's OK. It's really good."

"I don't know, Georgia. I've got some moral issues with vegetables. Sometimes, I just plow under the peas and beans because I can't bear to see anybody eat them."

"Yeah, I know. It seems to be a local thing around here. I've been in restaurants where I don't believe they serve vegetables at all."

"Are you counting hushpuppies? They're made from corn meal, you know."

"Sure. Why not? And, I think if you cook just about any vegetable around here with about half a pound of pork fat, it eases most people's consciences."

By the time John Kennedy Locklear became a part of her father's world, Georgia was long gone. Since Littlejohn McCain's death, they've seen each other on her rare visits and talked occasionally over the phone, mostly about the house. The man before her now has skin slightly darker than hers, seasoned by the sun. His black hair is cut to within a quarter-inch of his scalp. He's showing some gray at 38, mostly in his '60s retro sideburns. He's not much taller than Georgia, maybe a couple of inches under 6 feet, and he can't weigh 150 pounds.

He is, she's been told, quite in demand among the single and divorced women of eastern Scots County. He gives off a sense of steadiness and gravity, but his brown eyes always seem to be broadcasting some secret amusement. In the 11 years he has overseen the many rentals, broken leases and unanticipated repairs, he has always refused to accept anything from Georgia other than the occasional check for a new appliance or a repair he could not do himself, of which there have been few.

"Hell, Georgia," he told her once when she wanted to pay him for fixing a leaky roof, "your daddy gave me everything I've got. A little sweat once in a while is getting off light, in my book."

Now, she tells Kenny that she wants to ask him about a few things, and he suggests that they take a walk.

"Daylight Savings ends Sunday. We might as well take advantage of the sunlight while we've got it."

"Make hay while the sun shines?"

"Yeah, whatever."

The weather has turned warm. Georgia resists calling it Indian Summer. Kenny is comfortable in just a shirt, and she rolls up the sleeves of her light sweater.

They walk across the long back yard, toward the rock. At each end of the grassy area is a red flag on a pole in the middle of a closely mown circle.

"My own private course," Kenny explains. "Pinehurst with sandspurs. This is the even-numbered greens, and that's the odd-numbered greens." He points toward the more-distant pole. "The view doesn't change much, but the price is right."

She tells him about Jenny McLaurin's house, about William Blackwell and David Sheets, about all her misgivings and especially her guilt. She's been talking for 20 minutes, and they've been sitting by the rock for 10, before she finally runs down.

"Do you think they just ripped Jenny off?" she asks him at last.

He's smoking a filtered cigarette and looking across cleared autumn fields toward the Blue Sandhills.

"I don't know, Georgia. William Blackwell's liable to do anything."

"Did you hear anything, before she died, about her not being looked after or not being treated right?"

Kenny exhales smoke and is quiet for a moment.

"Hell, Georgia. You know people talk. That's the main sport around here."

"About how Jenny had been abandoned by her no-good, shiftless relatives?"

"No, not like that. No. They just, you know, worried about her."

"Well, why didn't somebody tell me? Why didn't you? You tell me every time a damn water heater dies or the roof springs a leak."

Kenny has a habit of waiting several seconds to answer, and Georgia has to tell herself not to jump in with another question or observation before he's dealt with the one already on the table. Breathe deep. Count to three.

"It's like this," he says at last. "I think folks figured you knew as much as you wanted to know."

"That's—that's so unfair," she sputters. "They just assume I'm a bad person, that I'd abandon my family."

Then she is silent. She has wondered for years what people really thought of the woman who let her father shift for himself long after he should have had some daily attention from someone, who let him go off into the woods on the hottest day of the year, daring the monkey. She never had the guts to ask, but she thinks she knows, now that she has made herself face the truth. Georgia McCain, they've been telling each other, wouldn't lift a finger to save her own father. Why would she care about a cousin?

41

"You're not a bad person, Georgia," Kenny says to break her silence. "They just do things different down here. If I didn't have an older brother who never left home taking care of my mother, she'd probably be living here with me. It's not wrong or right, just expected."

"Wouldn't that drive you crazy? I mean, you've got a pretty active social life, I'm told."

He gives her a sharp look. "Who told you that? No, it wouldn't drive me crazy, because I wouldn't let it. It's just something you have to do, like breathing or eating. Sometimes you don't get what you want, you know? If the doctor tells you you've got cancer, it doesn't do much good to throw a fit about it, you just deal with it, you live or you die.

"Not," he says quickly, "that having my mother move in here would be like getting cancer."

"Perish the thought."

The air is getting cooler, and Georgia pulls her sleeves back down.

"One other thing. Jenny seemed to have a million friends. I mean, the church was packed at her funeral. Why couldn't some of them, even if they didn't want to tell me about it, have helped her? Taken her to the doctor's, or picked up her groceries, just visited more often."

"Did you see how old those ladies are? Most of them are older than her. I guess, though, that there's more to it than that. Around here, there are things friends do, and things family does. It would have been almost an insult to step in like that. And, the Blackwells were related to Harold. Maybe most people thought she was being looked after."

"And how about you? What did you think?"

Kenny throws a cigarette butt down and squashes it under his boot heel.

"That's a tough one, Georgia. The Blackwells aren't famous for their charity around here. I didn't know about the will. But I wondered. I still wonder."

"I just wish you, or somebody, had called."

Eventually, they start back.

"If somebody had called, Georgia," Kenny asks her, stopping after a few steps, "what would have been your reaction? Would you have been put out? Irritated?"

Georgia knows she probably would have been both. She has trouble hiding her immediate reaction to unpleasant news; it is a failing she supposes she will never overcome.

"Maybe. But I'd still have done the right thing."

"Well, people—or at least, most of the ones I know—don't want to be beholden. They don't want to think that they're begging somebody for something they don't want to willingly give."

"So, if they thought I didn't want to do anything about Jenny, they would just not call me at all."

"They might."

"But that just hurts Jenny. I could've done something."

She remembers another phone call, one she got less than three months before her father died. It was from Jenny, who was still healthy, still delivering meals and paying visits to shut-ins all over the eastern half of the county. She saw Littlejohn, her uncle, at least once a week.

This call had come at a particularly bad time. Georgia was packing for a trip to Europe. Justin was 15 and was behaving badly because she and her boyfriend weren't taking him. And here was Cousin Jenny telling her, in that flat, irritating country accent that Georgia had tried all her life to escape, that they needed to do something about her father.

"He forgets things sometimes," Jenny said. "Important things. I'm afraid he's going to hurt himself."

Georgia told her that she had already bought non-refundable plane tickets and was going to be out of the country for the next couple of weeks, that she would call her father and go see him when she got back.

Georgia tried to assure Jenny and herself that Littlejohn McCain would never let strangers look after him.

"I'm not talking about strangers," Jenny said, and there was long silence. Finally, Georgia lied. She told her cousin that she had a meeting to go to in 30 minutes and had to get dressed.

They are already at the steps to Kenny Locklear's back porch when Georgia remembers her sunglasses. She had them on against the afternoon glare, then laid them down on a hacked-away flat spot on the Rock of Ages. She has left her regular glasses next door—she's proud that she still has 20-40 vision and doesn't really need them, except for driving, movies, television and a few other things.

"I'm sorry. I've left my shades out there."

"Want me to come with you?"

"No. I know right where they are."

"Well," Kenny says, "come on in when you get back. I'll fix you a drink. Coke? Beer? Something stronger?"

She tells him a beer would be nice.

She's been gone 10 minutes, and Kenny wonders if she needs help in the fast-dying day. He gets a flashlight and is opening the door to his porch when he sees Georgia coming toward him through the gloom.

She seems about to walk past the door entirely when he calls to her. She jumps and turns, then corrects her path.

"What's the matter?" He shines the light on her face. "Couldn't you find them?"

She looks down as if surprised that her hands are empty.

"No. I know where they are, though. I'll get them in the morning."

"Well, come on in. You look like you could use that beer right now."

He insists that she take the best chair in his living room, a recliner that she falls into gratefully.

He hands her the beer, in a cooler cup, and notices that her hand is shaking. When he turns on the light beside her, she looks pale.

"What's the matter?" he asks, moving close and feeling her forehead the way he used to check Tommy's when he suspected he was running a temperature. Georgia's skin is cool and clammy.

Georgia is not a superstitious woman. She wonders how she really can be, in good conscience, since she isn't even really religious. If I can't believe in the Lord Jesus Christ, with all those

44

disciples and such witnessing on his behalf, she said to Phil once, how can I believe in poltergeists and hobgoblins?

She thinks now, though, that ghosts might be the most positive spin she could put on the situation. The logical conclusion, the one she'd rather not consider, is that she is losing her mind.

Maybe, she thinks, I can believe in just one ghost.

A mist was starting to rise as she walked briskly back across the yard. The sun had already gone down, and she was admiring the pinks and oranges just above the horizon.

In Kenny's back yard, the long-abandoned pea and bean rows have never been completely flattened, giving the land an almost undetectable rise and fall that can trip the unsuspecting. Georgia stumbled as her toe caught the slightly higher ground of one of those phantom rows. When she looked up again, now no more than 100 feet from the rock, he was there.

Georgia stopped, not daring to move, the way she had acted the time a deer somehow found its way into their Montclair back yard while she was coming out at sundown with thistle for the birdfeeder.

The figure in the near distance did not seem to notice her. He was leaning against the rock, hands in his pockets, facing 90 degrees away from her, toward the lush land now owned by Annabelle and Blue. She was marginally aware of the low, mechanical hum of traffic from the interstate.

He sat like that for at least 5 minutes, neither he nor Georgia moving.

Then, he eased up to his full height and turned toward her as if he'd known she was there all along. The light was almost gone, but she was sure she could see him smile. He might or might not have motioned to her.

Georgia croaked his name out, once, and the figure moved slowly behind the rock. The only sound, other than the distant traffic, was a beagle barking in the next field.

She moved a few steps closer but could not work up the courage to go farther and retrieve the sunglasses.

45

She knew the posture, the shy grin, even the shirt and overalls.

She called his name again, and when there was no answer, she turned and walked fast, chilled to the bone now, forcing herself not to run.

"You're still cold," Kenny says. "I probably ought to get you some coffee, something warm. Want a blanket?"

Georgia shakes her head.

"What is it? Did something scare you?"

She takes another sip of beer.

"Kenny, do you ever see anything—anybody—out there at the rock? I mean, just standing there?"

He gets up and walks halfway across the room, his back to her, then turns around.

"You know what they say about it, Georgia?"

She shakes her head.

"They say that you can see just about anything you want to see out there. At least 10 times a year, people, almost all Lumbees, will come here—usually they ask me first—and spend the night out there by the rock. You saw where the grass was worn down around it? That's from the people spreading out on blankets and waiting out the night, thinking they'll see their ancestors."

Georgia puts down the beer.

"And do they?"

"See their ancestors? Some say they do. Some say they didn't see anything. And there's always kids around here, raising Cain, sneaking down there and trying to scare folks who are already half-sure they're going to see a ghost."

"How about you? You live here all the time. Have you ever seen one?"

"Ghosts? Nah, not really."

"Not really?"

"Well, there was one time. It's been at least 4 years ago. I was out trying to get one of my dogs back. I turn 'em loose to run rabbits and sometimes they decide they'd rather run half the night than eat. Then, they come back here about midnight, sit under my window and howl until I feed 'em.

"Anyhow, this one night, I was walking out there, between the rock and your family's old graveyard, the one where your daddy's buried, whistling for the dogs. And I saw a man—I'm sure it was a man, kind of old and slow-moving, walking away from the rock, away from me. I called out to him. He looked back, and then—and this was the strange part—despite the fact that he seemed kind of old and creaky, he somehow put distance between me and him. The last I saw of him, he was headed toward the woods over on Blue's land."

"What did he look like?"

"I don't know, Georgia. I don't even know if I saw anybody or not. It was almost dark, and I'd had a few beers after work. I was not what you would call a reliable witness."

"Did he look like anybody you knew?"

"It was too far to tell."

Georgia refuses another beer, and Kenny sees her to the door.

"Sure you won't stay and talk? I can rent a movie or something."

"Rent a movie? On a Friday night?" Georgia laughs. "Maybe I did get some bad information about you."

"Don't believe everything you hear," he tells her as she walks down the front steps.

She laughs, but after Kenny closes the door, she feels the goose bumps. They run up her arms to the back of her neck, up to her scalp. They don't go away until she is back inside her late father's house, breathing hard.

CHAPTER FIVE

October 31

Georgia removes the hymnal from its rack and thumbs her way to No. 47, "Sweet Hour of Prayer."

The last few years in Montclair, she never went to church, except sometimes on Christmas or Easter, and then just for the pageantry and nostalgia. She and Jeff had taken Justin. They had even been moderately, disinterestedly involved themselves—drafted into the choir, or to help coach a youth basketball team.

All that changed with the divorce. It was all up to Georgia after that, and she just didn't have will or faith enough to keep going.

She went to Geddie Presbyterian for homecoming two weeks ago because she thought she might see old friends, back visiting from some other city, shamed there by aging parents. There were a couple, but none of the ones she really wanted to see. Mostly, there were older people she had never really known that well, the ones who would come up and say, "I'll bet you don't remember me."

The morning of Halloween, though, brings a strange craving to go back. Getting to the 11 o'clock service is no problem; she's been awake since 4:30.

The monkey has been riding her harder than ever the last two nights. She retrieved her sunglasses yesterday morning, and there were no footprints she could discern other than hers and Kenny's, but there had been a brief shower Friday night.

She knows she stands an almost 100 percent chance of seeing Forsythia Crumpler if she goes to church, and that's part of the pull, she supposes. One more chance.

Justin and Leeza rise at last and come downstairs at 9. Georgia asks them without any expectations if they'd like to come with her, and after they surprise her by saying yes, she wonders what all the church ladies are thinking about Leeza's little coming attraction. It doesn't bother her that much that her first grandchild's parents are not married. But what about the congregation of Geddie Presbyterian Church? She can't ask Justin and Leeza to lie. And the ones at the funeral probably know, anyhow. Finally, she realizes that her stock can't fall much lower among her father's old friends and neighbors, and that she is a hypocrite for worrying about it in the first place.

Justin's idea of church wear is a blue shirt and leather jacket, no tie. His Top-Siders look as if they won't last out the fall. Leeza has on a loose-fitting everyday dress that accentuates her pregnancy. Georgia chose the one item she brought along in her hurried packing that fits her idea of church clothes, a jewel-necked, rust-colored Ann Taylor dress with long sleeves, almost new.

"Believe it or not," she tells them, "this is what people used to wear when they went to church."

"Back in the day," Justin says, laughing.

Geddie Presbyterian sits on the south side of Old Geddie Road, a graying piece of asphalt that long ago was the main road to Port Campbell. The church is equidistant from East Geddie and the mostly black community of Old Geddie. The two towns, and Geddie itself, to their north, inch closer together every year but stubbornly resist merging.

Now, there are houses on both sides of the brick church, mostly black on the west side, mostly white on the east. A cluster of more expensive homes, aimed at city people yearning for two acres of land and 2,500 square feet for under $150,000, as long as they don't mind putting in their own wells and septic tanks and hauling their own garbage to the dump, winds around back of Old Geddie.

Any new blood that has infiltrated the area has either flowed to the Baptist church near the center of town or to the AME Zion church half a mile to the west. Georgia counts 36 worshipers this

49

Sunday morning, including the three visitors. At least 25 are past retirement age. Of those, only two are men.

Well, she thinks, you don't have to live on pork fat for the wives to outlive the husbands. Happens everywhere.

The choir is the saddest thing of all. When Georgia was a girl, there were a dozen members, and most of them were competent. Her father sang bass, and five other men, all with voices that filled the old church, also were regulars. Her mother was usually among the women, harmonizing well, a team player. The choir would rehearse on Wednesday nights, and there was a certain amount of jollity, even horseplay, involved, something not easy to sustain in a country Presbyterian church. She heard the story many times of how her parents had their first date after a choir practice.

What stands before her now, moving turbidly through "Sweet Hour of Prayer," is something else entirely. There are four of them, and three were choir members when Georgia was in high school. Alberta Horne and Minnie McCauley are both nearly 80, stooped over so much that they seem in danger of tumbling down into the pulpit, where Rev. Weeks sits looking off into space as if willing himself somewhere else, perhaps in a church with two full choirs and an organ instead of a barely-tuned piano. The only man, Murphy Lee Roslin, is older than either of the women. His voice is weak and reedy, and he has to hold the hymnal so close that his face is obscured.

The one younger woman is the minister's wife, referred to by all, even the women more than twice her age, as Mrs. Weeks. Her voice is the best by far, but it has no connection with the other three. She seems to be trying to drown them out.

When the tithes and offerings are collected, by two deacons who are father and son, Georgia fishes around in her purse for something suitable. The father, waiting patiently at the end of the aisle, mouths "Thank you" and winks when she puts in a 10-dollar bill.

The sermon itself is mercifully short. Afterward, some of the church members come over to speak. She tells Alberta Horne how much she enjoyed the choir, and the old woman blushes. She compliments Rev. Weeks on his sermon.

No one is paying very much attention to Justin and Leeza, but no one is shunning her son or his pregnant girlfriend, either.

Georgia tries to make her way toward Forsythia Crumpler but is intercepted twice by older people wanting, it seems, just to squeeze her hand and tell her how pleased they are that she came again.

Justin and Leeza stay close to her. As they are all heading out the door, a woman Georgia doesn't remember, with snow-white hair and bright blue eyes, asks Leeza how long they've been married.

Georgia, in spite of herself, feels a little sorry for the girl.

"Ah," Leeza says, "actually, we're not married yet." She smiles and shrugs. There seems to Georgia to be a sudden stillness.

But the white-haired woman is not fazed.

"Well," she says, patting Leeza's full front, "you've still got a little time."

The woman totters off, and another, at least as old, and no more than 5 feet tall, reaches up and pats Leeza on the back. "Don't pay her no mind," she says. "You get married if you want to. My grandson, him and his girlfriend didn't get married, and they got the cutest little baby you ever seen. I wouldn't take nothing for him."

"Jesus," Justin says, and chuckles. Georgia shushes him, and they slip away.

She sees her old teacher getting into a car three down from Justin's.

"Wait here a minute," she says.

"Mrs. Crumpler?"

The woman turns toward her.

"Do you think . . . I mean, would it be all right if I came by your house sometime? I wanted to talk to you."

Forsythia Crumpler shrugs.

"I'm usually there."

The older woman looks at her for a second, then turns to get into her car.

After a roast-beef dinner, Leeza and Justin offer to do the dishes. Georgia thanks them and goes back to her bedroom to change. She wonders if getting a dishwasher would make the house more attractive.

51

There is a mantel across from her bed, above what once was a working fireplace. On the mantel is the old clock that goes back at least as far as her grandparents. She never bothered to take it with her to Montclair after her father died, and neither set of thieves bothered to steal it, perhaps because it hasn't worked for years. The last tenants did not even use this room, and Georgia appreciated the fact that Justin had it cleaned and ready for her when she arrived. Some day soon, she promises herself, she'll take the old clock to a shop in Raleigh and have it repaired.

Tunes get in her head and won't leave. Her mind seems to be completely indiscriminate. It could be a jingle on TV advertising toilet paper, or it could be Mozart on public radio—just whatever gets there first.

Today, the tenant is "Sweet Hour of Prayer." She isn't conscious of having heard the hymn in the last 20 years, and perhaps she never really listened to the lyrics, just mouthed them impatiently when she was young, waiting for the final stanza to end.

Now the old hymn won't leave her alone: "In seasons of distress and grief,/ my soul has often found relief,/ and oft escaped the tempter's snare/ by thy return, sweet hour of prayer."

Seasons of distress and grief. Well, she thinks, been there. Not since her mother's death and the breakup of her marriage in the same year, followed by her father's passing the next August, has she experienced such a season of distress and grief as has visited her in the last year of the century.

She supposes her tempter is the thing that whispers in her ear in the darkness, telling her to abandon all hope. Her monkey is a persuasive little beast. You've lost another husband, it says. You're going through the change. Most of what you loved is gone. It won't get better. You're probably losing your mind, too. Why fight it? Do a swan dive into your grief.

She envies anyone who can chase all that away with an hour of prayer. She remembers praying, as a little girl, and even then not being able completely to suspend the disbelief she could never admit to her parents.

The last time she tried it was on the frantic trip back to East Geddie that summer, after they had gotten home and learned that her father was in the hospital, near death.

She thinks she must have been delirious, because she let Justin, who had only barely gotten his license, drive part of the way. She sat there, in the passenger's seat, closed her eyes and silently asked God to spare Littlejohn McCain's life. She was apologetic about having the gall to ask for anything after so long an absence, and she could not make herself really believe Anyone was listening. She wondered, after they got to the hospital and learned from a dispassionate nurse that he was gone, if more faith could have saved him.

The monkey talks to her about that, too. Faith and acts, it says. You're not much on either one, are you?

CHAPTER SIX

After Phil died, I soldiered on through the rest of the spring semester. I was handling it well enough, I assured myself, even if I did sleep in our old bed only once in three months, preferring instead to curl up on the big leather couch, wrapped in the wool blanket we'd bought on our trip to Scotland. The couch was where he and I would half-sit, half-lie and read or watch television. I would sink back into his big, comfortable body, and his sure, wonderful hands would caress my hair, massage the back of my head, rub all the knots out of my neck, and sometimes slip smoothly down my blouse and stroke me until his intentions were hard to hide, and we would adjourn to the bedroom or the floor. Fifty-one years old and borne away by lust for my husband. You never appreciate your own luck sometimes until it's too late.

For weeks afterward, I could smell him, or thought I could, when I buried my face into the couch's wrinkled leather. I'd leave the television on like a night-light, waking sometimes at odd hours in the middle of an infomercial or a movie so bad I'd have to check the listings later to make sure I hadn't dreamed it.

True, I was losing my temper more than before. There seemed to be no penalty attached. Everybody was either too kind or just plain afraid to deal with the bereaved widow. My graduate students in particular gave me a very wide berth.

I should have been thrilled when Justin asked if he and Leeza could move into the big house in early June, about the time summer school was starting. They had been living with her parents, in a three-bedroom Cape Cod on 15th Street, and Leeza still had a younger brother in high school. We're talking five people, 1,600 square feet.

Truthfully, though, I was afraid. Didn't want company; didn't want to be alone. What a bitch.

As usual, I taught one summer school course, on short stories from *The New Yorker*. I loved that course and had taught it for eight years, in the fall and again in summer.

This time, though, I found I was tired beyond redemption of all the fine-boned, delicate stories I'd always enjoyed. Somehow, I got through, and then it was vacation time.

I turned down two offers from friends to spend a week with them at the beach. I was afraid to let myself be in a place where enjoyment was expected, where not smiling would have been ill-mannered.

By the Fourth of July, Justin and Leeza were giving me a lot of space. She was selling cosmetics at the mall, and he was doing manual labor, working with a construction crew building houses. I would mention to him occasionally how unbefitting this was for a summa cum laude graduate from the University of Virginia.

"I've got plenty of time, Mom," he would tell me, and it reminded me of the way he used to put off homework.

And what to make of Leeza? She is a pretty girl, I'll grant you. Beautiful hair the color of a new penny, the kind most girls are trying to get from a bottle, eyes full of fun, bubbly personality, loves dogs and cats. She's probably great at selling lipstick and eye shadow. She certainly knows how to use it.

Maybe we would have gotten along better if she had more than a high school diploma and some random courses at Montclair, which was more college than the rest of the Calloways could boast, granted. Maybe if she hadn't had that unjustifiably confident Attitude of the Young, exuding certainty that her ideas and beliefs had to be superior to those of old hags like me.

Maybe, if Justin hadn't told me she was two months pregnant right after they moved in.

"What are you going to do about it?" I'd asked him.

"Do?"

"Yes, do."

"Like get married? Or what?"

"I don't know." He was itching for me to say the magic "A" word, I could tell. But I wouldn't.

"I'm not going to do anything right now but be there for her," he said after a short silence. And we left it at that.

By August, they were back in Chez Calloway, in a 10-by-12 bedroom. We'd had an argument on Justin's 27th birthday. My fault. Another crack by me about the sands of time and summa cum laudes doing grunt work, and then they double-teamed me, and I made some remark about matrimony. We all apologized, but the general consensus was that it was time for somebody to go.

* * *

The first day of fall classes, late August, I was standing in this room with 12 graduate students, most of whom I knew. We were going to spend a semester studying the short stories of F. Scott Fitzgerald. I was not really pumped for doing this, but it was good, I told myself, to do something other than sit around on the screen porch and alternate between reading and staring unfocused into infinity.

And it might have been good, for someone who wasn't already going as crazy as a shithouse rat.

The classroom we were in could hold 60 students. Combine that with its high ceilings, and our little group huddled near the front seemed lost, swallowed up.

I had just gotten into my spiel about how much Fitzgerald's short stories were bringing in the '20s, in 1999 dollars, and how much he was driven by the economics of this, when I realized someone else was in the room.

He was sitting in the back. I don't know where he came from; I never heard the door open. But he was there. He didn't look the way he did as an old man. As a matter of fact, he looked a little like

Justin, and my first, split-second thought was that Justin had slipped into my classroom, maybe come over from the construction job he was on, still in his work clothes, although the bib overalls were a little over the top.

I must have been just standing there with my mouth open, and the looks I was getting indicated at least some of my class knew this had gone somewhere beyond quirky old English professor. They looked uneasy.

He didn't move, until I did. I started to walk slowly, past the little clump of scholars and toward the back of the room, where he was sitting with a slight smile on his face, his hands folded in front of him. By the time I'd taken four steps, though, he got up and was gone, before I'd come within 30 feet of him. He glanced back once on the way out, and when I looked out into the hallway, of course nobody was there. But I swear, I could smell him, some mix of sweat and Old Spice and the scent beneath that, which I always identified with the farm itself.

I did not go back into that classroom. Stella Greenleaf got my things later. I went directly to Hubert Lefall's office. It was Hubert's turn to play department head, and so he had to deal with my nervous breakdown on the first day of the fall semester. Poor Hubert: Nobody would have been less capable of dealing with my wild-eyed ravings and my tears. He'll probably use me in one of his novels some day, to get even.

We did finally get it straightened out. I cheated two classes of graduate students, although what I had to give them at that point was less, I am sure, than the gifts of the relatively enthusiastic doctoral candidates who took over for me. The good thing about academics: A certain amount of lunacy is expected, so it was fairly easy to set the wheels in motion and cover for one addled English professor.

I am now on sabbatical, supposedly wrestling with a scholarly paper on a set of short stories that the author never wanted read again, let alone dissected by English scholars. When I told Hubert Lefall in October that I was going to North Carolina for a few months, he just patted me on the shoulder, as if I might break, and told me to take all the time I needed, it being understood that "all the time I need" must not go beyond the start of classes next fall.

I didn't tell Justin about what I saw. What's the point? I just told him I needed a break. Hell, he ought to know about breaks. So I spent September alternating between my bed, the den and the screen porch, reading, drinking, staring into space and, I suppose, waiting for something to speak to me.

The only trouble with seeing your dead father in the back of your classroom: You kind of half expect to see him again, most anytime. You know anything that happens once can happen again.

Part of the flight to East Geddie, I'm sure, was a realization that you can run, but you can't hide, not even from people who have been dead 11 years and are buried 200 miles away. Might as well come on down, Georgia McCain. (I kept the name, by the way, for my third marriage, because I'd changed it twice already without a hell of a lot of luck. Maybe I ought to get a rabbit's foot.)

* * *

By early September, Justin had made good on his offer to go down and help get Daddy's old place in shape to sell, and I'm sure Leeza was glad to have someplace they could at least temporarily call their own.

I am not sure my appearance, a month later, was the thrill of their young lives. But I've been trying to play nice. Really.

CHAPTER SEVEN

November 5

W hat is now Blackwell Road, repaved so recently that the tire tracks of individual cars are still visible, was an unnamed dirt path when Georgia was in high school. Beyond William's house, it turns to dirt again before continuing on toward the swamp.

The house, on a small rise, is not much different from the one Georgia is trying to sell—wooden, two storeys with a rusting tin roof, surrounded by the various outbuildings of a working farm.

Near the main house are at least six other dwellings, all modular, every one occupied by William Blackwell's relatives, including his three sons and daughter and various grandchildren. Around it, in all directions, is cultivated land resting for the winter.

Georgia called yesterday, to see about picking up what few items Jenny left her. William himself had answered the phone and told her she could come by any time. They settled on 3 o'clock. As Georgia gets out of the van, her watch reads 2:58.

A large tan-and-black dog, mostly German shepherd, comes charging toward her, barking and baring its teeth, as if she is either a dangerous intruder or a very large pork chop. She is pinned against the van, afraid to turn around long enough to open the door and get back in.

This is how Pooh finds her. He walks up to the dog and kicks it in the ribs, sending it yelping away to safety behind the house.

"He won't hurt you," Pooh says. "He's just a big pussy." And he grins, the gaps between his teeth, like the rest of him, larger than life.

Georgia takes a deep breath.

"Thank you. Is your father home?"

"He's around here somewhere," Pooh says. "Go on inside."

Georgia walks onto the screen porch unescorted and knocks on the door that seems to lead to the kitchen. A minute later, a small woman who appears to be at least 60 opens the door cautiously and stares as Georgia explains what she's doing there.

Betty Blackwell, Georgia finds out later, is an Autry from the other side of Cool Spring, two years young than William. Farm life seems to have aged her. The two women sit in the living-dining room for several minutes, the silence broken occasionally by Georgia's attempts at conversation and Betty Blackwell's one-word answers, before William walks in.

"Sorry," he says, taking off his Dale Earnhardt hat. "I was looking after one of the horses. We keep 'em for the grandkids to ride, and sometimes they're more trouble than they're worth."

He looks sharply at his wife. "I hope 'ol Betty here has been keeping you entertained. She's quite the talker."

His wife blushes and frowns, then gets up silently and goes back to the kitchen, where much banging of pots and pans can be heard.

William rolls his eyes. Georgia tries to make her smile as non-committal as possible. She looks out the double windows and sees two preschool-age children playing in the side yard. They seem to be chasing a three-legged cat, circling around and trying to trap it. William tells her that they're his grandchildren. His sons, Pooh, Ike and Angier, and the one daughter, Sally, are all between 24 and 29, and among them they have made William Blackwell a grandfather five times over.

"The oldest one starts first grade next year. They might have to rebuild the school by the time they get all of 'em in there at the same time." William laughs, then bangs on the window glass and yells at them to leave the cat alone. "You want him to bite you again? You want some more shots?" The children, a boy and a girl, stop momentarily to stare at their grandfather, then go back to their pursuit of the cat. The boy has a stick in his hand.

William shakes his head.

"So, I expect you're here for Miss Jenny's stuff."

"I suppose so."

"I reckon we can get it all in that van. Nothing much of any size except the dresser, of course. Come on."

Georgia follows him into the hallway and eventually into a back room that is dark even in the middle of the day. William flips a light switch hidden away behind one of the many piles of cardboard boxes carelessly stacked and climbing high along every wall.

"Excuse the mess," he says. "It seems like we pack everything in here that we don't know what to do with. Jenny's stuff, or at least what all she left you, is over here."

He leads her to a far corner, through a narrow corridor bordered by more of the boxes. There sits the dresser, a homely pine construct to which age has not been kind. Someone, at some point, painted it a color of green not seen in nature. One of the four drawers has a knob missing. It might be considered, within the generous parameters of a modest farming community, an antique. Georgia knows she will have to take it or seem callous.

"We just put the letters and all the pictures and stuff in here," William says, opening a middle drawer. "And the jewelry box."

The portrait of Jenny and Harold leans against the dresser. It was done more than 40 years ago, when they were both in their 30s. Georgia hasn't really looked at it for many years, although it must have been in Jenny's house during her infrequent visits. She is surprised at how young they look. Harold is thin with dark, wavy hair; he reminds her of John Garfield. Jenny's curly blonde hair frames a face that seems almost free of worry lines. She looks happy.

Georgia has heard the story many times:

A man had come walking up their driveway, working his way along Route 47 from Port Campbell east, offering to do "artistic paintings" of couples, families, anything you want, for whatever he could get. The man came late on the same Thursday afternoon on which Harold had been paid 50 dollars—nearly a week's salary at the sawmill—by Parker Vinson for the use of his land. Parker Vinson made moonshine and preferred not to make it on land he actually owned, choosing instead to give people like Harold McLaurin 50 dollars here and there for certain concessions. Once, a still was found and destroyed on Harold's land, but no one had ever seen Harold near it. Actually, there were certain parts of the 120 acres he owned on the edge of Kinlaw's Hell that Harold made certain he never set foot on. So, the portrait man's timing was perfect. Harold paid him 20 dollars and a bed for the night in exchange for what had to have been a frivolous expenditure in eastern Scots County at a time when most people were more than happy to immortalize themselves via photography. It was the year before their son was run over by the train, and Jenny wanted Wallace in the painting, too, but Harold said no, he wanted this one to be just the two of them. It was a small thing. How could Harold know? But Jenny blamed him for that more than she did some of his larger, more obvious failings in years to come.

Georgia pulls the portrait out into the dim light of the naked overhead bulb.

"I can't believe Jenny and Harold were ever this young," she says as much to herself as to William Blackwell, who only grunts.

William gets his second son, Ike, to help him move enough boxes so that they can get the dresser out. Georgia brings the van around to the porch behind the storage room, and in half an hour, her meager, undeserved inheritance is, as William says, "good to go."

He seems sincere in inviting her to stay for supper—"Hell, I bet we could even scare up a beer or two if you want to sit and talk"—but Georgia says she'll take a rain check.

More like an ice check, she mutters to herself as she backs out of the driveway, trying to avoid children who don't seem disposed to move at all as she eyes them in the rearview mirror. When hell freezes over.

The boy she saw earlier, no more than 5 years old with white-blond hair, stands in the dirt, picking his nose. They make eye contact and he gives her the finger, then finally runs to the other side of the yard when she stops and opens the door.

The big part-shepherd chases the van for half a mile. He seems to actually be trying to bite the tires. Georgia has the sense, as she turns on to the state road, that she is leaving a foreign country.

"Blackwells Über Alles," she mutters.

Back at the house, Leeza is in the kitchen, leaning against the counter and holding a recipe book she must have brought down with her. She's frowning.

"Oh, hi," she says when she sees Georgia come in. "I was just looking for something good to cook tonight."

Georgia believes she manages to catch the grimace before it reaches her face. The last time Leeza "cooked" for them, there was a scene involving bloody chicken, tears and a quick call to Pizza Hut. Leeza has not had much experience cooking; she's been taught most of what she knows from Justin, who learned how to render several classes of plants and animals appetizing during his Peace Corps days.

"What're you thinking about fixing?" Georgia asks.

"Oh, I dunno. Here's one I've always liked. We had it once in this cool restaurant when Dad took us to New York. Beef Wellington."

"Hmm. Beef Wellington." Hell, Georgia thinks, why not try something hard? "Well, that's always kind of intimidated me. Tell you what: If you'll wait until I get my shiftless son to help me move this stuff out of the van, I'll show you a great recipe for roast beef. It's a no-brainer.

"I mean," she says quickly, gun-shy about accidental insults, "even I can do it."

Georgia, who has made a passable beef Wellington on a handful of occasions, has faced the sulking (Leeza's) and wrath (Justin's) before when feelings were hurt over kitchen prowess. As she walks out the screen door in search of her son, who is supposed to be "doing something with Kenny," she sees her possibly-future daughter-in-law still poring over the cookbook, perhaps ready to take on beef Wellington just to show Georgia she can, which she can't.

As the day fades, the wind has picked up and the weather has turned chilly, as if November is finally bringing fall to the Carolina coastal plain. Georgia's sweater is overmatched, but she doesn't want to go back inside just now.

She spots two figures across the field and sees that Justin and Kenny are playing golf on the little two-hole course Justin has taken to calling Little Augusta. While she is still 100 yards away, Justin takes a swing and they both yell "Fore." The ball is invisible to Georgia, who's staring into the low-hanging sun. She can only put her hands over her head and turn away from them until she hears a "thunk" in the near-distance.

"Sorry," Kenny says as they walk toward her. "We weren't expecting an audience today. The gallery's usually not much of a problem out here."

He and her son seem to genuinely like each other. They do have some history, although it's pretty much ancient history by now. Kenny did teach her son how to drive the unsettled summer he turned 16, the summer she abandoned him and he ran away to be with his grandfather. They haven't really stayed in touch over the years, but something's clicking. Maybe, she thinks, shared blood.

Some of it, she supposes, is the farm.

She teased Kenny gently about his love of farming the week she arrived, wondering if there possibly was a more unlikely way to get rich.

"You know what they say," she'd told him. "The way to make a small fortune is take a large fortune and go into farming."

"Or," he said, "you could teach English."

"I guess we're just not genetically disposed to make money," she said, then blushed as he offered an uncertain laugh.

But what to make of Justin? He never showed any desire to get dirt under his fingernails until he was past 22, but he has come home from Guatemala with what Georgia not-so-secretly hopes are only temporarily different priorities.

Of all things, they taught him just enough about agriculture to make him dangerous and sent him out to show native farmers how to build better storage bins for their grain so the rats wouldn't eat it. This seemed wrong to Georgia, when she first heard of it, in so many ways. How arrogant for the Peace Corps or anyone to come into another country and presume to tell people who had been farming the land since well before Columbus that they had been doing it all wrong. How ridiculous to send a sociology major from the University of Virginia, born and bred in the suburbs, to break

64

the news to them. How outrageous that they couldn't have him teaching them English or something he actually knew.

"But, Mom," Justin had written, "some of it they *are* doing wrong. We can learn a lot from them, but they can learn something from us, too. And if they don't have grain, they have to starve or give up their land and move to some shantytown on the edge of a big city, where they'll be worse off than they are here. Besides, I'm teaching them English, too. Or at least their kids."

So, Justin came back with more of an affinity for the land than Georgia has ever been able to conjure. To her, the farm was something to escape. There was no poetry in the land where she worked as little as she could, dreaming of a day when her world would be all tidy lawns and suburban streets and rooms that smelled like books.

Once, the last summer before college, her father asked her to take a ride with him in his old pickup. He was going out to look at the lush acres where he was making a good living growing strawberries, blueberries, cantaloupes, watermelons and a wide variety of other food that enticed city people from Port Campbell and travelers off what was then the closest road leading to and from Florida. It is land from which Annie Belle Geddie and her son, Blue, still prosper, according to Kenny, "in spite of what they tell you."

It was June of 1966, and everything was thriving. There had been enough rain but not too much, and early summer had been mild by North Carolina standards. He drove them over the fields, through dirt lanes crisscrossing the land, waving and occasionally chatting with the men and women working there. He stopped the truck beneath a lone shade tree, a sycamore, beside the creek.

"Listen," Littlejohn McCain had said to his daughter, after they had sat there for several seconds. "Just listen."

Georgia listened, and then shrugged and looked at her father. "What?"

He seemed genuinely disappointed that she couldn't hear it, too.

"If you sit real still," he said, "you can hear things growing. I don't know what it is exactly, but there's a hum almost, underneath everything else, like the land is alive."

Georgia was only wishing by this time that the truck had a radio, and air conditioning. They were starting to attract mosquitoes and gnats.

She really did try to listen, though. She wanted to at least humor her father, whom she loved but who represented The Farm and thus must be escaped.

But she couldn't hear it, and she told him so.

"I reckon you hear it or you don't," he'd said, speaking softy and looking across in the eastern distance to the Blue Sandhills. "It ain't possible to make somebody hear something if their ears can't pick it up."

They sat quietly for a few more minutes, hardly talking at all. After what seemed like a decent interval, she asked if they could go back to the house, that the bugs were eating her up.

He started the old truck.

When they returned, and before she could escape the great outdoors, he put his big, freckled right hand over her small, tan left one.

"I know this isn't what you want," he said. "It's probably good you're going off to school and all. Some people's got a life for themselves that's somewhere else altogether, and they've got to go find it. I was lucky, I reckon. I didn't have to move.

"You're going to do just fine, whatever you do. But I want you to know, if things ever get tough, and sometimes they can, you've always got you a home, right here. Don't forget that."

She said she wouldn't, and she was moved to kiss his stubbly cheek. He already seemed so old to her, just turned 60, and this was his benediction. He'd hardly ever said so many words to her at one time. He tended to hoard them for special occasions.

She understands now, and has for a painful while, what he meant about tough times, how they come to everyone. She's always been proud, though, that she never did come limping back home, no matter what. She's here now, she assures herself and everyone else, to sell the farm and get the hell out.

So why does her son, so removed from all this, seem somehow drawn back to a world he only experienced peripherally, for one brief, needy summer?

Maybe, she thinks, it skips a generation.

Maybe East Geddie is just another foreign culture to absorb.

Maybe, he just wants to drive me crazy.

When you were down in Guatemala, she wants to ask him if the time is ever right, and you were helping those farmers keep the rats out of their grain, did you ever hear things growing?

She'd like to know.

The three of them, with Leeza opening doors and helping as much as she can, get the dresser moved into an unused back room. Georgia invites Kenny to stay for dinner, but he says he can't, that he has to go somewhere.

"I'm sure," Georgia says with a smirk. He shakes his head, almost smiling.

To Georgia's relief, Leeza does decide that beef Wellington might be too ambitious, and she does let Georgia show her a tried-and-true recipe for roast beef that involves little more than opening a can of mushroom soup and slicing an onion.

While they wait for the roast to cook, Georgia suggests that they play Scrabble. She and Justin have always enjoyed it and are well-matched rivals. Leeza has played with them on a couple of occasions, but not well. It will do her good, Georgia thinks, to be challenged, expand her mind with something besides television and poorly written thrillers.

Justin is lukewarm to her suggestion, and Leeza seems chilly to the idea.

"Come on," Georgia pleads. "Just a quick game. We're not playing for money or anything."

"Just blood," Leeza says, and then laughs nervously when Georgia looks at her.

Justin and Leeza finally consent, and Georgia retrieves the faded set she found in the attic her first week down, the same one she and her mother once used. Littlejohn would play, too, on occasion, but he'd been illiterate for the first half of his life, and despite his late-quenched thirst for knowledge, he never was more than token opposition.

She and her mother did play for blood, Georgia has to admit, challenging questionable words, sending each other to the dictionary, sometimes outright arguing about the legitimacy of a word, dictionary be damned.

But she and Justin don't play that way. At least, she doesn't think they do.

Georgia has to start peeling and mashing the potatoes 20 minutes before the roast is done, and she will admit later to herself that she does chafe a little when Leeza takes so much time to come up with what often turns out to be a depressingly simple word.

There are only a few letters left to be uncovered when Leeza's turn comes around. Georgia, poker-faced, is trying not to look at the bottom middle triple-word space. She is trailing Justin by only 10 points, and he's just given her an unexpected chance at salvation by putting "bush" horizontally in such a position that the "u" is two letters above the triple word and one below a double-letter space. Q-U-I-T. Sixty-nine points, and dump the Q to boot. Game, set, match.

She has already won, in her head, when Leeza puts the S and the E beneath the U. "Use," she says, smiling apologetically. "Nine points. Sorry, that's all I can do."

"Well," Georgia says, feeling her face flush, "it's enough. Enough to keep me from using this damn Q. Well, that's it for me. You all finish up. I've got to fix those mashed potatoes."

She knows she's being childish, and she knows she's put a damper on what was a pleasant interlude with her son and the mother of her grandchild, but she can't help it.

"I didn't do it on purpose," Leeza says, but Georgia wonders.

She can't resist scratching the forbidden itch.

"You know, Leeza," she says, "if you've got a S, you can do so many things. You can get, what, 22 points by putting one of the end of this word here, even if you don't make up another word. Or you can get probably even more over here. Just *think*."

"I am thinking," Leeza says, and Georgia sees that she has bullied the girl nearly to tears. "But I never played this damn game until you and Justin showed me how."

"I'm sorry," Georgia says. She truly is, but it's a case, she suspects, of too little, too late, mouth outdistancing brain again. She doesn't know why Leeza sometimes sets her off. She is one of the most open, sweet-natured people Georgia knows. She sometimes suspects that she is predisposed to take advantage of such guilelessness, disrespecting it as a character flaw rather than the product of a conscious effort at goodness. And then, Georgia thinks, there's the daughter-in-law thing, *assuming she ever is my daughter-in-law. If she's so sweet and innocent, why'd she let my son knock her up?*

"You know, Mom," Justin says, a hard edge to his voice that cuts through Georgia and makes her draw up inside, "being queen of Scrabble doesn't exactly make you ruler of the world. I mean, the last time we played hearts, Leeza kicked your butt, I believe."

"Yeah," Leeza says, timidly.

It's true. Georgia never has been a great card player. She's never really liked card games that much, has always told herself they were too simple, not mentally stimulating enough.

"Well, anyway," she says, retreating with her glass of white wine to the kitchen, "I'm sorry."

They have a too-quiet dinner, a good roast wasted. Afterward, Justin does the dishes and Leeza says she's tired and wants to go to bed. It's almost nine o'clock. Georgia volunteers to help clean up so she can join him, but he declines her offer.

Self-defeated, Georgia retreats to her own bedroom. First, though, she goes to take a quick look at her small inheritance from Jenny McLaurin.

She takes out the old photo albums and flips through them, taking much more time than she had planned, because the past keeps coming up at her from pictures that go back more than a century. Jenny has scribbled names in barely legible pencil on the back of most, but some of them will never be identified.

There are brownish-yellow photographs of her father as a boy, one of him standing next to his brother Lafe, the one he accidentally shot and killed. Lafe's resemblance to Justin, the way she remembers him when he was 14 or 15, shakes her. They're all there: the frowning grandmother she barely remembers, old Red John McCain, the grandfather who fought in the Civil War and died more than 20 years before Georgia was born, all of Littlejohn's brothers and sisters, including Century, Jenny's mother, who doesn't look much like her at all. There are no photographs of Wallace.

"I would've done that, too," Georgia mutters.

In another drawer, there are what seem like hundreds of letters, saved for decades. Letters from the '30s, from World War II, from distant, now-dead relatives in Georgia and Florida and California, from people whose names in careful cursive script on the envelopes ring only the vaguest of bells.

Georgia has been known to read letters and postcards sent to and from total strangers when they fall unwanted into the world of estate sales and cheap antique stores. She knows she could all into a bottomless pit here, waking up face-down on the bedspread tomorrow morning with the soothing scent of old paper all around her.

When she looks at her watch, she sees that it's almost midnight.

Then, as she is about to tear herself away from it all, she sees her own name and address. It's a Christmas card, she can tell from the envelope, sent five years before, when Georgia still sent Christmas cards. She reads her own barely legible handwriting: "Best wishes. Hope to see you over the holidays. Love, Georgia." Not that they had any plans of coming down to East Geddie that Christmas. She can remember that December, how tired she'd become of writing "all these goddamn cards," swearing she'd never do it again. And she didn't. But Jenny had saved it.

Shuffling through the old stacks, she finds three more, all Christmas cards from earlier years. She remembers that they'd usually consign Jenny to the 'B' stack, sending her the cheaper, more treacly, more (God forbid) religious cards while saving the more expensive, more ecumenical ones (Season's Greetings; Happy Holidays; Peace), for other, more important people.

Georgia sighs, then starts trying to stuff all the loose letters back into the drawer. Finally, she has to put some of them in the next drawer down, and that's where she sees the jewelry box.

70

She had forgotten it, and now, finding it, she has no great curiosity. It isn't likely that Jenny McLaurin left her any precious gems.

Then, Georgia remembers something.

She opens the box, but all she encounters is a collection of earrings, necklaces and bracelets that could not possibly be worth $300 total.

Well, she probably would have been wearing it, anyhow. The sheriff and the funeral home just forgot to mention it. Or she lost it. Or sold it because she was broke and her sorry-ass nearest kin didn't even ask if she needed help.

"Good Lord," Georgia says. It's after 1 o'clock. Fatigue dampens her frisson over this minor mystery, one she's sure Forsythia Crumpler can easily clear up.

CHAPTER EIGHT

November 10

At church Sunday, Georgia learned that her old teacher was away visiting a cousin in Goldsboro and wouldn't be back until sometime Tuesday.

Now, on Wednesday morning, while Justin is taking Leeza to the obstetrician they've found in Port Campbell, Georgia calls her.

"Mrs. Crumpler?"

"Who is this?"

"I'm sorry. This is Georgia? Georgia McCain? Sorry to disturb you." She's always apologizing to this woman, always reduced to seventh-grade status by her. "I was wondering if I could come by. There's something I have to ask you, if you could spare a couple of minutes."

There's a short pause.

"Give me two hours. I'm doing laundry. Come about 1."

"Thank you, Mrs. Crumpler. I won't take up much of your time."

There's no answer on the other end.

"Well," Georgia says, "goodbye."

"Goodbye."

"Jesus," Georgia mutters as she hangs up.

Thinking about Jenny's wedding ring, she looks down at her own, which she perversely continues to wear, despite the fact that it can sometimes send her mind tumbling back where she tries very hard not to let it go.

She was 41 when she married for the second time, in May of 1989. Mark Hammaker was 49.

"In fun years," one of her friends told her, "he's about 87."

The marriage had not been the best of ideas. After a trip to Europe the summer before – with Justin shipped off to his grandfather's farm – had ended with them going their separate ways, they both thought that they might be, at best, occasional lovers. He was too anal. She was too irresponsible.

Maybe it was loss that brought them back together. Her father died that summer. Mark, also an only child, lost his mother unexpectedly in November. Maybe it was just mutual sympathy. Georgia thought she saw a more flexible man after his mother's death. She had been happy to have strong arms in which to fall, and happy to nurture him when it was his turn to mourn.

One thing that made it at least possible was what Georgia thought of as the new, improved Justin. His dislike for Mark ebbed after his summer of exile in East Geddie, at least partly because there was nothing much now for the man Justin had called "Mark the Narc" to carp about.

Justin came back to Montclair more focused, less rebellious. It was as if a switch had been turned on, or off. Georgia wondered if the precocious university brats didn't just grow up more quickly, fast-forwarding through all the angst and mess, turning unexpectedly adult at 16. She knew it didn't happen that way with all of them, though.

Maybe he was just—like her—getting over the divorce. Jeff Bowman's departure had really kick-started that very bad year-and-a-half in which Georgia lost both parents and her first husband.

There was no more talk by Mark of Justin going to some military school, of "straightening him out." Georgia never would have let that happen, but now it was a moot point. Justin had self-corrected, and while he would never really bond with Mark, there was a truce.

"As long as you love him," Justin told Georgia when she asked permission to marry from the only other male who mattered to her anymore, "I'll keep my mouth shut. I promise. Just don't try to make me call him Dad."

It wasn't a problem for very long. Actually, for the 13 months she and Mark were married, Justin was no problem at all. He made only one B his junior and senior years, got into the University of Virginia and was her rock.

She needed a rock. Mark Hammaker, it turned out, was more of a dead weight than something on which to lean.

They had their first married argument on their honeymoon. On a cruise of the Greek isles, he was appalled when he learned that Georgia had signed up for the optional parasailing excursion. He acted as if she had lost her mind, and he sulked when she floated back down, landing softly as a leaf on the small boat that had launched her.

"It's just like being strapped to a kite," she told Mark. "You need to loosen up, sweetie."

"You need to tighten up," he responded.

Good God, she thought when they went back, silently, to the cabin, what have I done? Jeff Bowman, for all his faults, at least was capable of having fun. He just had a zipper problem.

They rode it out, and when they couldn't stand it any longer, they got a divorce that involved considerably less blood-letting and paperwork than her first one. They had agreed it would be wise to have a pre-nuptial agreement "just in case."

By the time Mark Hammaker moved out, Justin was ready to graduate from high school and leave, too. He had a job that summer at a record store, and Georgia spent a lot of time getting used to, for the first time in her life, an empty house. She had gone from their old farmhouse in East Geddie to dormitory rooms and apartments to married life with hardly a night spent by herself, it seemed to her in 1990. After Jeff left, there was Justin to take care of, to keep her company.

Now, she was alone.

She got a cat, and while it was rather companionable, for a cat, it was not much of a conversationalist. Get used to it, she told herself. Be a big girl. This is how it is.

And that was how it was, for most of the next four years. She bought a new, smaller house, a mile from the university. She went out with old and new friends, she managed to get laid occasionally—it was easier now, with Justin gone at least nine months of the year. She threw herself into teaching. She took trips to Europe,

74

using some of the money she inherited from her father. She even had a book published, by another university press, on Fitzgerald's short stories.

By the time she met Phil Macomb in January of 1994, she was not entirely unhappy with the thought of never again sharing her bed on a full-time basis. Only occasionally, on such occasions as snowy evenings or when the first dogwoods started blooming, did she think freedom might be overrated.

He was not part of her usual crowd. He was not part of any crowd with which she had ever associated. He could, she told friends, actually do things. He ran his own home-construction company that specialized in renovating the old redbrick Virginia houses in the Montclair area that were drawing the come-heres from all over the East Coast. He was a genius at doing small, creative work.

Georgia first met him when she decided to get gas logs for her fireplace. She needed someone to repair all the damaged walls and ceilings left after the gas line had been run from her kitchen to the living room. A friend said Phil Macomb was the man, if you could get him to come. He was very busy.

It took her two months to lure him out. He'd canceled twice by then, and she was not disposed to like him very much. She had told herself she would give him one more chance. She didn't want to be rash. Good home-construction help was hard to find.

She'd only talked to him on the phone, knew only that he had a thick, old-Virginia accent, the kind you usually heard among the idle rich rather than blue-collar types.

When she answered the door that day, a tall, somewhat heavyset man with red hair and a neatly trimmed beard stood, holding his toolbox in one hand. He was not unhandsome, with a good nose, good chin, broad shoulders and blue, untroubled eyes. He had an easy smile and an outdoorsman's tan.

He spent five hours there that day, constructing three different covers for places where the pipes wouldn't go inside the thick terra cotta walls. He went out once to a local hardware store and came back with just the right materials to build her a cover for the shutoff valve. He even painted everything. When he was through, the violence visited upon her house by the gas man was invisible.

She'd been home that day, and they talked. Georgia didn't usually do that. She usually felt uncomfortable among the various plumbers, tree surgeons and air-conditioning repairmen whose services she needed from time to time. But Phil Macomb was easy to talk with. Mark had said on more than one occasion that the best reporters who worked for him at the paper were all good listeners. She thought that Phil Macomb would have been a good reporter.

He was from a reasonably well-off family that had made such fortune as it had on real estate, but he'd married young, divorced and managed to flunk out of VMI, James Madison and Randolph-Macon over a five-year span.

He had always been good with his hands, he told her. ("Only thing between me and the poorhouse.") He had been running his own company for more than a decade.

"I doubt if my momma will ever think I've amounted to anything, though," he said. "She thinks you have to have a couple of degrees on the wall to be a success." He looked at her own wall, with the three diplomas hanging there, and blushed. "No offense."

"None taken. My father was one of the smartest men I ever knew, and he didn't even learn how to read until he was older than you."

"Lot of that going around. I don't suppose they even called it a 'learning disability' back then. 'Course, I had a judgment disability, too."

They made eye contact for no more than a second, but there was something she saw, some question that needed answering. It was a strange thing, Georgia thought later, how you talked to people all the time, face to face, without really making that one laser-sharp connection. Then, out of nowhere, a guy like Phil Macomb shows up, and there it is.

She got him a beer, after he was done, and they sat and talked for a few minutes more. He said he had another job to do, and when he waved goodbye, she supposed that she might see him again, the next time something needed fixing that was beyond her meager talents.

Two nights later, he called her.

"I don't suppose you have a lot of free spots on your dance card, pretty as you are," he said, with almost no preamble, "but it occurred to me after I left that I'd sure like to see you sometime. Socially, or whatever."

She told him that, actually, she hadn't been doing a lot of dancing lately, had turned into kind of a wallflower.

He said he hadn't been doing much shagging either, but he thought he remembered how, if she'd like to join him.

"What kind of shagging are you talking about?"

"Aw, Miz Georgia," he said with an exaggerated drawl. "I love it when you talk dirty."

She went out with him two times before the night they slept together, once to a county high school basketball game because his son was the coach at one of the outlying schools, once to dinner. He turned down her invitation to come back to her place for coffee both times, kissing her goodnight at the door as if she were 17.

He'd been married and divorced before he knew where babies came from, he told her on the first date, when she expressed surprise that he could have a son in his mid-20s. He kept up with his two children from a reserved, polite distance.

"It isn't much to brag about," he said, "but I am a little better person now that I'm fully grown. I don't suppose my son and daughter have a lot of great memories from back then. It wasn't exactly the Waltons."

He had sent them checks and Christmas presents, mostly.

After the basketball game, which his son's team won, Georgia asked him if he wasn't going to go down and speak to him.

"No," he said. "He doesn't need me right now. When he needed me, I wasn't there. I'll talk to him later."

The third date, they went to a movie, one with more dialogue than action, recommended by Georgia. She moved close to him in the dark and chilly theater and felt for a moment like they should be doing at least some light petting. His body was warmer than hers, and she leaned into it.

She had asked a friend who knew the Macombs how old her new boyfriend was. The friend said she wasn't sure, but she thought he'd graduated from high school in 1969. Georgia wondered if she should lie about her age. Three years might be enough to scare even a seemingly good man like Phil Macomb away.

That night, after the movie, they were sitting at a table in one of Phil's hangouts when he took her hand in his and she realized that the hard piece of metal pinching her finger was his class ring from high school. She picked it up and looked at it as if admiring its workmanship.

"Class of '68," he said, looking her in the eye, amused. "I'm two years younger than you. Cradle-robber."

"How . . . How do you know how old I am?" She realized she was blushing and hoped the lights were low enough to mask it. "And what's it to you?"

"Asked around," he said, grinning. "After all, I need to know these things. I wouldn't want to do something to get a senior citizen overexcited. Not sure your poor old body could handle a lot of vigorous activity."

She'd had a couple of drinks already, and she supposed that loosened her tongue a little.

She told him that she was sure she could handle any vigor he might be willing to throw her decrepit way.

"I might take you up on that," he'd said, playing along, moving his head closer to hers across the table and lowering his voice. "You'd have to sign a release form, of course. Wouldn't want you on my conscience."

She took her shoe off under the table and ran her foot up his pants leg.

"You're not just offering an old lady a mercy fuck, are you?" she asked, looking him right in the eye, smiling just enough to indicate that she might be kidding, or she might not.

She didn't know what made her say that. She didn't want Phil Macomb to be some kind of one-night wonder. She'd had three of those in the last year.

She'd heard the joke about a guy's perfect date being one that turns into a pizza after sex. She was too kind to tell any of the men with whom she'd slept that it could work both ways, that she had a strong urge to call Domino's after they had fully explored the only subject in which they both were interested.

But Phil Macomb wasn't like that. She thought he might be a keeper.

He looked stunned, for a couple of seconds, and then he burst out laughing, drawing the attention of people at the tables around them. Most of what he did, Georgia was learning, he did loud.

"Old lady," he said, lowering his voice again, "if that were to happen, the one showing the mercy would be you. It would be one of the most merciful things anybody had ever done for me."

"Call me Mother Teresa," Georgia said, never taking her eyes off his.

She had to concede that it might have been nothing more than pheromones that first drew her to him, although she had come, by the third date, to appreciate his sense of humor, his ability to listen and what appeared to be a basic decency.

Nevertheless, there was the sex. She didn't remember having a better night in bed, and he swore she was the best he'd ever had. " 'Had?' " she'd said. "You make me sound like dinner." But she was secretly pleased. She hoped he wasn't just being kind.

And, after two hours of pleasantly wearing each other out, they found that neither wanted the other to turn into fast food. They talked about things that Georgia had never talked about with Jeff, and certainly not with Mark. In the weeks to come, they explored each other like children with new toys, playing sexual games they would never reveal to anyone else.

By April, she was more or less living in the old farmhouse he'd fixed up. She sometimes missed the comforts of solitary life, being able to do exactly what she wanted, dress how she wanted, eat what she wanted, but by May she wouldn't have gone back for anything and accepted that some people are supposed to live with other people.

They were married that June, in a very simple ceremony attended only by a few close friends. Justin came up from Atlanta, where he was in the first year of a master's program in sociology that he still hasn't finished, to give her away.

It all seemed to Georgia like payback for a lifetime of struggling with bad marriage karma, or bad judgment. She and Jeff Bowman had been too immature. She and Mark Hammaker had been too ill-suited.

79

But she hadn't said yes at first. Phil Macomb had to truly beg her, sure as she was that she was doomed to suffer in marriage. Why, she asked him, can't we just live together?

"We can live together," he said. "We can do that. But what I really want, more than I want food or air, is to have you with me in every way possible. I've been waiting my whole life for you, and I don't want to cheapen it, don't want to cheapen you."

Georgia thought the whole idea of cheapening anything was quaint, after everything that had gone before, but she came to see that he wanted her so much, that he wanted to always be there, that he would always be there. By the time she agreed, two weeks before the wedding, she was sure that he always would be.

* * *

She pulls into Forsythia Crumpler's driveway right on time and walks with no little trepidation toward the house.

Her old teacher answers the door on the third ring and lets her in.

"I'm sorry to disturb you like this," Georgia says, "but there's something I have to ask you."

"Before you do," the older woman says, holding up her hand, "I've got to say something. I was wrong the other day, raking you over the coals and all, especially after all you've been through this year."

"It's . . ."

"No, I've always had a bad habit of butting into other people's business. I don't think you did Jenny wrong. I know you'd have helped her if you'd known. I ought to have told you. I was just so upset."

Forsythia Crumpler seems to be near tears, something Georgia hasn't seen before.

"No," she says, putting a hand on Forsythia's shoulder, "you were right. I've been thinking about it. I asked myself what Daddy or Mom would have done, and they wouldn't have let this happen."

"People are busier today, get distracted more. They don't live in the same town."

The old woman grows silent.

80

"Thank you," Georgia tells her. "Thank you for your forgiveness. It means a lot to me."

They go inside and sit down to tea cakes and coffee. They talk about old times, former teacher and star student again. Forsythia tells her how sorry she was to learn about her husband.

"I heard about it from Jenny," she says. "I should have sent a card."

"Lucky in something, unlucky in love," Georgia says with a shrug. "I can't remember what it is I'm supposed to be lucky in, though. Maybe I ought to start playing the lottery."

"Lottery!" her host says, some of her old vinegar returning. "They're trying to get it down here. A tax on morons.

"Well, what was it you wanted to ask me about?"

So Georgia tells her about the ring.

* * *

Jenny McLaurin didn't have much that the world might have called valuable. The house and land were about all she and Harold ever possessed. There was one thing, though. Harold had given her a wedding ring that was her pride and joy.

He'd won it, she would find out later, off a rich young man in one of the Saturday night poker games that were held in the back of Dawson Autry's store. The games were very egalitarian affairs, a chance for the dirt farmers and laborers to rub shoulders with lawyers and prosperous businessmen trying to show they had the common touch.

They way it usually worked out, the rich got richer. It was much easier for a man with $200 in his pocket to bluff than it was for one with twenty that he really needed to turn into forty. If one was a politician or wished to be one, it was wise to lose a little back at the end, though, a gesture as close to *noblesse oblige* as one was likely to find in eastern Scots County after the war.

One November night, though, Harold McLaurin's luck turned temporarily good.

He was in a game of seven-card stud, deuces wild, with two men he'd known since they were children, plus a barber from

Geddie and a newly minted lawyer who'd come out from Port Campbell. The lawyer was the only son of a state senator, and everybody figured the boy would be one someday, too. He even had his father's name, with just another roman number attached. They called him Trip. People in Scots County tended to vote for familiar names, preferring the devil they knew.

The young lawyer had been drinking. What he'd had before he arrived, no one knew, but they'd encouraged him to try some of Parker Vinson's moonshine, and he no doubt thought that was part of the whole slumming experience, something to talk about after church the next day with other young members of his father's club.

He was winning at first, and then he was losing. One man who was watching said he had $300 on him when he came in. By 1:30 that morning, he was down to a few dollars he'd fished from his pockets, the detritus of 20-dollar bills he'd broken much earlier.

The last hand he played, he bet almost all of that on a pair of kings, a 5 and a 7, with two cards down. Only he and Harold McLaurin were still in the game and eligible to get the last face-down card. When he put the rest of his money in and got a third king, he knew he would win and have a great story to tell. One of his other "down" cards was a deuce.

When Harold anted up five dollars on the strength of his last card, the young lawyer couldn't find anyone to loan him the five he needed. There were a dozen people watching, and they were mostly pulling for one of their own.

"Give me one minute," the lawyer said, and he stumbled out the door to his car.

He returned carrying a small velvet box.

"Bitch gave it back," he'd said. "What'm I gonna do with a used diamond ring?"

He'd been carrying the two-carat ring around in the glove compartment of his car for two weeks, since Betsy McNeil found out who he had really visited on his last trip to Raleigh. (They would later marry anyhow after he bought her another, larger diamond. Then, a year later, they would divorce. The young lawyer would die a decade afterward in the snow outside a bar in Lincoln, Nebraska, shot through the heart, disbarred and disgraced.)

Nobody in the back room had ever seen a diamond that big. A couple of the spectators, if the conditions had been right, would have bashed his skull in for it.

"Tell you what," he said over the raw pine table to Harold McLaurin, who had more or less quit drinking two hours before, taking only the tiniest sip when the communal jar came around. "I'll bet this ring here against 50 dollars. If you've got the balls."

No one had ever accused Harold McLaurin of lack of nerve. His faults lay more in the area of patience and compassion. He might have slapped the lawyer across the room, but he knew what that diamond was worth, how painful it would be in the morning for the city boy to realize he'd lost it in a poker game to some redneck. It would not be a story he would repeat at the club. He would be glad none of his friends had come slumming to East Geddie with him.

Harold McLaurin was showing a jack, a 10, a 9 and a deuce. He counted his money, and all he had was 46 dollars.

One of the men who had refused to loan the lawyer a five handed one to Harold and got a dollar bill back.

To the lawyer's hurt, accusing look, he shrugged, "Well, I didn't think I could afford to lend five. Four, though, that's another matter."

There was rough laughter around the room.

"Let's see what you got," Harold said.

The lawyer showed the deuce and the king to go with the other two.

"Four kings."

Harold didn't say anything, just turned over the pair of face-down aces he'd drawn first, to go with the wild deuce that was showing. Then, he flipped the last card to reveal the other deuce.

The lawyer looked at the four aces. He looked at Harold, looked around the room, looked back at the table. His options seemed to be limited.

He was still sober enough to grasp what he had done.

"Tell you what," he said to Harold. "If you'll let me pawn this thing tomorrow, I'll bring the fifty right to your house, have it in your hands before you go to church."

83

"I don't go to church," Harold said. He reached for the ring when the young lawyer did, and the lawyer yielded first. "We didn't play for no IOU. We played for this"—he pointed to the velvet box, now closed—"and my fifty dollars."

There was unanimous agreement around the table, and Dawson Autry himself, who had suffered some property damage in the past from disagreements over cards and money, gently but firmly helped the young man back to his late-model car and pointed him toward Port Campbell.

The lawyer actually did come to see Harold the next day, at his parents' house, where he was living until he and Jenny could get married. He was sober and hinted at legal ramifications if Harold didn't take the hundred dollars he had in his hand, five crisp twenties, double what Harold had bet.

"You're on our land now," Harold told him. "You'd best be going. You go on and sic your daddy on us, if you want, but I don't expect it'll be worth it. I don't think he's a good enough lawyer to get that ring back, do you?"

He'd moved very close to the young lawyer, almost but not quite touching him. The other man backed away.

He promised that Harold hadn't heard the last of it, but Harold knew he had.

The next week, he gave the ring to Jenny, who would have married him anyway.

* * *

"So," Georgia says, "the ring always meant a lot. Somebody would always bring that story up, although I don't think Jenny liked to tell it as much as Harold did."

"I expect not."

"But I don't remember seeing it, and nobody from the sheriff's department or at the funeral home mentioned anything about a ring being on her hand. Did they to you?"

"No."

"And you were the one that found her? They said you identified her."

"I identified her, but I wasn't the first one there."

"You weren't?" Georgia wonders how it is that no one told her that before.

"No. I thought you knew. It was that big fat boy of William Blackwell's, the one they call Pooh. He came knocking on my door, all out of breath—which wouldn't have taken much—and said 'Miss Jenny has drownded..'

"So, he found her."

"Yes. They did come by once every blue moon, to keep her from changing the will, if nothing else. I called the rescue squad and went out with him, and there she was. By the time I got out there, he had managed to snag her dress, I suppose, with a stick and dragged her to the edge of the pond . . ."

Forsythia Crumpler stops and pulls out a Kleenex.

"I just feel terrible about not checking on her after church. I just assumed she didn't feel like coming to services that morning. Sometimes she didn't."

"Well, the coroner said she'd been dead several hours. There wasn't anything you could have done."

Then Georgia tells her about the jewelry box she inherited, how it occurred to her that the ring might be in there, but it wasn't.

The older woman frowns and is silent for a few seconds before speaking.

"Yes. Goodness, I hadn't thought about the ring. She was very fond of it. I remember she told me once, must have been two or three years ago, that sometimes her hands swelled so much from the arthritis that she couldn't wear it. She said she took it off at bedtime every night and then would see the next morning whether that was going to be a 'ring day' or not.

"Maybe she put it in a safety deposit box."

"There's no record of her or Harold having one, at least not with their bank. I checked. You know, Mrs. Crumpler, I don't care about that ring, for me. I hope you know that. Daddy left us more than we deserve. But it's just eating at me that it's disappeared. She loved that ring. She wouldn't have been careless with it."

Forsythia Crumpler nods and then frowns.

"Well, if it wasn't on her finger and it wasn't in her jewelry box . . ."

Exactly, Georgia thinks. Exactly.

When she gets back to the house, she calls the sheriff's office, where a secretary tells her Sheriff Hairr is busy "presently" but will call her back "directly."

She only has to wait 15 minutes. Apparently, old classmates do get some special treatment.

"Thank you for returning my call so soon, Wade, uh, Sheriff. Sorry."

"Not a problem, Georgia." He has his sheriff's voice on, a mix of Gary Cooper and Buford Pusser. "What can I do for you?"

She tells him about the ring, asks him if anybody recalled seeing one on Jenny's finger or anywhere else, either at the pond or in the rescue vehicle or at the mortuary.

"Well," he says, after a pause, "now that you mention it, I don't think anybody said anything about a ring, and I sure don't remember seeing one. What kind was it? I mean, how big was it?"

Two carats, Georgia tells him.

He whistles.

"Well," he says, "there are some folks around here who are full of meanness, I won't argue that point, but I can't imagine somebody stealing a wedding ring off a drowned woman's finger. . . . no offense."

"And I understand Pooh Blackwell, William's boy, was the first one to find her."

"That's the way I heard it."

"And he didn't see any sign of it, either?"

"Not that I know of. I can ask him."

"Would you?"

"No problem. You know, he's just about completely moved into Jenny's place. Saw him the other day, burning some stuff out back. Had to remind him to get a fire permit."

Georgia thanks Wade Hairr again and hangs up.

Just then, Justin and Leeza come in.

"They say it might be a Christmas baby," Leeza says, her excitement evident.

"Wouldn't that be something?" Georgia says, still preoccupied. She sees Justin looking at her the way she used to look at him when she would catch him picking his nose in public.

"That's really great," she says. "Christmas. Wouldn't that be amazing?" She flounders around for something that will show interest in her first grandchild. She really does care, but she's a little distracted right now.

"Ah, have you decided on a name yet?"

Another sore point. After they told her they wanted to be surprised, didn't want to know what the baby's sex would be, they'd also given her their list of boys' and girls' names. One of the female names had been Alysyn. Another had been Maree.

Georgia had looked at the list of names and could not stop herself from remarking that a girl bearing either of those names was going to spend a lot of her life spelling it out.

"Like Leeza with a 'z'?" Leeza had said.

Leeza tells her that they have pared the boys' names down to Gregg ("Three g's," Justin says, daring his mother to challenge it) and Mack. "Just Mack?" Georgia wants to say, but doesn't. One small step for diplomacy.

CHAPTER NINE

November 13

It might have been better, a couple of people suggest gently, to have had the yard sale in October, before the weather turned.

The few bargain-hunters who have come are walking around the big table on the screened back porch, their only refuge from a drenching, bone-chilling rain that has hammered the tin roof since before dawn. Georgia, Justin and Kenny have crammed the hallway and one of the back bedrooms with things that should have been sitting in bright sunlight.

The would-be buyers are as cautious as if they were assaying diamonds. They carefully evaluate mismatched plates and glasses, pots and pans of every size, and a large variety of tables and chairs no one has yet chosen to steal. There are three beds there, a lifetime supply of mason jars that never got refilled with grape preserves or apple jelly, and a thousand knickknacks of unknown origin.

Georgia has left untagged only what the three of them need until someone buys the place and she can concentrate on the future. *Whatever the hell that might be.*

She has to rescue the dresser filled with Jenny's letters and photographs. It is as worthless as the rest, and uglier than most, but Georgia has no intention of getting rid of it, at least not for now. She makes Justin and Kenny haul it back into her room.

The two men are spending most of their time in the old two-car garage, where the tools are. She let Kenny take some of them, but there are plenty left—axes, chisels, hammers, levels, manual drills, screwdrivers, a baffling variety of saws. She was struck, walking through last night, with how sufficient her father and his parents before them had to be. There were tools enough there, she saw, to build a house, and some probably were used to build this one. She is surprised that so few of them were stolen by a long line of tenants. Probably, like her, they had no clue what to do with most of them, and no inclination had they known.

The yard sale goes better than she might have expected, considering the weather. A few sharpies show up a full hour before it is supposed to start and walk away with a couple of hundred dollars worth, mostly tools. The people who come when they are supposed to, at 8, take care of another 500 dollars or so. At the end of the day, the final sharpie, what Justin called the closer sharpie, comes by and offers 150 dollars for the majority of what is left.

"Pretty good," Kenny says, when he's counting it up. All of them, including Leeza, are sitting in the living room, exhausted. "More than eight hundred and fifty dollars. That's a good haul for a yard sale around here."

Georgia is thinking that, after a couple of centuries of McCains accumulating things in East Geddie, the final tally comes out to a little over four dollars a year. But she keeps such depressing thoughts to herself. She is delighted, really, to see the stuff hauled away. What she needs to remind her of her father and mother, she already has.

Alberta Horne and Minnie McCauley and some of the other church ladies come by, and all of them shake their heads in sadness to see the last of Littlejohn and Sarah McCain's worldly possessions (other than the house itself, of course) going off in bits and pieces. It doesn't keep them from buying a collander, a set of glasses and an iron wash pot at half the asking price.

The house itself seems to be less desirable than the items inside it. It is on the wrong side of town, away from the hills and hardwoods that draw most of the Scots County population that can choose where it lives. Despite what they've done to modernize it, it is still an old, wooden house with a lush piece of land around it and a decent view.

The real-estate agent says she's committed to selling it, but Georgia wonders.

"We just have to find that right person," the agent says, as if she is running a dating service.

The ad doesn't run in the *Port Campbell Post* any more, because it was more efficient to run it in the free publication the Realtors themselves put out.

"Cheaper, she means," Kenny said when he heard that.

The agent's contract runs out in early December. Maybe, Georgia says, she'll change agents if she hasn't sold it by then.

"Maybe," she says now, "we're asking too much. A hundred and twenty thousand might be too much for the market."

"Damn the market," Kenny says, surprising her with the heat he brings to the subject. "This place is a steal for $120,000. Don't let anybody beat you down on that price. Besides, if you drop it ten thousand, some wise-ass will come in here and think he can get it for even less. Tell 'em all to go to hell."

"Well," she says, "you know, Kenny, we might have a little better luck if we didn't have to check the wind direction every time somebody came out to look at it."

Kenny is quiet.

On a day like this, with the clouds suffocatingly close and the air thick with mist and fog, you can smell the hogs, even indoors. Everyone tells Georgia she'll get used to them. Justin and Leeza seem to have; at least, they don't complain. Georgia will forget about them for several crisp, clear days, and then she'll wake up as she did this morning and think she's choking.

One of Georgia's least favorite childhood experiences was hog-killing. Everyone on the farm and whatever help they could lure in from outside would spend a cold, windy November day turning the McCains' hogs into bacon, ham, sausage, souse meat, liver pudding, pigs' feet, fatback, crackling and other things that nurtured the expression "everything but the oink."

In those days, though, a farm family would keep four or five hogs around, enough for meat, even if they had pork three times a day—which they sometimes did. The hog pen itself was always a proper distance from the house and thus not very offensive. Only on that day when the fattest, most luckless hogs were slaughtered did it become an unpleasant part of Georgia's world. The rest of the time, she just tried to avoid their pen.

It isn't so easy now, though. Hog farms have gotten larger, and while John Kennedy Locklear doesn't own anywhere near the largest hog farm in the county, he has used a small fraction of his 160 acres to house and fatten 500 of them, which are then hauled away to the slaughterhouse.

The smell of 500 hogs, their containment pond and the buildings where they are fattened for slaughter is enough to make Georgia's eyes water when the wind and the clouds are just right.

It has been like that the last two days. Yesterday, the agent brought a pair of potential buyers out to East Geddie. They were moving down from Akron, Ohio, and thought they could make their money go a little farther if they could forgo hills and hardwoods.

"My God," the young woman said. "What the hell is that?"

The agent had taken the only tack she could take. She couldn't very well claim she didn't smell it, too. She was holding a tissue near her nose as they walked up to the house.

"It's the smell of money," she said, daring them to refute it.

"Well," said the husband, "I knew money talked, but I wasn't aware until now that it smelled bad, too."

They had been polite enough, showing mild enthusiasm about the house ("It's so spacious, if we could just knock down a couple of walls. . . ."), about the screened porch and the various outbuildings. But the agent knew it was a lost cause, and she told Georgia why.

When Kenny learned what the agent had said, he told Georgia he was sorry, but that he needed the hogs.

He hadn't really wanted to get into the pork business. He'd had a decent tobacco allotment, although he could see the handwriting on the wall there. He made some money off soybeans and even that old standby, cotton. He grows watermelons and cantaloupes, and even some strawberries and blueberries, although Annabelle and Blue's land is the best for that.

But, in the end, the hogs were what made it possible for him to keep farming. To Kenny Locklear, hogs didn't smell like money so much as they smelled like solvency.

He told Georgia that he could have brought in four times that many hogs, with a little sweet-talking and arm-twisting at the county political level, and the Smithfield people who bought them would be more than happy to help him out there.

"Well," Georgia said, "I thank you for that, at least. I can't imagine what four times that many hogs would smell like. I'm about at the threshold of nausea already."

Now, it's on the table again. It is a dilemma none of them knows how to solve. No one wants to hire lawyers to destroy a friendship.

"Maybe," Justin says, "you can advertise for potential buyers with head colds."

Kenny has never even liked hogs, wonders who would have something like a pot-bellied pig from Vietnam or wherever as a pet. He wishes he had a choice.

"I'm sorry," he says, taking in Justin and Leeza, too. "I'm sorry that hogs don't smell so sweet. Hell, I can smell 'em. Blue complains about them, too. Their places are closer to it than yours, even. But the only thing between me and spending the rest of my life leasing land and teaching ag at the high school is those hogs. When you're back in Virginia, I'll still be here, grateful as hell to Mr. McCain for giving me this and trying the best way I know to hang on to it.

"If I lost this farm, Georgia, I'd feel worse than the man in the Bible that squandered all his talents. I'd feel worse than if I'd never had anything at all."

For Kenny, it's a very long speech.

"OK," she says, holding up her arms in surrender, "forget it. You're right. You'll be here to savor the sweet smell of success long after we're gone. It's your call. Somebody'll buy it."

She wishes she was sure of that.

Georgia hasn't thought much about Jenny McLaurin's ring the last couple of days. Getting everything together for the yard sale has commanded most of her attention and energy.

She is unprepared, when she looks out the window, to see a large red truck, with a cab deep enough for a second row of seats, come to a stop straddling a mud puddle in their side yard. It is so tall that it blocks their view of the garage.

They don't get many visitors. Anyone going down this road is likely either going to see Kenny or one of Annabelle and Blue Geddie's family. Georgia, Justin and Leeza haven't been around long enough to have a lot of outside visitors, just a couple of Georgia's old school friends who never left.

Even in the fast-approaching, cloud-obscured twilight, she can see that it's Pooh. When he eases himself down to first the running board and then the ground, the big truck visibly sways to the left. He walks around the pump house, toward the back porch. Hardly anyone comes to the old house's front entrance.

Georgia gets up to go to the back door and let him in, but he's just standing in the sandy yard, looking off into the distance. The rain has stopped, and the sun is making one last feeble effort to break through just before it disappears, imbuing the land and the trees beyond it with a buttery kind of light, both optimistic and mocking.

Georgia doesn't even know if he prefers to be called Pooh or not.

"Ah, would you like to come in?" she asks.

He doesn't answer at first, just shakes his head. Then she hears a low, "No, ma'am."

She stands there for a few seconds, stymied.

"Well, what do you want . . . Pooh?"

He says nothing else.

Georgia puts down her drink and walks down the steps into the yard. She is bone-tired and somewhat irritated with the large lump of humanity before her. William Blackwell's son is an unsettling presence to her, but he is on her turf now, and she wants to know why he is making a tedious day just a little longer.

In the fading light, he seems even larger than she remembers, perhaps because he's wearing boots and a baseball cap and she's wearing the slippers she put on after the last bargain-hunter left. His head is wider than it is tall, and wider by far across his jowls than at his cranium. His eyes are squinched little slits above a pug nose and a dentally challenged mouth encircled by a Fu Manchu mustache. His neck does not seem to exist, as a neck. His head sits, like a snowman's, directly atop the larger mass of his body. His arms are like a pair of fat sausages poking out from the gray, armless sweatshirt he's wearing without a jacket in the 45-degree gloom.

"I don't have all day," Georgia says. "Now, again: What do you want? I . . ."

"What I want," he says, turning to face her, "is for you to leave me the fuck alone."

"What. . . ?"

"You talked to that sheriff, that Wade Hairr. I didn't steal no goddamn ring off of Miss Jenny. I wouldn't of done that."

"I didn't say you did. I just said it was missing. I wondered where it had gone to."

Pooh gives a short, humorless laugh.

"They sent Pooh to the work farm once. She set me up. They always tryin' to set me up. Ain't goin' back again. No ma'am."

He leans closer to her and almost whispers it.

"You understand me, bitch?"

Georgia feels a chill raising the hairs on her arms and the back of her neck, but she's damned if she's going to be intimidated on her own land, by some tub of shit inbred second-generation bully.

She takes a step back.

"Now you listen to me," she says. "I don't think your father would appreciate what you just said, and if you don't get the hell out of here right now, I *will* have you arrested."

She hears footsteps behind her.

"Georgia? Everything OK?"

"Fine," she says, but the tenor of her voice causes Kenny to come into the back yard, too.

"Pooh," he says, his voice not hard and not soft, as neutral as he can make it.

"This is between me and her," the big man says. "Ain't got nothing to do with you."

"He thinks I'm accusing him of stealing Jenny's ring," Georgia says, shaking her head. This sudden violence has ambushed her the way the summer thunderstorms used to. She feels flustered and out of control.

"She just wanted to find out where it went, Pooh. That's all," Kenny says.

"Wasn't no cause to get the sheriff on me. Him and Daddy are buddies, and now Daddy thinks I'm a thief. Because of her."

"Nobody thinks you're a thief," Georgia says.

"We looked out for that old lady," Pooh says, beating one of his meat-heavy arms against his thigh. "We was her family."

Georgia can't stop herself. It's just too damn much.

"And now you've got her house and her land," she says. "I think you all made out pretty well. What did you do for all that—buy her groceries once in a while, come by and see her every month or so? You keep this crap up, and I'll show you some real trouble. There'll be lawyers inside your shorts."

Pooh moves toward her, his face so red in the dying light he looks like some comic-book devil.

"It's *my* house!" he screams at her. "First you accuse me of stealing from that old lady, and now you want to take my house. Goddamn you!"

Kenny steps between them, but he is backhanded to the ground by Pooh's left arm. Georgia is backpedaling toward the porch steps. Behind her, she hears her son open the screen door, his yelling merging with Pooh's and her own.

She half-falls backward and is sitting on the second step from the bottom. Justin steps between her and Pooh, who throws him aside.

Then Georgia, trying to get up, sees Pooh's head go back slightly, his slitted little eyes suddenly bulging out from all that fat, visible at last. And then she sees the small flash of metal, shining in the kitchen light. *First star I see tonight.*

Kenny has to stand on tiptoes to reach around the big man and hold the carpet knife effectively to his throat—found somehow in the rolls of fat—while his other hand pulls back hard on Pooh's scruffy black hair. Pooh's arms flail uselessly at his sides, and then he is still. Perhaps he has been in this situation before. He seems to understand the gravity of it.

"Now," Kenny tells him, "I wish I had my gun with me, so I could shoot you dead on the spot, Pooh, but this'll have to do. If you don't get the hell out of here, right now, I'll make you wish I had've shot you. I'll make you bleed to death right here in this lady's back yard, and I won't do a day in jail because of it, I can assure you. I'll let you die before the police even get here, so nobody will ever hear your side. Now, make up your mind, Pooh."

He says it calmly, oblivious to the trickle of blood running from his nose.

Pooh nods his head, as much as he can.

"OK? Now, I'm going to let you go. I'll decide later whether to have your ass arrested or not. Assault. Trespassing. Whatever. We'll at least get a restraining order. Enough to make your parole officer sit up and take notice.

"But what you've got to decide is whether you want to stop there or go for the big prize. Gotta decide whether you want to go all the way. I'm gonna walk you over to your truck, and you're gonna get in and drive yourself off this lady's property, and you're not going to bother her any more. Am I right?"

He asks it twice, pulling a little harder, pushing the knife a little deeper. Georgia thinks she sees the first trickle of blood.

Pooh nods, short and quick.

"And assume," Kenny says, "any time you see me from now on, that I'll be armed."

He walks the big man over to the truck like that, a strange, violent dance in the fading light, the two men in murderous rhythm.

There is a moment when Pooh might have tried to take the knife away from him. Kenny has to push him forward, toward the truck door, releasing him from the blade's threat. Pooh could have taken his chances then, maybe even pulled a gun from beneath his front seat. If he has one there, he doesn't go for it, and he doesn't charge Kenny.

He wipes the blood from beneath his chin as he starts the engine and rolls down the window.

"It ain't over," he says, staring hard at Kenny Locklear. "Ain't no damn Indian going to treat me like that."

"Yeah, you're right," Kenny tells him. "It ought to be over, but it probably ain't. Don't make me do this, Pooh."

There is no answer, and the big red truck backs, fishtailing wildly, out to the circular drive, then roars away, throwing wet sand into the night.

The silence is overwhelming. It used to be quieter, of course, before you could hear the distant swoosh and grind of cars and trucks on the interstate. But still, Kenny would live here just for the quiet.

"Well," he says, retracting the carpet knife blade, "I think I've done enough damage for one day."

Georgia falls against him, almost knocking him over, because, truth be hold, he's a little shaky himself. She's crying. Justin stands back a little, holding Leeza.

"Where. . ." Georgia says, between sobs, "where did you get that thing?" She points to the pocket to which he's returned the knife.

"It's just something you carry around," he shrugs. He doesn't want to tell her about Saturday nights in the Lumbee bars and nip joints, something he doesn't do any more, but it's where he learned his manly etiquette. There were a lot of Indian carpet-layers, and somehow the light, deadly, nasty, cheap little tool became the thing any grown man had in his pocket, just in case everyone wasn't as sweet-natured and fair-minded as he was. Sometimes, you just couldn't depend on justice to be as swift or sure as a carpet knife. There was something mature about it. It wasn't like some kid just pulling out some toy of a gun and spraying the room, killing two or three people he'd never even touched. If you were driven so far as to use a carpet knife, you were committed. You didn't cut a man's throat or slit his gut on a whim.

And now, he knows he's going to have to start carrying a gun, something he hasn't done in years, something he thought he had left behind when he went away to college, when he moved out into the longed-for solitude Littlejohn McCain has afforded him.

"I'm sorry I got you into this," Georgia says, still crying. "What in the world are we going to do? Why did he do that?"

He did it, Kenny tells her, because he's a sick puppy, always has been. The two years he did for rape should have been more, but there were only two of them out there, and William Blackwell used all his clout, and maybe the girl broke her own cheekbone and left arm in the throes of passion. The jury didn't believe that, of course, but they believed enough of it, blamed the girl for even being in a pickup truck with Pooh Blackwell.

97

"This place is crazy," Justin says, his arm awkwardly around his mother now.

"Nah," Kenny says, shaking his head. "It's no more crazy now than it was yesterday. It's just Scots County on a Saturday night. Everything'll be better tomorrow morning. Old Pooh will probably come by and apologize."

When my pigs fly, he thinks to himself.

CHAPTER TEN

November 14

Georgia is sure she slept no more than three hours. The monkey had a good night.

Now, lying on her back in the stillness of Sunday morning, with the storm passed and a weak sun illuminating the curtains beside her bed, she wishes she could skip church.

Why the hell not? She's 51 years old, and she's skipped church on a regular basis for much of the past 15 years. When Justin turned 12, she and Jeff told him it was up to him whether he wanted to continue going. No more nagging. They hadn't wanted him to reach adulthood completely ignorant of the possibility of a Higher Being, unaware of the Golden Rule and the Ten Commandments. Georgia thought there was even a literary aspect to it. Like most children growing up when and where she did, she received most of her spotty classical education from the Bible.

Justin went more than they did, to Grace Presbyterian three blocks away, but he quit entirely after their marriage broke up, as if that failure was brought about by some structural flaw in the church, some fallibility by the Infallible.

Still, Georgia thinks joining the Peace Corps after college and grad school was a kind of church for him, a way of meeting God halfway.

These days, she thinks that Justin, with his ready-to-pop-any-minute girlfriend, his dope she's sure they'll be smoking again as soon as the baby is born (please, God, not before), his lack of reverence for the church of his fathers, is more godly than she.

Which, she knows, is damning him with nearly inaudible praise.

She has been in a sulk equal to the one that led to Justin abandoning organized religion. After years of sleeping late on Sundays, she had become an important part of the little Methodist church Phil and his family attended, singing hymns amid a congregation so elderly that she and Phil were part of "the young folks." But, after March, she felt she had a right to be pissed off at Whoever is in charge. After the funeral, she never went inside his old church again.

Why, then, not roll over and give sleep a chance in broad daylight?

The answer, she supposes, is Forsythia Crumpler.

The real answer, she worries, is that she is still, after 51 damn years, too eager to please, still a slave to praise. If she worships a graven image, if she has broken that commandment, too, on her golden calf is chiseled the word "Approval."

On Wednesday, in the process of them making their peace, her old teacher had asked her if she was coming to church on Sunday. Happy to be back in the good graces of her oldest living mentor, she had said yes.

Truth be known, she does enjoy some aspects of the services.

The Reverend Weeks is the kind of pastor that a church like Geddie Presbyterian—older even than Phil's was, and much more needy—tends to get. He seems a good enough man. He is in his mid-40s, five years into the ministry after abandoning a career in hospital administration. The kind of light he must have seen, grumped one of the deacons after a sermon during which two elders began snoring at separate times and had to be elbowed awake by their wives, was not exactly the wattage of the one that blinded Paul on the road to Damascus. "It seems more like a night light," the deacon muttered to his wife on the way home.

In addition to being an uninspiring speaker, he does not have the natural gift for remembering names. Even after two years at Geddie, he struggles when greeting his small, ancient flock after services.

But there are other elements of Georgia's few Sundays at the church that almost salvage it for her. She does find a peace that passes at least her understanding in going through the routines, not changed much since she was a girl here, fidgeting and flirting. The church had been larger then, with many more young people, and there was a social aspect to it.

She falls into the rhythm of the call to worship, the Gloria Patri, the reciting of the Apostles' Creed, the tithes and offerings, the small choir's thin, enervated musical interludes and all the other stops on the way to a 10-minute sermon that always seems longer. (An asterisk beside each hymn asks, "Those that can, please stand." Georgia wonders if it is meant to be puckish. Considering Rev. Weeks and his wife, who produce the program, she thinks not. Most but not all in the congregation are still able to rise.)

The service reminds her of t'ai chi, which she found gave her an inexplicable rush of well-being when she embraced it after her first divorce and her father's death. There was no logical reason why it helped her. But it did.

She also wonders if it isn't just nostalgia.

The three of them have established a routine in which everyone gets his or her own breakfast and lunch, with dinner their only truly communal meal, even on Sundays. (The older people here still call it "supper"; dinner is the large meal they used to eat in the middle of the day, sometimes starting before noon, when they were all farmers or farmers' wives.)

Getting everyone to the table at the same time was difficult before nightfall, and it led to unnecessary friction. Georgia would rise late for Leeza's eggs. Leeza and Justin would oversleep Georgia's French toast.

Today, Georgia finds the house empty when she comes into the dining-living room at 8:45, looking for cereal and orange juice. Dirty dishes, glasses and silverware sit in the sink, and Justin's Toyota is gone. She is still a little shaky from last night, and she considers calling Kenny. He left soon after Pooh did, probably in the service of one of the young women who seem to occupy his time. He said to call him on his cell phone if there was trouble, quick to add that he was sure there wouldn't be. The rest of them ate a dispirited meal, then watched TV for a while, stricken mostly mute by the attack they could neither predict nor defuse, wondering if Pooh was coming back.

Justin, she feels sure, was and is upset that he could not protect his mother adequately, that even with his hard-earned Guatemalan calluses, he still needed Kenny and his carpet knife. And Leeza has tended, as her first child's birth looms, to expect smoothness and treat the bumps as personal affronts.

Georgia regrets getting Kenny into the middle of something so idiotic, yet so threatening. She fears that this is one of those situations she remembers from her youth here, in which logic and patience always seemed to get drowned out by some bloodlust, the dimensions and protocol of which she has never really understood. Part of what she found appealing about the leafy, corduroy-jacketed world of academia was the absence of such explosions. Her colleagues might harbor grudges and turn pettiness into an art form, but there was never the necessity to carry a carpet knife.

She played it over in her mind endlessly after Pooh's departure, and she continues to do so this morning. What did she do wrong? How had this gotten so out of her control? Should she go see Pooh, or William? Should she—and she can't believe she's even considering this—get a gun?

She realizes that she needs a local guide, the same one who rescued her last night.

She decides, finally, that she should wait. Kenny might be a late riser, especially on a Sunday morning. He might not even be alone. She'll call him after lunch.

She does feel better after her two hours at the old church. Even Sunday School, taught by a sweet-natured young woman who stumbles so hopelessly over the lesson plan that Georgia wants to snatch the book from her and do it herself, is at least bearable.

Several people ask her how the yard sale went, and they seem impressed that so much of the house's furnishings sold.

"I hope you didn't let that Jimmy Cole come up at the end and get everything for nothing," Murphy Lee Roslin says loudly. He says everything loudly, because he is mostly deaf. Georgia wonders why he doesn't make this much noise when he sings.

"Well, Mr. Roslin," Georgia says, forcing herself to speak up, "he did get a few things, but you know, it isn't like we were going to take them up to Sotheby's and get a million dollars for them."

She gets puzzled looks from Mr. Roslin and others within earshot, but nobody asks her what she's talking about.

Sotheby's, she thinks. Jesus. She wonders if she will ever relearn the language down here, if she ever knew it at all. Even as a teen-ager, and certainly as a college student, she found so much of what she said was, to the ears of Geddie Presbyterian's faithful, a string of non sequiturs.

And then, there's the cursing. She's always had what her mother would have called a trash-mouth. She's never really considered four-letter words to be the devil's instruments. When she uses the F-word in public, she thinks of herself as colorful, sassy, irreverent, uninhibited—traits that do not seem to command respect in East Geddie.

When she came out of Sunday services three weeks earlier and saw that one of her tires had gone flat, she exclaimed "shit!" before she even thought about it. There was an uneasy silence behind her before two of the deacons came over and helped her put the spare on.

She hasn't mentioned last night's confrontation. She is so uneasy with it that she doesn't even feel comfortable talking about it among these quiet, peaceful people.

She does talk with Forsythia Crumpler, though, as they are both going to their cars.

Forsythia asks if she has found out anything else about Jenny's ring. She asks it in a low voice after the others are out of earshot.

Georgia tells her that all she knows is that Wade Hairr didn't remember seeing a ring, and neither did anyone else between the pond and the morgue.

"Well," the older woman says, "like I told you, she was so crippled with that arthritis. She might have just not worn it that day."

"Wade Hairr said he would ask about it, ask the Blackwell boy."

"And has he?"

So Georgia does what she didn't really plan to do. She tells her old teacher about Pooh's visit. When she is through, she finds that she is shaking. Forsythia leans against her car, looks up at her and frowns.

"I probably ought not to say this, but that one scares me. He gets an idea in his head, and it seems as if he can't get it out.

"I remember, must have been four or five years ago, he thought one of the Gibbs boys had cheated him in some kind of business deal, the kind of thing the Blackwells are usually involved in. You know, two cats for a dog, or some such. I don't even know all the details, but he beat that boy so bad he had to go to the hospital. I think he moved away from here not long after he got out. I knew that boy. There wasn't a bit of meanness or dishonesty in him. It was all in Pooh's head."

"Well, I wish I could get this particular idea out of his head. The last thing in the world I want to do is make enemies around here."

Forsythia rises up from the car.

"You know, I guess I've taught just about everybody between Pooh's age and 65 who grew up around here. You teach elementary school, you see them for seven years. It wasn't that big a school. And you can't help but have impressions. After a while, you can get a good idea, just from remembering their older brothers and sisters and observing their parents, and from seeing them grow up, how they're going to turn out.

"Some of them, it just seems like they were born a certain way, and they are bound for a certain fate, and about all you can do is try to alter their course a little. You don't give up on them, but you know pretty much how it's all going to turn out. It can be a terrible thing, teaching at one school that long."

Georgia smiles a little.

"So, how did you think I was going to turn out?"

The older woman gives her an inscrutable look.

"Well, I guess you turned out about the way I figured. Thought you'd move away and not come back, thought you might have become a writer. Didn't think you'd get married three times, but who can predict that?"

Who indeed, Georgia thinks.

The older woman opens her car door, then turns stiffly around to face Georgia again.

"We're glad you came back, though," she says, dispensing a small smile. "And we're glad to have some young people here, too. Bring them with you next time."

"Yeah," Georgia says, shaking her head. "Maybe they'll even get married here. Maybe they'll get married somewhere, I hope."

"Don't worry about that, now. They'll either get married or they won't. You can't bully them into it."

"It's just that I never imagined that my first grandchild would be born out of wedlock."

Forsythia frowns as she turns to go.

"It'll work out," she says. "It'll work out. And the baby will be loved, I can tell that. That's what counts."

* * *

Georgia phones Kenny, but no one answers. When she walks over, his car is gone.

Justin and Leeza don't return until after 3. They've been visiting the Geddies, they tell Georgia, who is getting ready to skewer them for leaving her at home alone.

"We told you that," he reminds her. "We told you last week that I'd finally gone to see Blue, and how we were going to their church today. Remember? We left a little early to run by that 24-hour drugstore in Port Campbell and get some things for Leeza."

Georgia pretends not to recall. She knows she probably would have declined if they'd asked her to join them. The AME Zion services, everyone knew, were interminable. Spirited, but interminable.

"Their church was so neat," Leeza says, as enthusiastic as Georgia has seen her lately, her belly so obscenely large that Georgia can't believe she's been up and about all morning and half the afternoon. "They sang, and got excited and clapped their hands. It wasn't like any church I've ever been to."

I'll bet not, Georgia thinks but does not say. She wishes she could infuse the good people of Geddie Presbyterian with some of the black church's spirit.

"Well," she says, looking for something to complain about, "why didn't you wake me up? I might have come with you."

"You looked like you could use the sleep," Justin said, "after last night and all."

"So," Georgia asks, "how is Blue? And his mother—Annabelle?"

Blue is married; he and Sherita have a boy and a girl. They and his mother live on opposite sides of Littlejohn McCain Road, in matching double-wides.

"And what was the other one's name—Godfrey?"

"Winfrey. Ah, he's in prison. Drugs, I think. He's supposed to get out next summer, Blue said."

"That's too bad. About him being in prison, I mean. Not the getting-out part."

She remembers learning about the wreck when she got to East Geddie to pick up Justin and take him back to Montclair that summer. She just assumed, her primitive brain overriding 22 years of sensitivity training, that the two black kids with her son had been the cause of it. Looking at her son's broken nose and scars, she was raving about pressing charges, but her father talked her out of it. On the way back home, Justin told her about the marijuana he'd provided and the damage he had done, and Georgia then understood the part of Littlejohn McCain's will that left 150 acres of prime farmland to an African-American family she barely knew.

She asks Justin if Blue walks with a limp. She is embarrassed that she hasn't been to see them herself, but she salves her conscience by remembering that they haven't visited her, either.

"Just a little," Justin says. "I wasn't even going to say anything about it, but he brought it up. It's funny. He said he thought that wreck was the luckiest thing that had ever happened to him. He said it made him grow up, forget about playing basketball and focus on something."

Winfrey, he tells her, did become a big high school basketball star, just as both of them dreamed they'd be, and he even played a year or two at Pembroke, but then he just drifted, never graduated.

"But you know," Justin says, "there's still hard feelings about the land, between Kenny and the Geddies. It's too bad. I mean, they live right beside each other and all, and they barely speak."

Georgia knows the basics, as told to her by Kenny and various other old acquaintances who talk of it obliquely, deftly dodging direct inquiries.

It seems obvious to her that her father meant to give some of the very best land to Blue and his mother. The land reaching over toward the Blue Sandhills was where he himself had made much of what money he made farming. It had never been planted in tobacco, and the berries and melons and cantaloupes they raised down in the bottomland flourished.

The interstate was foreseen before Littlejohn died, but the final route had not been determined. Those plans were announced within a year of his passing.

The road they finally built took away a few acres of the best land and more or less ruined a dozen more, cut off now from the rest of the farm by the raised highway.

In the meanwhile, Kenny had traded three acres of his land south of the still-rut road to the Geddies in exchange for three acres on the north side that included the Rock of Ages, where he would build his home.

It hadn't seemed important at the time. Nobody had any problems with it. They didn't even call in a lawyer, just wrote it out on a piece of paper and got it notarized. They sealed the deal with a handshake.

But then, after they became aware that they would soon be losing almost 20 acres of prime berry land—the money they received for it didn't come close to equaling its long-term value—Blue and his mother came to Kenny Locklear one day and told him they had changed their minds, that they were going to need that good land where Kenny had already laid the footings for his new brick rancher.

It was a mess, everyone agreed. Kenny's dream was to build within eyesight of the old Indian rock, to actually own the land on which it sat. Blue and Annabelle suspected Kenny had known all along that they were going to be losing a valuable little triangle of their land to the new highway.

What really tore it was when, on the occasion of their second meeting, Kenny said he didn't think they should renege on the deal they'd already made.

107

Neither Blue nor Annabelle were familiar with that verb, but they sure as hell knew what it sounded like.

"You can't talk to me like that," Blue had said, and the two of them walked out on a startled Kenny, who became aware later and second-hand of the faux pas he had committed.

He came to them and tried to explain, but then, when it seemed as if they weren't in the mood to listen, he became exasperated and angry, and he wound up storming out of their tarpaper home that the double-wides soon would replace.

The lawyer Blue threatened to bring in never materialized, and so the feud just festered, fed by crowds of Lumbees who sometimes parked on Annabelle and Blue's land when they came to see the rock, and by friends of Blue's who were prone to throw their empty beer cans into Kenny's yard as they drove by.

In general, though, it has been a quiet grudge, gradually receding. They don't actively hate or even harass each other. Kenny admonishes his visitors to respect the Geddies' property, and Blue tells his friends not to be throwing their trash in his neighbor's yard.

The old scar, though, has not completely healed.

Kenny says the Geddies have made a pretty good living off what's left of their inheritance, and he can't be blamed if they pissed away the right-of-way money, mostly on things they bought for their worthless relatives.

"But we're going to try to get them together," Leeza says.

"Well, we hope maybe we can," Justin says, looking more doubtful. "We had this idea."

"What?" Georgia asks.

But her son doesn't want to say.

"It's kind of half-baked, and I'd rather wait and see if we can do it or not."

Georgia is determined not to press him, not to be overbearing. She even understands her son's reluctance. She knows she is prone to throw cold water on youthful dreams.

She is sure he will tell her eventually. He's never been able to keep a secret for long.

"Oh," Leeza says, "and Annabelle—that's what she wants me to call her—is going to teach me how to make biscuits, from scratch."

Well, Georgia thinks, that shouldn't be much harder than beef Wellington. She herself never really gained the knack for making biscuits. Her mother, an orphan reared by an older couple, had barely known how to do it. Her father actually was the family biscuit-maker.

It was not something the future collegian and world-traveler dreamed of doing—making the perfect buttermilk biscuit. It was one of those skills that was highly treasured around East Geddie but did not travel well.

She had tried, though, attempting in vain to turn self-rising flour, shortening, a pinch of baking of soda and buttermilk into something light as air and capable of absorbing twice its weight in molasses. Hers usually bear a depressing resemblance, in shape and heft, to hockey pucks.

"Well," Georgia says, "that ought to be interesting. That's no easy feat, making them from scratch. I'm looking forward to you learning that trick. I haven't had a good scratch biscuit since homecoming at the church."

"She spent about an hour showing me how," Leeza says, and Georgia notices the smudges of flour around the parts of her an apron would not have covered. "She's a nice lady."

As opposed, Georgia is sure she is thinking, to the mean asshole who keeps busting my chops every time I do something wrong around here.

Just then, Georgia detects a flash of movement and turns to the window to see Kenny's car coming down the road.

"Oh, good," she says, glad for the excuse. "Kenny's home. I wanted to go over and talk to him about last night."

They haven't mentioned it until now. Georgia finds that it embarrasses her, makes her blame herself for somehow letting such ugliness burst into their lives. Justin, she's sure, feels the same helplessness she does in the face of such black and unassailable rage.

She goes to get her coat, telling them she will be back in a few minutes.

"Want us to come with you?" Justin asks.

"No, that's OK. You all can just, ah, practice making biscuits or something."

She doesn't know why she said that, and she leaves before anyone can accuse her of meanness or sarcasm.

Kenny is getting ready to wash his car, an old Nissan that seems not to fit what Georgia imagines as his mid-life single-male lifestyle.

"Hi," she says, coming up behind him as he is bending to turn the hose on. "I called earlier, but you weren't here."

He turns and nods, squinting into the afternoon sun. He shuts the water off again and wipes his hands on the sides of his jeans. He is still a handsome man, Georgia thinks, really seeing him now. Her image of him, imprinted long ago, seems to need updating. There is more substance there, or maybe it was there all along and she didn't notice. It helps that he talks occasionally now and seems more comfortable in her presence. She used to think that she scared him, and he certainly disconcerted her.

She is relatively certain that Kenny is her never-known half-brother's son, issue of Littlejohn McCain and the dark and beautiful Rose Lockamy Locklear. Despite this, she wonders if she hasn't consigned him, all this time, to the general subset of "Lumbee," as if he were of a different species altogether.

He is tan and fit from making his living at least partially with his muscles, but he isn't worn out the way Georgia remembers the old-time farmers, who worked like the mules with which they ploughed and were heavy on sweat, light on knowledge. Any of the latter that had come from books instead of being passed on, right or wrong, from father to son was viewed with scepticism.

He offers no explanation for his absence today.

"I figured maybe you just had a hot date last night and didn't make it home," she says, trying to make it into a joke.

He shakes his head.

"I had a hot date all right," he says. "Tommy."

She knew that he had custody of the boy one day a week, plus two weeks in the summer, when they go on vacation together. She's never seen Tommy, though, and tends to forget that Kenny has a son. All she knows about him is that he is supposed to have some kind of developmental problem.

Kenny usually likes to make his day with his son either Saturday or Sunday. The boy is inside now, watching television.

"Why don't you ever bring him over to see us?" she asks. "I'd love to meet him."

"Maybe I will sometime," Kenny says. "Maybe I will."

Georgia thanks him again for saving her, thinking as she says it what an old-fashioned, non-feminist notion that is. Nevertheless, he did. So there.

"I've got something I want you to have," he tells her, a hesitant tone in his voice. "I hope you won't just dismiss it out of hand."

He goes to the trunk and brings it out, so small it might be a child's toy, ready to squirt water on her. He hands it to Georgia, who has never held a gun before. She stares at it and wants to hand it back but is afraid of offending Kenny.

"I know it's not your style," he says, holding his hands up to ward off the argument, "and everything will probably just smooth over, water over the dam. But it's never a bad idea just to have one around."

He tells her it's called a Ladysmith, chauvinistically small, tiny enough to fit into a purse. It only weighs about a pound and a half empty, he tells her, but it feels heavier, as if its serious intent adds to its bulk.

"I . . . I can't," she says, thinking what a betrayal this would be of every word she's ever uttered or written against an out-of-control gun culture. "I'd probably wind up shooting myself."

"Bull," he says, and, taking the gun from her, motions her to come with him.

Across the collard patch behind the barn is a lone pine tree, and on the tree is a target. Georgia has heard what she thought were gunshots occasionally across the field, and she guesses, from the Swiss-cheese condition of the paper, that this is where they came from.

He gives her the gun. His hands are rough but warm.

"Now, just aim it. Take in a breath, then let it halfway out, and pull."

She does it, with him helping steady her arms from behind. She closes her eyes in anticipation of the sound, which is not as loud as she had feared. She is surprised that there is not more kick. She has actually, Kenny tells her, hit the edge of the target 30 feet away.

"You'd be using this a lot closer than that if—God forbid—you ever had to," he tells her. "Here. Try again."

She shoots at the target 20 times and is ashamed at how good, how empowered she feels. When she has used up what ammunition Kenny brought with him, she tries to give it back again.

"Nope. It's yours."

She doesn't argue, for now.

"Well, what do I owe you?"

"You don't owe me anything. A man owed *me* something, and I had him pay me back."

He shows her how to load it.

"Eight rounds, no safety. Just keep pulling the trigger. And don't worry. It won't go off if you drop it or something."

She can imagine the small, serious piece of metal falling to the floor and discharging as she reaches for her offering money at church.

"I'm never going to use this," she tells him.

"You already have. Just remember how easy it is, for better or worse. Bad things don't always happen, Georgia, but they can happen, and it doesn't hurt to be prepared."

"Like a Boy Scout."

"Yeah. Right."

She asks him if she can talk to him about Pooh, and about Jenny McLaurin's ring.

He frowns but says sure, tell me about Jenny McLaurin's ring.

She puts the little gun, no heavier than a small flashlight, in her purse, and feels changed by its weight.

CHAPTER ELEVEN

November 16

Kenny's pickup almost never touches asphalt, seldom leaves the clay road and dirt paths of the farm. Georgia suggested taking it, because it would arouse less suspicion than the Nissan he usually drives.

"You've been watching too many *Magnum* reruns," he told her before they left. "I mean, we're just going to drive up there, right? We're not trying to sneak up on anybody."

But he does indulge her.

She's instructed him to pull off the state highway, alongside the Campbell and Cool Spring railroad tracks. They are no more than a couple of hundred feet from the driveway to the late Jenny McLaurin's home. The yard looks neglected, especially compared with Forsythia Crumpler's next door. Georgia notices that no one has taken "The McLaurin's" off the mailbox yet. There is no sign of Pooh's big truck in the driveway, but it could be around back.

"OK, now," she says, and then stops.

"OK, now," Kenny repeats, as if to prime her.

"He's probably not even there, but we just park in the driveway and walk up to the front door, and, if he is there, we tell him we want to make peace, that we don't want any trouble," she says, looking to see if Kenny approves.

A shrug.

"Whatever. Maybe we'll catch him in a rare moment of sanity. Maybe he'll just shoot us. Kidding."

Georgia does have the little gun, though. She's carrying it inside one of the pockets of her leather jacket, wrapped in a rag like

Kenny told her, so it won't show. She doesn't even want to know what he's carrying.

She finally called William Blackwell yesterday. The conversation did not go as well as she had hoped.

"Well, Georgia," he said, "the boy was a little upset. He thinks you're trying to get the house back somehow. He thinks you're trying to get the law on him again."

"I don't want to cause any trouble." She realized that she sounded like the boys William Blackwell used to torment before he beat them up.

William broke a long silence by telling her that maybe it would be a good idea if she came out and talked to Pooh herself.

"I expect he'll be there tomorrow morning," he said. "He's about moved in and all. It's a real nice place, although Jenny did kind of let it go there towards the end. It was real good of her, though, to will it to us."

"She was a saint," Georgia was proud of herself for stopping at those four syllables when so many others yearned to free themselves.

She looked up the phone number, but no one answered, just Pooh's ill-tempered voice on the recording, inquiring of all callers, "What the fuck do you want?" followed by a beep.

Georgia didn't leave a message. Instead, she talked Kenny into accompanying her to her cousin's old house. She wanted to go at 9 in the morning.

Kenny convinced her that 11 would be a better hour.

"You're not likely to wake him that late, and the bars won't be open yet."

Now, as Kenny's pickup rises over the single set of tracks and then dips into the yard itself, she feels her stomach sink along with the truck.

She gets out and waits for Kenny, and they walk up to the front door together, neatly dressed like some couple trying to lure a sinner to their church.

Kenny rings the doorbell three times, then knocks twice.

He starts walking around the side of the house, headed for the back yard. Georgia scurries after him, staying close.

114

No one answers the back door, either, and after a minute or so, Kenny shrugs and turns around.

"Can we just take a look at the pond?" Georgia asks. "I haven't even been here since the day she drowned."

"Don't see why not. I didn't see any no trespassing signs."

"Actually, I think there is one, over there in the weeds, but Harold put it up. Can you be arrested for disobeying dead people's trespassing signs?"

Kenny laughs.

"Come on."

A faded green rowboat sits upright and exposed to the elements on the raised bank, one of the few evidences, other than broad-based neglect, that someone of a different nature has taken over Jenny McLaurin's home. The boat has water standing in it from the weekend's rain. Kenny turns it over, as if he can't bear to do otherwise, and lets the dirty water out.

They walk along the edge of the pond and are halfway down the side nearest the house when Georgia sees something.

She walks out through the weeds where Harold and Jenny used to raise tomatoes and beans. Just as Kenny is about to ask her what she's doing, she reaches down into the vegetation and comes up holding a shoe.

It is a sensible shoe, of the kind that would have been worn by an older country lady with bad feet and not enough money, flat-heeled and apparently of a dark blue color originally, although the elements have taken their toll.

"A dog probably drug it up," Kenny says. "It looks like it's been there awhile."

Georgia doesn't say anything at first. She doesn't even know what drew her to the pond, other than a chance to see it one last time, unlikely as she is to be invited to brunch or cocktails by the present owner.

She carries the shoe with her as they do a full lap around Harold McLaurin's prized pond. In the distance, across the road and in the direction of Maxwell's Millpond, she can hear a loon's sleepy call, as languid as if it were a July day instead of the week before Thanksgiving. Georgia looks down into the brown water, seemingly too stained and debris-filled even for the catfish it allegedly still sustains. All she sees are two reflections—hers staring into the pond, Kenny looking into the distance as he jingles the change in his pocket. And the carpet knife, she's thinking. It doesn't hit her until they are almost back to the house.

"Kenny," she says, stopping and grabbing his arm, forcing him to make a whiplash stop, "when I went over to the funeral home, after Jenny drowned, I took over the burial clothes, and they gave me a bag with what she had on when they brought her to the undertaker's. I thought it was such a crazy thing for them to do."

Kenny nods his head, waiting.

"I never opened it, but I know this much: There was a shoe in there. One shoe. I guess she'd had it on when she went in the water, and I figured she just lost the other one when she was thrashing about, as much as I thought of it at all."

"There are a lot of shoes, Georgia."

"Well, maybe I have been watching too much television, but I swear that shoe looks just like this one."

"Well, even if it is, which it probably isn't, she could have just, you know, kicked it off when she started to fall."

Georgia shakes her head.

"It was at least 20 feet from the bank," she says. "And how come if one shoe just flies off like it had wings, the other one stays on all the way to the bottom, like it was glued on?"

"Well, it might not be a match at all. I'll bet you could go to just about any old place like this and find all kinds of things in the weeds out back that didn't look like they belonged there. It's like those kids' shoes you see thrown over the power lines for some damn reason. Or you'll be driving down the road and there'll be one just lying there in the middle of the highway."

"Well, I'm going to see." And she puts the shoe into her jacket pocket, opposite the Ladysmith. The shoe doesn't quite fit; its toe sticks out, pointing upward.

"OK. You know best," Kenny says, in a voice that suggests the opposite. "Come on, let's go before the fat boy gets back. We're just not destined to be graced with his company today. Maybe he's actually gotten a job."

They are walking back to the truck when Georgia hears Forsythia Crumpler calling.

She waits at her hedge, unwilling to trespass.

"I saw you all walking by the pond," she says, nodding to Kenny. "Can't help but keep an eye on that place, I suppose. Habit."

"We came to see Pooh," Georgia says, "but he wasn't at home."

"Come to make peace?" Forsythia offers a slight smile, then turns to Kenny.

"Mr. Locklear," she says, "I hope you're taking care of this girl. That Pooh Blackwell scares me. I tell you, Georgia, I used to not lock my doors at night. I do now."

"Mrs. Crumpler," Georgia says, "does this look like one of Jenny's shoes?"

The older woman takes the shoe, examines it from all angles.

She shakes her head.

"I don't know. Lord, it looks like some she had, but I can't say for sure."

Georgia thanks her, then thinks to ask if she's all right.

"I'm fine," the old woman says, then hesitates before she speaks again. "I'm just sorry to have that boy living next door to me. He comes tearing in and out of here all hours of the night, and he's got all kinds of no-account friends that like to visit him."

"You want me to talk to him?" Kenny says.

She looks alarmed.

"No. No, don't do that. That'll just make it worse. Let's just wait and see how it works out."

They leave it at that. Georgia promises to check up on her, and promises herself that she will call her every day.

Kenny drops Georgia in her driveway. Before he leaves, she walks around to his side of the truck and thanks him for his time and support.

"Nothing to it," he says. "You know, though, Mrs. Crumpler is right about watching out for yourself. I'm pretty sure I can take care of that fat tub of crap, if it comes to it, and I'd rather make peace than war, but you ought to be careful."

"Hey," Georgia says, forcing a smile, "I've got my trusty friend here." And she pats her pocket.

"If you take it out," he tells her, as he's already told her twice, "use it, early and often. That's important."

She holds up her right hand.

"I promise. Scout's honor."

He shakes his head and drives off.

Justin and Leeza are there when she walks inside, along with another man she doesn't immediately recognize. The darkness of his skin is accentuated by the white of the apron he's wearing. He's standing next to Leeza, who also is wearing one. Hers is yellow with blue flowers, once worn by Georgia's mother and now appropriated by the girl who soon will give her a grandchild. Four generations involved, more or less, she thinks. Justin stands to one side. They all seem to have been laughing, and her expression sets them off again.

"What?"

Justin finally controls himself enough to tell her that Blue has come by to visit, and Leeza was trying to make biscuits the way Annabelle taught her, without much luck. And so now Blue is helping.

Georgia shakes Blue Geddie's hand. It has flour on it, as does his face and everything else the apron does not cover. Georgia thinks, despite herself, of Al Jolson in reverse.

She hasn't spoken to Blue in years.

After her father's death, when everyone knew about the will (she had rebuffed a local lawyer who tried to convince her Littlejohn McCain didn't truly mean to give nearly half his farm to "those people"), she visited Blue and his mother a couple of times, but it was awkward.

They seemed afraid that their good luck was only an illusion. They couldn't make themselves believe that she meant them well, that she was not seeking, after all the nice words and genteel manners, to take back from them their godsend. She couldn't have convinced them that she thought land she never wanted was just compensation for her son's careless act and Blue's shattered leg. They kept waiting for the other shoe to drop, and when it didn't, they always bid her goodbye with obvious relief.

After that, Georgia thought it would be better to just let it lie and stop scaring Blue and Annabelle to death.

She would see one or the other of them from time to time over the years, but it has been the better part of a decade since she has had a face-to-face conversation with Blue Geddie.

He has grown into a handsome man, with a strong, full nose separating eyes and mouth that obviously are accustomed to laughter. His flawless, unwrinkled skin is a rich mahogany seldom seen even one state north, in the Piedmont of Virginia. His head, shaved and darkly shining, shows off its perfect proportions. He and the red-haired sunburn-magnet Leeza, who can barely reach the counter, actually has to turn a little to give her swollen belly room, are so different in color that Georgia wonders if they don't represent the extremes that human pigment can attain.

"Well, Blue," Georgia says, raising her arms, "I'm sure you're a better biscuit-maker than I am. Your kids are probably better. The dog is probably better."

"Well, Miss Georgia," he says, "my momma used to say I was so ugly, she figured I'd better learn how to cook, since no woman was likely to ever do it for me."

Georgia tells him he must have been the ugly duckling, then, turned into a swan, and when he gives her a polite but blank look, she says, "What I mean is, you've grown into a handsome man. And stop calling me 'Miss Georgia.' Just Georgia will do fine."

It's impossible to tell, but she thinks he is blushing.

Leeza does seem to be getting the hang of biscuits. After they've talked for a while, she produces a baking sheet full of them. They look and smell almost like some of the better ones Georgia remembers from her childhood. There is ham left from breakfast, along with molasses and syrup and butter, and the four of them make a lunch that, while lacking in variety, is as good as any Georgia can remember in some time.

Blue's visit, it develops over the course of their impromptu meal, is more than just a social one.

"One of the guys I worked with in the Peace Corps, his family runs a big distributorship up in Manhattan," Justin tells her. "They buy fresh fruit and vegetables all over the Southeast and haul it up there, the same day. He used to tell me about it all the time when we were in Guatemala. They were always looking for the best way to get some of the great stuff they grow down here up there.

"They just have to have reliable sources for everything, stuff ready to go when the truck gets here. I've been talking to him, and he's going to come down and check it out. Selling produce to rich New Yorkers will beat the hell out of selling berries to people a bucket at a time."

"Although," Blue says, "we'll still do that, too."

Justin nods.

Georgia wants to ask her son, just shy of a master's degree, what in the world he thinks he's doing, how he could consider such a boneheaded move, how he could think about embracing the very thing she went to college to escape, how he could so blithely embrace downward mobility, and what exactly in the hell does he knows about farming.

She is becoming adept at holding her tongue.

"Part of it," Justin says, "is we've got to get Kenny on board."

Kenny's land turns out the sweetest cantaloupes and watermelons, a big mover, Justin tells her, for the city people up North. Georgia remembers that people did brag on her father's melons when she was a girl. She never developed a taste for them, herself.

And the McCain farm has always produced more than its share of greens—collards, mustard, kale and turnips—well into the winter.

"If we can get all of this tied together," he adds, "we can have something to send up there just about all year."

"What does Kenny say about this?" Georgia asks them.

"He's studying it," Blue says, in a tone that might have some disapproval in it.

"Why hasn't anybody mentioned this to me before?"

"Well," Justin says, when the other two look to him, "I guess we figured you'd just clear a space on the floor and have a shit-fit. We wanted to have a good plan before we told you about it. We've still got to figure out who gets what, assuming we make anything."

"But I'm not having a shit-fit," Georgia says, forcing a smile. "I'm calm. I'm not judgmental. I'm not asking you if you've lost your mind. Excuse me."

She gets up and walks out, leaving silence and then low talking behind her.

The shoe is still sticking out of her jacket. She walks to the back room where she put the plastic bag containing Jenny's possessions.

She takes the other one out. She puts them both together, under the brightest lamp in the room.

They are both beyond repair, but as Georgia looks at them as closely as she can, she comes to the conclusion that fills her with dread and, she must admit, excitement.

She calls the sheriff's office. This time, Wade Hairr is in, although she waits five minutes for him to come to the phone.

"Sure, Georgia," he tells her. "Come on by. What is it you want to show me?"

"I'd rather just show it to you, Wade."

"This doesn't happen to have anything to do with Jenny McLaurin's death, does it?"

"Well . . . Yes, it does. But this is important. I know you think I'm fixated or something, but I think you're going to want to see this."

He sounds like a man seeking to let someone know he's trying to be tolerant and not quite succeeding.

"OK, then. When?"

"How about now?"

A short silence.

"I reckon that'd be OK."

She thanks him and hangs up, then puts both shoes in the same bag, emptying Jenny's other possessions on the bed.

The heft of her jacket as she removes it reminds her of the gun.

She takes it out and puts it in the top drawer of Jenny's dresser, holding it with the same care and trepidation she might have afforded a non-poisonous snake.

121

CHAPTER TWELVE

November 19

This has ceased being funny.

I am tired of seeing things other people aren't seeing, and pretending I don't see them.

My old classmate the sheriff was concerned enough, I suppose, considering he thought he was dealing with a lunatic.

I showed him the two shoes and explained their provenance—surely not a word I would have used around Wade Hairr.

It wasn't just the shoes, I explained. It was the shoes and the missing ring.

"Well, Georgia," he told me, digging into his right ear with his index finger while I tried to look somewhere else, "it isn't much to go on, you've got to admit. God knows where that ring went to, and God knows how that shoe got in the middle of that field, or even if it is the match of the one Miss Jenny was wearing."

He made it clear that, if I were to find some more evidence, something that would actually meet Wade Hairr's definition of evidence, I should call him.

I hadn't planned to mention anything about Pooh's visit Saturday night, and I still haven't seen that eminent personage. Kenny's been busy, and I haven't really wanted to go back by there since I found the shoe.

Wade brought it up.

"Pooh didn't seem too happy when I asked him about the ring, by the way."

"I know."

And then I gave him the watered-down version.

"Well," Wade said, with a smile that was just a notch shy of rueful, "he gets things in his head."

"Gets things in his head like what?" Although I thought I knew.

"Well..." Wade started most sentences with that word, and he could turn it into three syllables if he was really stalling for time, "he seems to believe that you're trying to get the house back from him. I told him there isn't anything to that. Heck, I even told William that."

"William thinks I'm trying to get the house back, too?"

"I didn't say that. It's just, well, they think it's funny that you would be coming to the sheriff's department about a missing ring nobody seemed to even think about until she'd been dead near-bout three weeks."

"Well, Jesus Christ," I said, and the woman clerk looked at me and frowned. "I mean, what was I supposed to do? He was the one who found her. I just thought he might have seen the ring, or at least noticed if she didn't have one on."

"Well, I'm just saying . . ." Wade held his hands up in defense. "Just let it die down, Georgia, would be my advice. Let sleeping dogs lie. You don't want to get the boy mad at you."

I had to admit I didn't want that. I also had to admit to myself that Wade Hairr was one sorry-ass excuse for a sheriff.

"OK," I said, getting up while Wade stayed seated, "forget it. Maybe the shoes don't match. Maybe it's nothing. Just do one thing, if you would. Don't mention it to William or Pooh."

That, of course, would prove too much to ask.

This morning, I was thinking about all that, while I listened to a smooth jazz CD. I was thinking that I might never really know whether Jenny died of neglect, in which I played a major role, or of something more exotic. I was trying to resign myself to that lack of knowledge.

There aren't any easy ways to lose someone.

With Daddy, it was neglect. I should have known he wasn't going to just let himself dwindle away to nothing, be a "burden."

Somebody would have had to step in and stop him by force, take him home with her to Virginia, say, or move back for a while.

Somebody didn't.

With Phil, it was the opposite of neglect, I guess you'd say.

Either one can leave you staring out a window at nothing, months or years later, until your coffee gets cold.

Phil was in great shape, I thought. Hell, we made love three and four times a week, a record among my little middle-aged group of over-educated, under-appreciated ladies, as far as anyone would admit. Phil had to know I talked about him, the way friends of mine would just sometimes grin and walk away when we'd run into one of them at a restaurant or a movie. He always made me come at least twice, and sometimes three or four times. He was very, very good, not just with his cock, but with his tongue and his hands, and with his mind. He had some imagination, something no one would have imagined in the gentle, steady self he presented to the world outside our bedroom (OK; maybe include living room, bathrooms, and sometimes the back porch, too.)

At 51, against all conceivable odds, I was having the best sex I'd ever had in my life, even better than when Jeff and I were young. (He came too fast or I came too slow. Story of my life: bad timing.) Phil was like Indian summer for me, I thought—a warm, exhilarating respite before the big chill.

He might have been just a little overweight, but not much. He liked to tell me he was built for comfort and not for speed. I was more than comfortable with comfort.

I could have put him on a diet, but I didn't want to do anything to Phil Macomb that might have caused him anything but pleasure. I thought I owed him that much. And he was a working man, for Christ's sake. Anybody who spent all day actually making his living by the sweat of his brow ought to be able to eat a steak and a baked potato with butter and sour cream.

That Friday night, we'd ordered delivery pizza and drunk three or four beers each, then retired to the bedroom. Beer never seemed to slow him down, but that night it did. We tried a couple of positions, lying there in the cool darkness, before he finally hit his stride on top of me with my legs thrown back as far as my poor old grateful body would allow.

124

And then he gave kind of a jerk, and I thought for an instant how strange that he was coming when I thought he was a good 15 minutes away.

He fell forward, pinning me there with my legs wrapped around him.

I called his name, and then I tried to get out from under. I couldn't, at first, his lifeless weight such a sudden burden. He'd always been so strong, no doubt doing the equivalent of pushups when he was on top, and I never knew how big a man he was until he died on me.

It took me five long minutes to get free and took the rescue squad another 10 to get there, and by then, it was too late. I had kept meaning to take CPR lessons.

I'd thrown on a nightgown and bathrobe, but there was little I could do to preserve Phil Macomb's dignity, other than throw a sheet over him. I guess the rescue squad had seen worse. They handled it with aplomb, trying their damnedest to bring him back, but failing. I know one history professor at Montclair who supposedly died on the toilet. So, yes, it can always be worse.

It was strange, thinking of it later, how nobody but the rescue squad was there with me. He died at 10:17, but nobody from any of the neighbors' houses came over. They must have seen that something was obviously, terribly wrong. Riding off, in the back of the ambulance, I actually saw one of them, two houses down, looking out through the living room curtains.

Maybe they just didn't want to intrude, but it did make me feel a little strange, later on. It might have changed my perception of who we all were to each other. It might have made me realize that reciprocal dinner invitations, house-watching and drunken New Year's Eve parties had not necessarily bonded us all for life.

The next few days have been all but expunged from my memory. Somebody took care of calling people and getting them to call other people. Somebody took care of funeral arrangements for a man who had never given a moment's thought to such things, who was sure, as I was, that he and I would be together for decades. (Hell, we thought we'd still be having sex for decades. It's hard to go directly from "Your fantasy or mine tonight?" to "Burial or cremation?")

Somebody took care of all the goddamned paperwork that won't wait sympathetically while you gradually became aware that you really have lost the love of your life, that he isn't coming back. It must have been me.

Montclair isn't that large a town. People are going to know things. Phil's family found out, somehow, that he had died in bed, and that he hadn't been sleeping at the time. And there was this sense of blame in the air, on top of everything else. I could feel it like the cold March wind whipping through that cemetery, where Philip Anson Macomb III was laid to rest among his father, his grandparents and apparently about every other Macomb who ever lived in or around Montclair.

It was a free grave site, waiting for a man who shouldn't have needed it for a very long time, so I accepted their offer, but there doesn't seem to be any place in that cemetery for me.

Georgia McCain Macomb, killer bride.

The breakdown, if that's what it was, was inevitable, I suppose. Friends tried to warn me it was coming, gently suggested professional help, tried to keep me from sitting around half the night with the lights out, just staring off into space.

. . . Like I've been doing this morning, when I see my father, or surely think I do.

Looking out the kitchen window, your view, across plowed-under corn fields and around the two chinaberry trees that stand defiantly if a little scraggly in an otherwise flat land, is of the backs of houses and the few commercial enterprises in East Geddie. Chain-link fences enclose cars and storage sheds long past any conceivable usefulness, rusting metal with no place else to go.

This early on a too-warm November morning, it all seems to be floating above a couple of feet of ground fog. I don't know if I have ever seen quite this exact scene before, in all the years I lived here. I never was one to bond with nature, though.

It does entrance me, and when I see the figure walking across it, left to right as if he were taking a shortcut through our field, going from nowhere to nowhere, it doesn't really seem odd, at first, just part of the same little tableau, laid out for my benefit.

In a few seconds, it dawns on me that the surreal and the not-real might be occupying my line of sight at the same time.

He does seem to be floating on the mist. I can't see anything lower than his knees. He's perhaps a hundred yards away, close enough to know it isn't Kenny, too far away to make a positive identification.

When he turns toward me, though, I know. He's looking right at me, and he's in better focus than he should be, considering the distance and my book-weary eyes.

He stands like that for a few more seconds, stock-still. Then, he turns and continues on his way. Toward the woods beyond the Rock of Ages, the fog has lifted a little, to more than head-high, and he walks right into it. I watch for another 15 minutes, until it clears, but by then there's no sign of him.

By the time Justin and Leeza come down for breakfast, I'm sitting at the kitchen table, holding a cold cup of coffee and staring at an interior nothing rather than an exterior one.

"Mom?" Justin asks, touching my arm.

I look up and ask him what he wants for breakfast.

He tells me that he and Leeza will just have some fruit and cereal.

"Are you OK?" Leeza asks. "You look, you know, a little pale. Can we fix something for you?"

I look at her and smile. She is a sweet girl, standing there so distended, looking so young that she appears to be wearing some kind of faux-pregnant Halloween costume, yet more outwardly calm than I could possibly have been the month before Justin was born.

She does mean well, I'm sure.

I tell her I've just got the November blahs. Nothing to be concerned about.

No reason to alarm people.

CHAPTER THIRTEEN

November 21

Sunday dawns bright and promising. It's supposed to be nearly 70 degrees, almost a record.

When the phone rings, Georgia is trying to find something clean and decent to wear to church, chastising herself for not going to the cleaner's last week.

"Have you ever been canoeing?" Kenny asks.

She has. It is another memory to jump out and accost her, just when she thinks they've all been beaten back.

Phil finally cajoled her into going with him, to a stretch on a small river he preferred, between Montclair and the mountains. It had just enough riffles of just enough magnitude to be challenging but not life-threatening. The scenery, with hills on all sides much of the way, was so stunning that Georgia would often quit paddling and insist they move out of the stream so she could just look for a few minutes. A 12-mile trip that might have taken Phil Macomb four hours by himself took the two of them almost twice that long.

"If you aren't going to stop and admire all that beauty once in a while," she asked him when he became impatient with her, "what's the point?"

He told her that he had done quite a bit of that the first hundred times or so he'd canoed the Little Bright.

"I could enjoy this stretch blindfolded," he told her. "I could get by just on the smell and sounds. I know all the hills and rocks by heart. I see them, but if I stopped every time I saw something drop-dead gorgeous out here, I'd never get where I'm going."

He told her he only paused when something had changed—a downed tree redirecting the current, a rockslide redecorating some obscure hillside, a new hawk's nest, flowers on a part of the bank where he'd never seen them before, their seeds washed up by the stream or dropped by some bird.

"Like new exhibits in one of your museums, you know?"

They'd done the Little Bright together half a dozen times in the two years before Phil died. She kicks herself now for every time she let him go alone.

Yes, Georgia tells Kenny Locklear, I've canoed before.

He wants to take her out on the Campbell River, south of Port Campbell.

Georgia demurs.

It isn't just Phil. She remembers the Campbell as a brown, torpid haven for water moccasins, a place used recreationally only by river-rat children whose parents couldn't take them to the ocean or a decent lake. As a child, she would watch from afar, horrified and fascinated, as they would swing into its foul broth from tree ropes or jump off the abandoned, half-submerged barge that sat below the Highway 47 bridge. One or two a summer seemed to drown in it.

She liked the Little Bright, once Phil had lured her into it, partly because it only resembled the Coastal Plains rivers of her youth in that both were wet. The Little Bright lacked the accompanying swamp, the earthy miasma that marked the Campbell, which boasted alligators not so many miles south of Port Campbell itself. A mountain-fed stream seemed less fearsome. You could see the rocks at the bottom, and though it might throw you from a canoe if you didn't respect its riffles properly, at least you could see where you might end up. To sink into the brown, catfish-infested Campbell was, to Georgia, to disappear from the Earth entirely with no hope of returning.

"You know," Kenny says, "it really isn't all that bad. For one thing, all the mills closing was bad news for Port Campbell, good news for the river. It won't even be that muddy today. All that rain last week is somewhere out in the Atlantic Ocean by now."

She doesn't know why she finally agrees. Maybe, she thinks, she trusts others to decide what she should do, going on the premise that they surely must have more sense than she. She knows this is a problem, having seen it in enough of her friends over the years as bad luck or bad choices beat them down. Still, she thinks, it's just an afternoon on the river. And she could use a little fresh air, a little exercise.

She goes to church alone, sitting next to Forsythia Crumpler and trying to stay awake during the Rev. Weeks' sermon, entitled, the church bulletin says, "Giving Thanks Every Day."

Georgia appreciates that the Presbyterians aren't as aggressively self-righteous as some of the evangelical churches she sees while running errands in and around East Geddie and Port Campbell, but her old church's quiet, sober mien has not exactly been the ticket for bringing in the multitudes, even from among the middle-class newcomers in the upscale development right behind it. Usually, the Baptists or the evangelicals beat them to the new families' front doors.

Georgia sighs as she looks around her at the old, familiar faces and the dearth of new ones.

She has promised Forsythia that she will go with her on Thanksgiving day to deliver meals to those who are ever older and more feeble than the small crowd sitting around them this Sunday morning. She doesn't know why she agreed: There are few people living who enjoy visiting the sick and shut-in less than Georgia McCain.

She wonders if this is because her father and mother made her go with them on such visits so often as a child. She has memories still of the sour-food and urine smell of the cheap nursing homes where the very old were warehoused, staring open-mouthed and toothless as their minds and bodies deteriorated from neglect and yesterday's soiled garments dried (or didn't) on a clothesline outside.

She thinks it might be because she knows this is just the sort of place in which she might have let her own father rot away had he not elected to sit outside in the hot Carolina sun the last day of July 11 years ago and make his own fate, or let God decide for him.

130

Georgia wonders if she is just giving in to Forsythia Crumpler the way she gave in to Kenny about the canoe trip. She wonders if she isn't just giving in—or up—period.

Still, though, when it was explained that there just aren't that many "healthy ones" left to make the rounds—and Georgia realizes that her old teacher, even at her age, is one of the healthy ones just by being ambulatory—she feels powerless to refuse.

"Not all of them are in nursing homes," Forsythia said. "Some of them that aren't, though, ought to be."

"What about you?" Georgia asks, clumsily. "I mean, do you have any plans?"

The old woman shakes her head, tightly and quickly, and the subject is dropped.

"Have you had any more trouble with that Pooh?" Forsythia asks her after they have paid their respects to the pastor.

Georgia shakes her head.

"Have you?"

"Not the last couple of days."

"Well, you tell me if he's a problem. I'll sic Kenny on him."

"He's a good man," Forsythia says. "You can count on him."

Every time Georgia hears anyone from East Geddie talk about someone's dependability, she clenches a little, hearing in her own mind the unspoken punch line: "unlike you."

Forsythia Crumpler probably means no harm or censure, though. She seems to have come around to a position of at least accepting her old student as she is.

"I'm going canoeing with him this afternoon," Georgia says, and then adds, "Kenny" when Forsythia seems confused.

"In the river?"

"Well, yeah. I mean, that's about the only place you can, other than Maxwell's Mill Pond."

"Well," Forsythia says, turning to go, "you be careful."

When Kenny comes for her, he has a smaller version of himself in tow.

"This," he announces to Georgia, Justin and Leeza, who are washing dishes, "is Tommy. What do you say, pal?"

Tommy is coerced into a mumbled "Hi."

He has his father's dark complexion, but his hair is reddish-blond, from either his mother's genes or the residue of a sunstruck Carolina summer. Or maybe, Georgia thinks, it'll just turn dark later.

"We're heading to Momma's, aren't we, buddy?" Kenny asks, and the boy nods with a lack of enthusiasm.

Yesterday was Kenny's day with Tommy, and they spent Saturday night camping out in the little stand of woods beyond the McCain graveyard.

"We saw a ghost," the boy says, but when Georgia tries to draw him out, he's already distracted by something she can't see.

She tells Kenny it's perfectly fine with her if Tommy comes with them canoeing. The boy looks up, and Georgia can't tell if she's seeing fear or hope. Kenny shakes his head, though, and mouths, "She'd kill me."

Georgia, trying to make conversation, asks Tommy how he likes school.

"It sucks," he mumbles, and is chastised by his father.

She is to follow Kenny in the minivan, first to Teresa's, where he will deliver the boy, and then to the river, where they'll leave her vehicle at a pickup spot 10 miles downstream from where they put in, then drive back to the starting point.

She stays in the minivan, behind Kenny's truck, with the engine running, while he takes his son to the home of his ex-wife and her parents. A head bobs out from behind the storm-door glass, then ducks back in again.

"Was she checking me out?" Georgia asks when they get to the landing.

"Who? Teresa? Hell, no. Why should she? Are we on a date?" He has turned his head toward her as he throws his arm over the seat and backs out of the almost-abandoned dirt clearing beside the river. He smiles slightly, almost shyly, it seems to Georgia, then looks away.

"I suppose," Georgia tells him, "if you had a date today, we wouldn't be going canoeing, would we?"

"There you have it."

He drives them back to the place where they'll enter the Campbell, just below the river bridge. This lot, larger than the one downstream, is also dirt and nearly deserted. From where they sit, almost level with the water in front of them, it seems a more pleasant river than Georgia remembers. The unexpected warmth of the day, magnified by the truck's windows knocking off the wind—what Phil used to call "the windshield factor"—makes Georgia so comfortable she wants to do nothing more than sit there, maybe doze off, listen to some oldies on the radio.

"If this doesn't beat watching the Redskins choke another one," Kenny says, looking out at the water, too, "I'll kiss your ass."

He glances at her.

"Figuratively speaking, of course."

Georgia laughs.

"Definitely figuratively speaking."

They get out, reluctantly, and manage to get the canoe, cooler, life vests and a couple of paddles out of the truck bed and into the water.

"God, this is great," Kenny says, and the way he says it, it almost sounds like a prayer. "No motorboats or Sea-Doos or any of that mess. It's worth coming out here sometimes even in December, just for that. Cold weather keeps the riff-raff out."

Georgia finds that she has lost most of whatever rowing muscles she had developed on the Little Bright. She struggles to help Kenny, and it takes them a mile or so to attain a rhythm, with him slowing his stroke as she speeds up a little. Finally, they are moving in something resembling a straight line.

She apologizes again as they find themselves pointing more toward the far bank than down river.

"Stop that," he says. "We aren't in a hurry to be anywhere. It's probably too late to make the Olympic rowing team anyhow."

"Sorry," she says, then laughs.

Almost as soon as they have achieved something resembling forward motion again, Kenny ceases rowing and motions her to do the same. They put the paddles in the boat and just drift.

"We'll probably get to the other landing in less than three hours if we just drift," Kenny said. He reaches for a beer and offers her one.

133

"Got Coke if you want one," he said. No, she says, a beer would taste good. The river reflects the bright sun that already is diving toward the trees on the other side. The double dose of sunlight and half an hour of rowing have made this feel more like a September day. Only the sycamores along the bank, mostly bare now, hint of impending winter, their mottled white trunks like a harbinger of snow.

Ahead of them, an island splits the river into two diverging streams that are reunited a hundred yards farther down.

"Peacock Island," Kenny says. He guides the canoe to its sandy shore with one paddle, then helps Georgia out.

"I'd always heard of this place," she says, looking around. "Something about a rich guy who owned it and brought all kinds of exotic wildlife out here?"

"Yeah. And the peacocks got loose. Some people say they can still hear one screaming now and then, but I think you'd have a hell of a time hiding a peacock on an island this size, or anywhere else around here."

Kenny has brought along some chips, and they sit under a live oak tree, legs crossed, passing the bag back and forth while they drink a couple of beers. To Georgia, who remembers the dry, blue-law Scots County Sundays of her youth, the alcohol seems like an illicit pleasure.

They talk about Pooh Blackwell, although Georgia doesn't mention her latest conversation with Wade Hairr. She hasn't told anyone, partly because no one, including Kenny, seems interested in Jenny McLaurin conspiracy theories.

They discuss Justin and Blue's plan to sell much of the farm's produce to northern distributors. As Blue had said earlier, Kenny is "studying it."

"There are so many ways for something like this to go wrong," he tells her, "and only one way for it to go right. It might work, but Blue, you know, he's had some crazy ideas. And Justin—well, he's a smart kid—smart man. But, no offense, he doesn't know much about farming."

"Well," Georgia says, "maybe among the three of you, you can conjure up one decent plan. Put all those big ol' manly brain cells together."

"Maybe we can. Who knows? Hell, I'm about one-third smart. Maybe Blue and Justin can fill in the rest."

They talk about her father, and, at last, loss.

"I don't know," Kenny says, when she asks him, point blank, why he and Teresa broke up. "I think most people just haven't completely grown up when they get married, you know? We just couldn't seem to agree to grow in the same direction."

And she tells him about Jeff Bowman, Justin's father, without mentioning how, with the aid of one of her graduate students, she managed to pay back his philandering in kind and complete the immolation of their marriage.

"And then," she goes on, "you jump from the frying pan into the fire, if you aren't careful. Strike two."

"And—Phil—right? That must have been tough."

She starts to tell him about Phil Macomb, but she can't do it. She has to turn away. It comes up on her all of a sudden sometimes, when she thinks she can talk about it more or less dispassionately.

"Anyhow," she says, composed again, "strike three."

Kenny puts his hand on hers, so softly that she can barely feel it.

"It isn't baseball, Georgia," he says. "You can keep swinging as long as you want."

She laughs.

"Figuratively speaking of course."

"Definitely," he says, smiling as he squints into the sun. "Definitely figuratively."

He asks her if she has the gun with her.

She bats her eyelashes.

"Not today. I've got a big, strong man to protect me today."

"Well," he says, "just don't be afraid to use it, is all."

"I hope it doesn't come to that. I really would rather go my whole life without having to kill somebody."

Kenny is silent. She wonders if he's asleep, but when she turns, he's just staring out across the river.

"What about you?" she asks him, trying to make him smile. "Ever kill anybody?"

He remains silent.

"You have." It isn't a question. "You have. Haven't you?"

135

She feels his hand leave hers. Through the narrow slits of her vision, she sees him walk off toward the east side of the island.

When he returns, he tells her that they'd better move on or plan to stay the night.

They have to hurry the rest of the trip, and by the time they reach the lot where Georgia's vehicle sits alone, the sun has disappeared below the tree line. The wind blowing down the river, an aid as they tried to make up for pleasantly lost time, now chills their sweat. The afternoon's warmth is a distant memory.

They realize that the canoe won't fit into the van, so they have to go back for Kenny's truck. As soon as she's stopped, he gets out and goes around to the driver's side door.

She offers to follow him back and help him put the canoe back into the bed, but he says he's fine, that she probably ought to be heading home. She can barely make out his dark face as he leans on the door frame. He seems to be smiling.

"They probably think you drowned or something."

"Well," she says, "anyhow, thank you for a very nice afternoon. Thank you for making me have a good time against my will. And I didn't mean to be nosy. None of my business."

"You're not nosy. Sometime, maybe I'll tell you a story."

She leans toward him slightly. Neither of them could have said who kissed whom. Probably, Georgia thought, it was some kind of mutual pull that wouldn't have happened if their faces hadn't been so close that they were pulled the last few inches by scent or whatever stimulus makes people do the unlikely if not unthinkable.

Whatever, Georgia thought, driving home alone, slightly disheveled and a little horny. It had been a hell of a kiss, her opening wide, without reserve, tasting him as he explored her mouth with a hunger she hadn't experienced in recent memory. Most men, she was sure, did not understand how a really good, tongue-swallowing, dental-flossing kiss could move women, or at least her. Maybe Kenny didn't know either.

It couldn't have lasted more than 10 seconds. When he pulled away first, he didn't say anything, but he looked as troubled as Georgia had ever seen him when he backed off into the dark. He tripped on something and almost stumbled, cursing as he caught himself on the hood of his truck.

"OK," Georgia said. "Thanks. See you."

She couldn't hear what he said.

Back home, she has to placate Justin and Leeza, who do indeed seem to have surmised that she must have drowned.

"You know," she tells them, "I am a pretty good swimmer. I can take care of myself."

"I guess," Justin says, frowning, and when she looks at herself a few moments later in the mirror, she sees that she does look like someone who has recently been in distress of some sort. Her sweater is bunched up badly from being thrown on in haste as the cold wind picked up. Her hair looks more than windblown. And her face, she feels, must be telegraphing, to anyone who studies it, Just Been Kissed.

She shrugs and stands there. She had almost forgotten the spicy sweetness of guilty pleasure.

CHAPTER FOURTEEN

November 25

The Indian summer sun of last week would have found a way to break through these early morning clouds, but this is a weak and sickly imitation, a portent of bleakness.

Leeza joins Georgia in the kitchen before 8, early for her these heavy-laded days. She seems ready to give birth any moment, although the calendar says it'll be another month. She makes herself some tea, then waddles across the room and manages to squeeze herself and baby Alysyn-Maree-Gregg-Mack between a chair and the table.

She answers Georgia's unasked question.

"I thought you might need some help."

There is no guile or irony in her face or words as she says it.

"Well, thank you."

Georgia does indeed need some help. She has been induced to promise more than she thinks now she can deliver this Thanksgiving.

There are four shut-ins that she and Forsythia Crumpler will be visiting today, sometime in the early afternoon. They will be bringing full dinners, prepared by others while Georgia is getting her own family's meal ready. She is not sure how she will manage to be in two places at once. Kenny is coming and is bringing, at Georgia's urging, his son. He gets Tommy on alternate holidays. She also asked Blue, Annabelle, Sherita and their children. They seemed to appreciate the invitation, but Annabelle is cooking for an extended family that, as she ticks off the names, seems likely to fill the adults' and children's tables, then spill out of the Geddies' modest home and into the yard.

Georgia has managed to get Forsythia to join them as well, finally worming out of her the information that she was not in anyone's plans for the day.

Georgia has written down everything she will need to make Thanksgiving dinner, and now she has assembled all the many parts on the too-small kitchen counter. She marvels at cooks who never seem to look at recipes, or even have recipes, outside their own heads.

- Turkey (almost defrosted; she will have to get Justin to reach inside the still-icy bird and pull out what her father used to call "lizards and gizzards").
- Makings for sweet-potato casserole, with note not to forget the little marshmallows this time.
- Makings for yellow-squash casserole.
- Pumpkin pie (bought).
- Cranberry sauce (bought).
- Dressing (bought).
- Rolls (definitely bought).

Kenny is bring field peas and butterbeans, canned by his mother and cooked by him with, he assures her, at least half a pound of pork fat for flavoring.

Even vegetarians, he tells her, have strokes down here.

Georgia asks Leeza to cut up the squash and onions while she reacquaints herself with the sweet-potato recipe.

"Would you like me to make some biscuits?" Leeza asks.

There is little Georgia would like less. She contemplates the neatly boxed, canned and organized bounty before her and knows that soon it will explode into a mess that will in no way justify the resulting meal. The last thing she needs, she wants to say, is biscuits, with flour and Crisco and buttermilk everywhere, one more large bowl, one more need for the lone chopping block.

But Leeza has become quite proud of her biscuits, which with more consultation with Annabelle have become, even Georgia must admit, quite acceptable, a welcome addition to her small domestic résumé.

"Sure," Georgia says, "biscuits would be great. Annabelle didn't show you how to make gravy did she?"

Leeza shakes her head.

"No, she didn't. Can't you. . . ?"

"Sometimes."

If they can get the two casseroles prepared, if the turkey is ready to go into the oven by 10:30, if somebody can set the table and keep an eye on the bird and put everything else in the oven at the requisite times, if nothing else happens, they might be eating at 3:30, the way it was planned. And that's counting on me to make the gravy, Georgia thinks. God help us.

"Shit," she says. "Shit!"

"What? What is it?"

"Beaujolais nouveau. I forgot the Beaujolais nouveau."

She always stocked up on a few bottles for Thanksgiving at home. Even if they were eating elsewhere, they'd bring the new wine with them. This year, in a strange setting, she has forgotten the Beaujolais nouveau.

Leeza giggles.

"What's so funny?"

"Well," she says, "I can't drink it. I doubt if Mrs. Crumpler will. I don't think I've ever seen Kenny drink anything except beer, and I doubt his son is much of a drinker. I'm sure Justin won't hold it against you."

I need it, Georgia wants to say. I wanted everything to be perfect. She remembers all the imperfect meals back in Montclair, the burned, underdone, oversalted, underseasoned, sabotaged-by-bad-recipes meals. She equates the mess of her life to some extent with her inability to make edible meals on a consistent basis.

But she can't say all that without sounding like the mental case she fears she has become.

"OK," she shrugs, "no wine. What the hell."

She has agreed to pick up Forsythia at noon. Their four stops shouldn't take more than hour, she thought at first, but she since has realized that she is on what she has always referred to, ever since she left, as EGT—East Geddie Time. Pleasantries will have

140

to be exchanged. The two of them will be obliged to sit down in a dark, overstuffed living room or, even worse, a bedroom smelling of Ben-Gay and night sweats. They might be there for only 15 minutes, but they will have to sit and "visit."

"I'll be back by 2:30," she tells Justin and Leeza, who assure her they have things under control.

Forsythia is ready when Georgia arrives, dressed as if she were going to church. Georgia is wearing slacks and a peasant blouse with a sweet-potato stain on the front.

They pick up the four complete dinners that the men and women of the Presbyterian and Baptist churches have prepared, everything from soup to nuts, they assure them. Georgia can smell the turkey and dressing under the tinfoil, much better than what is cooking back at Chez McCain, she's sure. She is tempted to steal one of the little tins of gravy.

"It's mighty nice of you to do this, Georgia," Minnie McCauley says conspiratorially while Forsythia is talking with one of the deacons about the best route for them to take. "She really hadn't ought to be driving all over the county by herself."

Georgia is lying when she says that she is glad to do it, but she doesn't really resent it, either, she realizes.

Forsythia's route takes them first to a trailer park on the back side of Geddie itself, where Mary Draughon lives alone, having, at 88, outlived two husbands and both her sons, one claimed by a heart attack and the other by colon cancer. Her three grandchildren are "somewhere," Forsythia says, snorting and looking out the side window.

Mary Draughon, who seems to Georgia to be at least 100, is ensconced in a recliner, and it takes her five minutes to get out of it and unlock the front door.

"Didn't used to have to lock everything," she says, by way of greeting, "before the niggers got so mean around here."

She notes that she doesn't like cranberry sauce, and she hopes out loud that the dressing doesn't have onions in it. She spends the next 10 minutes talking about her health, her family and her neighbors. None of the news is good.

141

Her complaints over, Mary Draughon asks them if they want some Russian tea, which is, Georgia sees, the opening for them to depart gracefully.

"No, honey," Forsythia says, "we have three more of these to deliver. Don't want to keep folks waiting for Thanksgiving dinner."

"Well, you all don't have to go so soon," she says, but after five more minutes of what Georgia used to refer to impatiently as mealy-mouthing, they are out the door. One down, three to go.

"She's had it tough," Forsythia says, when they're back in the car and she sees Georgia shaking her head. "But, you do have to take charge of your own fate, make people want to come see you. The thing is, I don't believe I can remember Mary Draughon ever being that much fun, and it sure doesn't get better when you're going on 90."

Forsythia Crumpler laughs quietly, almost a giggle.

"That's un-Christian of me," she says, shaking her head.

"Well," Georgia says, "you can't please Jesus all the time."

She thinks she's being far too flip for her old teacher, but Forsythia looks sharply at her and then breaks out laughing.

"No, I don't suppose you can."

Their next stop, almost to McNeil, is a little house, not much more than 1,000 square feet, Georgia estimates.

Sam Lacy doesn't go to Geddie Presbyterian. He used to go to the Baptist church, Forsythia says, but he hasn't gone anywhere that anyone knows of for a few decades.

"He's had a stroke," she adds. "I suppose he gets by on Social Security, such as it is."

Sam Lacy takes a long time to come to the front door. He drags his left foot, and his left arm hangs useless at his side. He mumbles his thanks as he leads them into his little kitchen, where he stands amid dirty plates and glasses while they unwrap everything. He looks as if he hasn't combed his dingy yellow-gray hair, and he smells as if he hasn't washed lately.

"Dinner's served, Sam," Forsythia says. "Happy Thanksgiving."

The man tries to say something else, and it's clear to Georgia that his speech has been impaired as well.

He seems shy, embarrassed in their presence. He doesn't insist on them sitting down and visiting, and they're out again in five minutes.

"Poor thing," Forsythia says, "I ought to come visit him once in a while. I taught him, too, you know."

"But he looks like he's 10 years older than you, at least." Georgia says it quietly as they're walking down the dirt path back to the van.

"The men around here age so fast, the ones that get to age at all. The sad thing is, I can still remember how most of them looked when I taught them, so I can see how far they've slipped."

"I guess that's discouraging."

Forsythia looks at her.

"Well, it happens. It's sad, but I don't know if it's discouraging. It's just what happens. People get old."

Their last two stops take perhaps 15 minutes each. One widow lives along the Ammon Road; the other has a trailer in East Geddie. By the last one, Georgia has the process down pat, is able to say all the pleasant and meaningless but essential things. She realizes that neither of the old ladies is going to complain about her having to leave to "get back and feed the hungry at my place." They understand that's what a woman does on Thanksgiving day, if she's lucky enough to have family.

"Well," the last one says, "you come see me some time when you can stay awhile longer, you hear?"

And Georgia lies that she will.

"So," Forsythia says when they're back in the car, "is everybody ready for the blessed arrival?"

"As ready as can be expected. A marriage certificate would've been nice, I guess."

Georgia doesn't know why she mentions it. She has promised herself to be supportive of her son, even if it kills her.

Forsythia smiles.

"I didn't know anybody even got bothered by that these days. Things have changed so much. But that kind of thing has always gone on, as long as there've been men and women."

Georgia looks over at her as they pull out of the driveway.

143

"Really? Were there women you knew who had children out of wedlock?"

"Bastards."

It shocks Georgia to hear Forsythia Crumpler say the word.

"That's what they called them then," the old lady continues. "Bastards. Such an ugly, hateful thing to label someone."

The look of Forsythia Crumpler's face keeps Georgia from questioning her further.

They are back by 2:45. Forsythia looks a little tired. Georgia asks her if she'd like an arm to lean on, and she is surprised when her old teacher takes her up on the offer. It worries her a little; Forsythia is not the kind of woman to accept help under almost any circumstances.

To Georgia's relief, Thanksgiving dinner is moving along smoothly, perhaps more smoothly, she thinks, than if I had been here to make everybody's sphincter a little tighter.

The turkey is well on its way to done, a little tinfoil tent on it now that it has browned enough. The side dishes are either in or ready to go in at the appointed times. The biscuits have been cooked already and smell wonderful, their scent mixing with the turkey and the pies.

Leeza and Justin both have on aprons. They work well together, Georgia can see, even in the kind of kitchen where two people have to turn sideways to pass each other. She tries to help, but it's clear that she would only be in the way. She says she'll set the table, but that's been taken care of, too.

Kenny and Tommy get there just after she and Forsythia. The four of them sit in the den and wait to be called to dinner. Georgia and Forsythia both keep offering to get up and see if there's anything they can do.

"Let somebody else cook today," Kenny says, after he's headed them off for the third time. "You all have done your quota of Thanksgiving turkeys, I'm guessing. You've fed enough people already today."

"Some sad people out there," Forsythia says.

Kenny agrees that there are. Asked how his mother's doing, he says that she's having dinner with enough children and grandchildren that he suspects she'll never even know he's missing.

"I doubt that," Forsythia says, and Kenny nods.

"We're going by later," he tells her.

Dinner is achieved with scarcely a hitch. Kenny's son doesn't seem to like much of anything that is offered, other than the two helpings of bought pumpkin pie, but he doesn't whine about it, and everyone else eats enthusiastically.

Georgia and Kenny do the dishes, while Justin lets Tommy show him the place in the near woods where he says he saw a deer last weekend. Leeza goes to take a nap. Forsythia, who wanted to help, also falls asleep, in a recliner in the den within eyesight of the two dishwashers. It pleases Georgia that her older teacher is comfortable enough to do that.

"So," Kenny asks in a muted voice, "what's the latest on Pooh?"

Georgia shrugs.

Since she found the shoe and saw that it matched the one Jenny McLaurin was wearing when she drowned, she has gradually given up on the idea of seeking Pooh Blackwell out. She wishes she had shown the matched set to Kenny before she took them to Wade Hairr. They are now property of the Scots County sheriff's department, and Georgia wonders if she will ever see them again. Telling Kenny they were a perfect match was not as good as holding them up in front of his eyes.

She hasn't even mentioned the shoe issue to Justin. She's not sure why. Maybe she doesn't want to involve him, pull him into what everyone else sees as a wild-goose chase, and a potentially dangerous one at that. Maybe she doesn't mention it for the same reason she doesn't mention seeing a man who died 11 years ago: She doesn't want Justin to think his mother is losing her mind.

She finally told Kenny on Tuesday. She had come over to bring him some leftover chili. She was anxious, curious to see if one thoughtless kiss had changed anything between them, but Kenny seemed the same as ever, to her relief and slight disappointment.

145

When she told him about the shoes, he listened to her, nodding his head, sympathizing, but he seemed willing to take the Occam's razor approach. Go with the simplest and most straightforward answer. Jenny McLaurin couldn't swim. She slipped in the pond and couldn't get out.

He suggested this to Georgia, as gently as he could.

She did not take his lack of enthusiasm well, especially when the only thing that really seemed to upset him was that she had told Wade Hairr something that she didn't want getting back to Pooh or his father.

"You might as well put it in the newspaper," he told her. "Maybe Wade Hairr won't tell William about it. Maybe he'll just tell one or two of his flap-jaw deputies, and one of them will tell William's cousin, who'll tell him, and he'll tell Pooh."

"Maybe I ought to just shut up and let that fat piece of shit get away with it," Georgia said, tears welling up.

He told her, pinning her with his fierce eyes, that if he truly believed Pooh Blackwell had murdered Jenny, he'd be at the head of the lynch mob.

"I think the Blackwells did what the Blackwells have always done," he said, looking out across his land. "They saw a way to steal something within the bounds of the law, and they did. I do find it hard to believe they just flat-out killed her.

"If they take it over the edge, you know I'm there. But I've got to live here, Georgia, right here, night and day. I can't be playing Columbo, chasing wild-ass theories around, making enemies out of everybody. I don't like carrying a loaded gun with me."

Neither, Georgia told him, do I.

Now, she doesn't know what to say. She is starting to doubt her own convictions. She knows it would be easier to just let it go. She knows she has always had trouble letting things go. Her analyst told her that, as did her first and third husbands.

The diamond ring, if it was on her hand that day, could have been stolen by any of several individuals in the employ of the sheriff's department, the fire department, the funeral home—God knows who else. The shoe could have been dragged there by a dog after it washed up on the bank of the pond, or it could have come from some other place and time entirely. They might one day drain Harold McLaurin's snake pond and find a single, sensible shoe in the muck at the bottom, where it sank after it left Jenny's thrashing foot.

Anything was possible. Her answer was but one of several theories, and far from the most straightforward and likely.

"I haven't tried again to talk to Pooh," she tells Kenny. "I don't know what to do about all that. I guess I just wish it would all go away. I'm sorry I got you into it."

"I'm here, watching your back."

As he says this, he puts his right hand on the nape of her neck and rubs it. She leans into him. She turns at the same time he does, and they are wrapped in their second long, wet embrace of the week, their tongues deep in each other's mouths. He pulls her away from the window, out of view of the recliner and Forsythia Crumpler. His hands are squeezing her bottom, and she is reaching for the zipper of his jeans. He grabs her hand and shakes his head. She nods hers but backs away. Neither of them says a word as they return to the dishes.

They are almost finished when they see Tommy come running from the woods, looking frightened. Justin, walking fast and calling after him from 20 yards behind, also looks shaken.

Tommy doesn't say a word, just runs to his father and puts his arms around his waist, burying his head in his stomach.

"What?" Kenny says, as Justin opens the screen door and stands there, looking as if he wants to hit someone.

"The cat," Justin says. "The goddamn cat. Nails. Jesus."

There had always been cats around the farmhouse, feral creatures living on the periphery, earning their keep by thinning out the rats and mice. Whatever humans were living there would feed them, leaving table scraps and water at the edge of the yard. No cat ever was allowed inside a house. Georgia was 24 before she realized she was allergic to them; she had not been in a culture until that time that regularly allowed them indoors.

Occasionally, a younger family member would try to tame one of them, with mixed results. Georgia herself can remember a tabby

147

kitten she once took in, when she was 10. It had been abandoned by its mother, and Littlejohn and Sarah let the kitten stay on the porch in the house they were living in, next door. Georgia could carry it around in her arms, as long as there were no dogs around. It was the only one of the woods cats in decades to have a name: Ginger.

Ginger reached adulthood and left one day, never to return except for meals. Georgia tried for weeks to coax the animal back in from the hubcap holding the cats' food, but it would never let her or another human come within 20 feet of it again.

Leeza had always lived among cats. When she saw the half-dozen or so that frequented the farm—fed now mostly by Kenny—she wanted one of them for a pet. Justin didn't remember that much about the farm, but he did remember the cats. He remembered picking one of the more careless ones up when he was 6 or 7 and getting scratched badly enough to require a rather painful shot.

They're wild, he told Leeza. They won't even let you get near them.

We'll see, she said.

She would wander out in the yard, into the fields and woods, sometimes carrying food with her, sometimes not. She would be gone for two hours or more, long enough to worry Justin.

Within a week, one of the cats, another tabby, barely more than a kitten, was following her back to the yard. Leeza would lower herself awkwardly to the ground and sit cross-legged, talking to the animal, and it would sit, not 10 feet away, watching her. Then it was 8 feet, then 5.

Two weeks after Justin told her the cats were wild, she was able to pet one of them. She would walk along with the cat rubbing against her legs. Justin worried that it would cause her to trip and fall.

She named the cat Nails, because of its scruffy, street-wise demeanor, and she has been feeding it separately from the others, sitting on the brick back steps. Sometimes, the cat would sit beside her, both of them looking out at the fields and woods, the other cats staring back at them from across the yard.

"Just don't let them in the house," Georgia said, the first time she saw this wonder for herself. Leeza never did, although with the weather getting colder, Georgia has figured it's only a matter of time. She knows from personal experience that a woman eight months pregnant can get about anything she wants.

Kenny leaves Tommy with Forsythia Crumpler, who has been roused from her nap by the commotion. Tommy wants to come with him, but when his father tells him to stay with Mrs. Crumpler, he obeys him. Kenny and Justin don't want Georgia to come with them, either, but she insists.

The cat is at the old tobacco barn, hanging by a cord from a hook over the door, its tongue sticking out like something from some sadistic cartoon, its legs dangling from its body, looking much smaller than it did when it was alive.

Kenny walks around the old farm every day or two. Even though the barn is on Blue and Annabelle's land, it's part of his route as well. He walked by here yesterday morning.

They huddle and devise a plan. If they can get back to the house before Leeza gets up from her nap, and if they can get Tommy out of the house, they might be able to tell her that the cat ran off, disappeared, turned wild, whatever. There is a precedent, Georgia tells them. It seems cruel, but less cruel than having to tell a woman eight months pregnant that somebody has gone to the trouble to hang her pet cat.

"Maybe," Justin says, "after the baby is born."

Justin goes to get a shovel, and Kenny and Georgia return to the house before Leeza awakens. Kenny takes Tommy home. The boy is sitting, watching television with Forsythia, when they return, sharing the recliner. She has her arm around him. He has his thumb in his mouth.

"I'm sorry," Georgia says as they both leave.

"Maybe it's some of the Armstrongs' kids," Kenny says. "This would be about their level of sorriness."

One look tells Georgia how little he believes this.

Justin is back in half an hour, just as Leeza is getting settled in the den, apologizing for being "so lazy," wondering where everyone has gone.

149

"Has anyone fed the cats? And Nails?" she asks, and they're silent for a couple of seconds.

Finally, Justin says he did.

"I just left some food for all of them in the hubcap out back. Nails got his share too," he tells her. Still waking up, she nods her head and smiles.

Georgia takes Forsythia home. They don't talk much about the cat, and they both tell each other to be careful. It seems to be their mantra these days.

When Forsythia makes no effort to get out of the car and go inside, Georgia starts to ask her if anything is wrong.

"I don't know why I'm telling you this," the old lady says. "But something's got me thinking about it today. Maybe it's Leeza and her baby."

Her lower lip is trembling. Georgia puts her hand on Forsythia's and listens.

Forsythia McDonald grew up in a family that was almost wealthy by Port Campbell standards. She would be the only girl in her class to go on to college.

James Gilley was the son of the town's police chief, a wild, handsome boy.

"I just loved him to death," Forsythia says, clutching a handkerchief.

They were 16, seniors three months from graduation, when Forsythia knew she was pregnant and had been for at least two months.

"We could have gotten married. It would have been a disaster, though, and I'm sure James Gilley didn't want to, not really. Nobody knew what to do. It was an awful time, and it should have been so grand, with graduation coming, and then college.

"Everyone was just so ashamed of me. They talk now about boys taking their share of the responsibility when something like that happens. That wasn't the way it was back then."

The chief sent his son away to live with relatives in Greensboro. Forsythia McDonald's parents sent her away, too, to Evergreen.

"It was a place for 'bad' girls like me. It was like a prison. I was able to graduate from high school there, among other girls waiting to have their babies, too. I was so scared. My parents came to see me twice the whole time, and it was only 60 miles away."

The baby was born in early September.

"I saw her just once, and I wish I'd never seen her at all. They wouldn't even let me touch her. I can see her face right now."

The adoptive parents took her away, and Forsythia came home later that month, to a household that never truly forgave but insisted on forgetting.

"We never mentioned it again, ever. The next year I started college, a year late, and I suppose, considering the times, I'm lucky they didn't just disown me or something. Everybody in Port Campbell knew about it, of course. You couldn't keep something like that a secret.

"They treated me like I was lucky, lucky to still have a life in front of me, not condemned to carrying some bastard child around like a mark of shame. But all I could feel was emptiness."

She went on to graduate with honors from the women's college in Greensboro, driven by a determination to erase the stain. Two years after she came back to Scots County to teach, she met and soon married Whit Crumpler, a prosperous farmer who adored her. He was a plain man in intellect and appearance.

She would see James Gilley from time to time, here and there, but he seemed to want to avoid her, and he eventually moved away for good.

"I never did right by Whit," she says, looking across the barren fields. "He seemed to worship me, but I never got over the loss— the losses, really. In spite of everything James Gilley did or didn't do, I never really got over him.

"But the baby. Oh, Lord, how many times have I wondered whatever happened to her? They had a fire at Evergreen some years back that destroyed all their records, and you couldn't find her now even if you wanted to."

Forsythia and Whit Crumpler never had children.

"I can go for a day sometimes without thinking about her, but that's about it. I even gave her a name, in my mind. Geneva. Sometimes, I talk to her. Isn't that silly?"

151

"No. That's not the least bit silly. Does anyone else know—I mean, I've never heard anyone saying anything—" Georgia struggles to find the words.

"Oh, they must know, or at least the ones in my generation do, even out here in East Geddie. But they don't talk about it. I suppose they afford me that courtesy. But they know."

"Well," Georgia says, "anyone who doesn't know will never know from me."

Forsythia pats her on her knee.

"That's why I told you, I guess."

Georgia has been home half an hour when the phone rings.

When she answers, there is no response for two or three seconds, and she thinks at first that the telemarketers are even working on national holidays. Then, just as she starts to put the receiver back, she hears the voice, low but distinct.

"Happy Thanksgiving, bitch. Sorry about your cat."

CHAPTER FIFTEEN

November 28

Georgia finds herself daydreaming in the mostly empty sanctuary. She wonders if this is part of what she is supposed to get out of organized religion—a small patch of peace that might carry outside the walls of the church. Like yoga, without all that twisting and bending.

The last three days have not been in the least peaceful.

She and Justin have both spent an inordinate amount of time looking for a nonexistent cat. Georgia would walk through the fields, within earshot of Leeza, calling, "Here, kitty, kitty. Here, Nails. Come here, boy," and feeling like an utter fool.

She asked her son if he didn't think it would be better just to tell Leeza about the cat's demise, but he told her he didn't think so, that he just didn't want to deal with that kind of drama right now.

Some day, he told her, we'll all laugh about this.

God knows, Georgia thinks, there is drama enough already. She has no doubt as to whose voice she heard on the phone Thanksgiving night. She hasn't told anyone except Kenny about it. When she told him, on Friday, he said it sounded about right.

She wondered if they shouldn't go to the sheriff, and realized how fruitless that would be even as she suggested it.

"I know you'd like to go over there and shoot his nuts off," Kenny told her. "It's going to take a little patience, though. We're going to have to have some kind of evidence."

"With the quality of local law enforcement," Georgia said, "he's probably going to have to make a confession in the middle of High Street and have it notarized. I don't know if that would do it."

Kenny had something else to say, too, and he said it carefully, back on his heels.

"I know you don't want to hear this, and I believe you totally when you say it was Pooh on the phone. It sounds like something the sick bastard would do. But, just because he's mad enough at you to kill that cat still doesn't prove he did anything to Miss Jenny."

"If he's sick enough to hang a cat," Georgia said, "he's sick enough to kill a defenseless old lady. Hell, the cat probably put up a better fight."

She is still furious at Wade Hairr and his useless, loose-lipped office, and furious at herself for giving them something they could blab to Pooh Blackwell and his father.

Kenny told her it would be easy for a person to park in a certain lane that leads into the woods off the Old Geddie Road and walk from there to the edge of the field, where the cats usually congregated.

Probably, Georgia realized, that person could see them clearly in the house from there, too.

"That one was probably easier to catch," Kenny added, "being half tame and all."

No good deed goes unpunished, Georgia thought. They'll keep that little bit of information from Leeza even after the baby is born and they have to tell her what happened to Nails.

* * *

This morning, her nerves are so shaky that, when one of the two children in Geddie Presbyterian drops a hymnal to the wooden floor in the middle of Rev. Weeks' tepid sermon, she jumps and turns to glare at the boy. The little pistol sits in her jacket pocket, wrapped inside a rag. Every once in a while, she reaches in to feel it there. She is ashamed of how much comfort it gives her, perhaps as much as she is getting from Rev. Weeks' half-heard sermon.

Neither Justin nor Leeza came this morning. Georgia sits next to Forsythia. Neither of them mention Forsythia's Thanksgiving revelation, and Georgia doubts they ever will.

Afterward she speaks to Minnie McCauley, Alberta Horne and some of the other older women.

"You're gettin' to be a regular around here," Murphy Lee Roslin says, and Georgia smiles. She wonders how long she can stay. Common sense tells her to get in her van and head north this very afternoon. Let Justin handle the sale of the house and land, if such a sale ever comes about. Something else, stubbornness, she supposes, keeps her in East Geddie. She wonders if she isn't staying the course just to make up for the times she didn't, and if she isn't compounding her problems by doing so.

On top of everything, it looks as if Justin, Kenny and Blue really are going to go into this blue-sky business venture, selling Carolina watermelons, strawberries, greens, pork and whatever else they can produce to Manhattanites. They've talked twice more, and they'll meet this afternoon to see if they can agree on enough things to take it to a lawyer.

If that happens, Georgia supposes, the idea of selling Little-john McCain's farm is a moot point. As much as she cringes at the thought of her well-educated son living permanently in this place, she won't sell it out from under him if that's what he wants. She's told him, after finally expressing her reservations, that she'll charge him some nominal rent if he wants to do this.

Part of keeping Justin in the dark about some of Pooh's mean-ness is the realization that, if her son really is going to live down here—night and day, as Kenny says—he's not going to need a blood feud with the Blackwells. She doesn't want Justin carrying a gun around with him, or a carpet knife.

Sunday afternoon, after all the dishes have been washed, Leeza goes to rest, and Georgia and her son are alone. One of the benefits of this self-imposed exile has been the occasional quiet time with Justin. They didn't have as many of those as she would have hoped when they were living in the same house in Montclair. Leeza wasn't taking afternoon naps then, for one thing, and Justin was working, and Georgia was still teaching. And, she thinks now, she was crazy. That didn't help.

Now, a few of those moments do ambush them and thus make them drop their guards.

They have the old fireplace working. Justin cut up some fallen pines back in the early fall and has been chopping them into more or less firewood-size chunks. He says it's good exercise.

They've only had three or four fires so far, and Georgia is still afraid that the chimney will catch from whatever they haven't cleaned out of there. She can still remember how the house in which she grew up was totaled by tenants misusing a faulty fireplace.

Today, though, it feels good. For all its improvements, the old house is drafty. She sits on an old sofa they've moved within 10 feet of the fire and puts her sock-clad feet on the coffee table. She has a book in her hand that she never gets around to opening.

Lost in thought, she is half-asleep when Justin flops down beside her.

"So," he says, "is this the way you remember the old home place? I mean, is this how it was when you were a girl?"

"You forget, I didn't live here as a girl. I was already in college when Mom and Daddy moved in here, after his mother and brother and sister died."

She wondered at the time if they had lost their minds, taking a couple of steps back in terms of modern comforts from their comfortable little house next door, but they—her mother, really—brought the old place back to and beyond whatever it had been in its so-called heyday.

"So you grew up in the other house, the one that burned down?"

"There used to be a crape myrtle out there to mark it," Georgia says, staring into the fire. "I guess it died, too. I don't remember when."

"I thought this place was so cool when I was a little kid."

Georgia looks at him in disbelief.

"You were bored to tears by this place, Justin. We had to threaten you or bribe you to get you to come down here."

"Well," he says, shrugging, "maybe when I was older. But I don't remember it like that."

"I hated it here," Georgia says. "I could not wait to get away. I guess those farmer genes just skip a generation."

Justin looks over at her.

156

"I don't think it's genetic. You know, I'd never grown anything in my life until Guatemala. We didn't even have a garden."

"That was the plan."

"But there was something about the way they were living down there. I don't mean the poverty and the oppression. The farming cycle, the seasons—I know you think harmony with nature and all that is a bunch of bullshit, but it felt right to me. I think that was what made life bearable for them in spite of everything else. I didn't plan on anything like this, didn't think about it until you decided to sell the farm, but it occurred to me more than once down there that, if you had your own place and some good topsoil and didn't have to live such a hand-to-mouth existence, working the land wouldn't be such a bad thing to do."

Georgia thinks it must be her and Jeff's total denial of the natural world when he was growing up that has made Justin see Littlejohn McCain's old farm, or what's left of it, as some kind of Eden. They'd both grown up in the lonesome, sandspurs-and-pines Carolina country and had had enough to last a lifetime, they assured each other.

"If your granddad had known you were going to become such a son of the soil," she tells him, "maybe he'd have left you a bigger piece of it. And we could have saved all that money on college tuition."

"Well," he says, "it might not work out. You've always told me that you shouldn't be afraid to try different things, otherwise how are you going to find what makes you happy?"

Hoisted, Georgia thinks, by my own petard.

"Some of it," she says, taking an intuitive leap, "might be the same thing that got you into the Peace Corps."

He looks at her, then back into the fire.

"Huh," he says. "I never thought of that. I mean, East Geddie isn't exactly Guatemala, and Kenny and Blue can teach me a hell of a lot more than I can teach them. All I'm bringing is a little bit of land and some contacts up north."

He leaves to bring in another log from the back porch and tosses it into the fire, making sparks fly out on the floor in front of them.

157

"But, yeah, OK. Maybe I like the idea that I'm not living some place where everybody is just like me. Maybe everything you always taught me, about everyone being equal, not looking down your nose at people just because they didn't pick their parents or place of birth better, maybe that does mean something to me."

Georgia wonders how he has managed to give her credit for instilling all the right values in him and at the same time make it seem like a rebuke of her entire life. You didn't have to *do* all that stuff, she wants to tell him. They were just general guidelines. Do as I do, not as I say.

Justin doesn't raise his voice during any of this. He is calm and determined, the way Georgia has seen him at times in his life since he was old enough to reason. He was like this before he decided he was going to play midget football, and he stuck with it through three seasons despite the fact that anyone could see he didn't even like the sport that much or have any aptitude for it. He was like this when he told her he was joining the Peace Corps.

Arguing won't do any good.

She can't resist one more shot, though.

"Why," she asks him, "weren't you listening to me when I would wail and moan about what a boring, dead-end place East Geddie was? Why didn't that take?"

He laughs.

"I don't know. There was always this feeling I had that you were protesting too much, like if you didn't keep up this barrier, you'd be drawn right back down here, and you'd feel like a failure, like you were trapped."

"And," Georgia says, holding out her arms, "here I am, God help me."

She could, she feels sure, live here if she had to, if there were no other place to go. The thing she doesn't have, she supposes, is that oft-referenced sense of place. She's never felt as if she was "from" Montclair, and she doesn't feel she's "from" East Geddie, either. The whole point, when she left home, was to be comfortable everywhere, be a citizen of the world.

The only problem, she thinks, is that sometimes she is not really comfortable anywhere these days. She almost envies Wade

Hairr and William Blackwell and the others who don't seem to have to go anywhere new, learn anything new, see anything new.

"How about Leeza?" she asks. "How is she going to take to all this?"

"She's more into it than I am," Justin says. "She's always lived in these little houses, smaller than ours, nowhere to be by yourself, nothing to call her own. She thinks she'll love it, our kids running all around the yard, lots of dogs and cats."

At the mention of cats, they both wince.

"I know you're not happy that we're not married," he says, and Georgia is quiet. "I know this isn't the way you imagined it would be. You probably saw me getting my Ph.D., maybe going to some Ivy League school, marrying somebody with two or three degrees."

Georgia tries to protest, weakly, but Justin continues over her.

"But I love her, Mom. And if she'll ever agree to marry me, I'll take her up on it in a heartbeat."

"If she'll. . . ?"

"That's just between you and me."

Georgia finds that, the older she gets, the more her assumptions about life are embarrassingly, achingly wrong.

Leeza, it turns out, is so soured on the whole concept of marriage after 19 years under her parents' roof that she is convinced a wedding will ruin whatever happiness they have.

"Her parents should have gotten divorced a long time ago," Justin says. "They made you and Dad look like great role models."

He looks over at her quickly.

"Sorry. I mean, you *were* great role models. Just because you didn't get along didn't mean you didn't love me. I know that now."

Georgia thanks him for that, patting him on his knee. She's truly glad that Jeff and Justin have stayed fairly close, although Jeff's second family out in California has put some distance between them.

We did get along, though, she thinks. If Jeff could have kept his dick in his pants when he wasn't in her company, it would have all been different. They'd probably still be married. It wasn't perfect, but it wasn't bad, nothing to break up a family over. Except for that. It isn't hard to understand, but she isn't up, even now, to explaining it to her son.

"Well, honey," Georgia says, realizing she hasn't called him that in years, "I hope this farming idea turns out to be the thing that makes you happy."

Although part of her hopes he's back in graduate school by the next fall semester.

* * *

By the time Leeza rises from her nap, Justin has gone over to Kenny's. Georgia can see Blue's truck parked in the driveway.

"Big business next door," she says as Leeza looks out the window, holding her hands against the wall as she leans forward. Georgia wonders if she will need help standing up again, she is so front-heavy.

"I think it's really neat," Leeza says, popping back to full vertical mode with hardly a hitch. "I mean, we'll be growing our own crops, selling food for other people. We're going to make it all organic."

Including the pork, Georgia thinks but doesn't say. Leeza, she thinks, should have come of age in the late '60s. She'd have been in her element in one of the communes, like the one a couple of Georgia's friends joined. They tried to get her to come with them to some place out in Oregon, but she told them she went to college so she wouldn't ever have to go back to the earth again.

She wants to give Leeza the benefit of the doubt, allow for the possibility that this could turn out well, somehow. She doesn't know when she got so judgmental, always thinking she knows what's best, always having to stifle herself from giving one and all unsolicited advice.

"Organic," she says, and nods. "That's good."

She gets up and makes them both some hot tea.

"Thank you," Leeza says when she returns.

"You know," she continues, sipping the tea, "Justin really respects you. What you say means a lot to him."

Georgia laughs.

160

"He hides it well."

"No, I mean, he worries that you think he's going to fuck—excuse me—mess up, that we won't be able to make a go of it, with the farm and all."

"Well, nothing's a lock." It's the best she can do. "I just remember all the hard work and dirt and chicken manure."

"He's not afraid of any of that," Leeza says. "Neither of us is."

I hope so, Georgia thinks.

The weather is perfect for sitting by the fire, drinking tea, reading a book. But Leeza decides she wants to go outside and look for Nails again.

"He might be hurt out there somewhere," she says. "I can't just let him suffer. Even if he's dead, he ought not to just rot away out there somewhere."

Her lower lip is trembling.

Georgia tries to talk her out of it, but she insists on going out into the cold to look for the cat they buried three days ago.

Georgia doesn't know why she does it. The only justification is her fear that walking through the woods on this cold, miserable day will somehow harm her grandchild, and maybe Leeza, too.

"Sweetie," she says, "sit down for a second, OK?"

And she tells her that Nails is "gone."

"Run away?"

Georgia has to stifle a laugh.

"No. He died. On Thanksgiving day. Justin didn't want to upset you by telling you. He was going to wait until after the baby was born. We found him out by the barn. It looked like he just lay down and died. Animals do that sometimes."

And sometimes they're hanged from a barn rafter like a piece of meat, by your friendly neighborhood psychopath.

"Show me where," Leeza says, and nothing will do but for Georgia to put on her heavy coat and take the girl to the place where Justin buried the poor tortured animal.

She takes it well, after a few tears. She seems to understand that everyone had her best interests at heart.

"Things do die on a farm," Georgia tells her.

161

"I know that!" Leeza exclaims. "I know that! I'm not an idiot. But Nails was going to be my pet."

There are plenty of cats, Georgia wants to say.

The only thing left for her to do now is walk over to Kenny Locklear's and tell her son and the others the official story on the demise of Nails the cat, so they're all on the same page.

The three men seem to be playing well together, but Georgia can tell there are issues not yet resolved. They seem relieved to have some excuse to break up their meeting.

She can't resist telling them about Leeza thinking "gone" meant "run away." Kenny and Blue chuckle; Justin frowns, and she knows she's stepped in it again.

"I thought we weren't going to tell her until after the baby came," he says.

"She was going to go trudging out through those woods, in freezing weather, looking for a cat that's six feet under."

"Maybe a foot and a half," Justin says, and everyone cracks up in spite of themselves.

"I guess she really felt for that cat," Blue says, "but, damn, cats don't rate much above chickens around here, in the pecking order."

"Pecking order," Kenny repeats it, then his face turns red and he starts howling with laughter, which sets everyone else off.

"Pecking order." Somebody will say the word again and start another round of laughter. Finally, they're gasping and wheezing, all glad Leeza is still next door.

It's funny, Georgia thinks, what stays with you. She has friends who mourn the death of a cat the way they would the death of a child. Some of them spend more on the veterinarian than they do on their own doctors over a year. But she has retained from the farm a kind of hardness, a callousness where it comes to animals. It isn't what she would have chosen to take with her, but she didn't get to choose.

"So," Georgia says, "how is the big business merger going?"

They're all silent, suddenly somber . Justin finally speaks. He tells her they still have some details to work out.

"Like what?"

He gives her a look.

162

"I'll tell you later, Mom."

Justin excuses himself and goes to comfort Leeza. Blue says he has to get back as well.

"I want it to work," Kenny tells him as he leaves. Blue nods.

While his truck is still backing out of the drive, Georgia is demanding that Kenny tell her what happened.

"It does concern me, you know," she says. "It determines whether I'm going to keep that damn white elephant in the real estate listings or not."

"Old business," Kenny says, and explains it to her:

Blue and his mother still harbor a grudge over the land they lost to the interstate. What the Geddies want in exchange for the three of them going into business together is a five-acre strip of land running along the eastern boundary of Kenny's part, from the clay road to the southeast corner. He says it's prime land for the berry crops and melons he wants to grow there.

"It's a holdup," Kenny says, shaking his head, seeming more puzzled than angry. "Justin's just about convinced me that we'll all do well working together on this. That friend of his in New York does have the right connections, it seems like, and the three of us can give them what they want. But Blue's got a burr up his ass about getting something back for the land the interstate took."

Georgia asks him if it would kill him to give him five acres.

"Georgia," he tells her, his jaw tight, "they aren't making any more land. Nobody ever gave me much my whole life until your daddy, and I don't aim to be strong-armed into giving it away. If we go out of business together, he'll still have that land."

"Well," she tells him, as she turns to leave, "you're a smart guy. You'll think of something."

"Some of the things I've done lately have been less than smart," he says.

"Yeah, I can relate," Georgia says. She walks out the door before either of them can do or say anything else.

163

CHAPTER SIXTEEN

November 30

An all-day rain has set in. The last leaves have been blown and washed from the Bradford pears, whose late-turning foliage had given the back yard a brief second burst of fall color.

The trees were planted by Georgia's father, at her urging, three years before he died. Already they are 20 feet tall, and within another decade, they'll start splitting and have to be taken down.

Georgia thinks of the ones back in Montclair, the ones that inspired her to impose them on her father's pine-dominated yard. They planted them in almost every median strip in town, 20 years ago. Now, the town is having to remove every last one and replace them with something slower growing but more lasting.

If she were a tree, Georgia thinks as she gazes out through the horizontal rain, she would be a Bradford pear—fast starter, lots of splash and dazzle, but not built for the long haul. Not something you could depend on for shelter from the storm. Hell, it doesn't even bear edible fruit. She realizes Littlejohn probably planted the pears to humor her as much as anything. His favorite tree was a bald cypress he had relocated from the swamp to a space near a wet-weather spring back of the garage. He'd planted it there when Georgia was 10 years old and they were still living in their little house next door. She and her mother would laugh about the little tree, which seemed to grow about four inches a year and would lose its meager needles in September. It bore a striking resemblance, Georgia liked to say, to Charlie Brown's Christmas tree. Now, though, the tree is nearly 30 feet high, almost majestic among the evergreens. It could last, Georgia read somewhere, 1,500 years.

She is washing the few dishes she has dirtied eating a haphazard breakfast. She is trying to decide what to do, where to go, how to do the least damage.

Every day she stays in East Geddie, she kicks herself for not leaving. She has managed to incur the wrath of the village psychopath, leaving a helpless cat as an innocent victim. She has no faith in her judgment and is on the verge of conceding to Kenny, herself and everyone else that Jenny McLaurin lost her balance, fell into her late husband's snake pond and drowned. Period. End of story.

She wonders if she shouldn't just go back to Pooh Blackwell's house and tell him how wrong she was, beg his forgiveness, and try to get along.

It would be the wise thing to do, especially with Justin's idea to connect Carolina produce with Manhattan consumers now sidetracked by the kind of long-simmering disagreement that has always made small-town life so unappealing to her.

She feels the need again to sell the damn farm. If someone offered her $20,000 less than the asking price right now, she probably would take it. Let Justin go back to the real world, forget a dream that would have worked better in the 19th century than at the tail end of the 20th. If the farm is ever going to get sold, she knows it would be in her best interests to stay in East Geddie for the time being, Blackwells notwithstanding, to keep the heat on.

She called the real-estate agent yesterday, and the woman gave her all the happy bullshit about "hard to sell just before the holidays" and "we're going to really push it in the new year; it'll sell before spring, I guarantee it." And, of course, the teensiest bit of pessimism. "We might want to, you know, maybe think about lowering the price a little come January." As if December, not even here yet, was written off already.

There is something else, too. She admits that she does feel some responsibility to stay with Justin and Leeza until the baby is born. It isn't as if she'll be boiling water and applying cold compresses, urging the first-time mother to push harder, like some Scarlet O'Hara thrown into the breach. Leeza has a perfectly good obstetrician in Port Campbell, one the two of them found on their

165

own. Georgia has always looked upon small-town doctors with a gimlet eye, but Dr. Haycock does seem to be competent enough, and very pleasant. The hospital, which serves four counties, appears adequate for birthing babies.

But there is this sense of cluelessness on the parts of her son and his girlfriend.

Georgia feels needed, even though no one has told her this.

It isn't just the Ouija-board names for the baby. They don't seem to be doing the requisite reading on how to keep a helpless, 7-pound human being alive until it gets old enough to feed itself. They have done hardly anything to prepare a baby's room.

She can take some of the blame for this lapse, she supposes. "How do we know the place won't sell next week, and we'll have to move back up to Montclair?" Justin asked her the last time she broached the subject. It is as good a reason as any to give up selling the place at all, but if Justin can't feed himself and his family down here, he's going to have to go somewhere else and get a job, anyhow. She has no intention of giving him the old farm and then having him get as bored with East Geddie as she used to be, abandoning it for her to try to sell again. If you can make this deal with Kenny and Blue work, she told him yesterday, I'll let you stay here. But you've got to do something. I'm trying, he told her.

There wouldn't even have been a baby shower if Georgia hadn't arranged one. It's set for Thursday night. Forsythia and several of the other women of the church will be there. Leeza's sister is coming down from Montclair, along with a couple of girlfriends. Her mother sent her regrets, saying she couldn't get off work. Leeza just shrugged when Georgia explained that as gently as she could. Annabelle Geddie and Blue's wife, Sherita, have been invited as well. They seemed pleased to have been asked and said they would try to come.

Georgia thinks sometimes that if she doesn't stay around until the baby is born, she will be responsible for anything bad that might happen.

Responsibility has traditionally worn on her like a 20-pound weight. She has shucked off more than her share. This time, though, she thinks she can carry it, if she can keep Pooh Blackwell at a safe distance.

So, the strategy, as Georgia sees it through the rain that streaks the double-pane glass, is to sell the house if someone offers a reasonable price—unless the Three Amigos can come up with a business plan—then hope the new owners can wait until sometime in the new year to move in. She supposes she soon will be looking for a Christmas tree and decking the halls in East Geddie.

Justin and Leeza have gone to the doctor's. Afterward, they plan to take in a movie and do some grocery shopping. Georgia thinks about visiting Forsythia, or taking a nostalgia trip to some of her old haunts, but the day is fit for nothing except watching an old movie on TV (thank God, Justin got cable installed) or taking a nap.

Georgia opts for both. Even though she's only been up for three hours, sleep finds her soon after she curls up on the old couch in front of the television.

She doesn't dream that much any more, and when she does, remembering the details is like trying to catch fog.

This one, though, is different.

She hasn't been inside Jenny McLaurin's former home in years. Awake, she could tell you very little about the house's layout. Her memories are more tied to senses other than sight—the fat-laden smell of country cooking, or the jarring horn blasts from the Campbell and Cool Spring engine as it hauled a dozen flatcars toward the lumber yard at noon, returning like clockwork at 2:30.

In the dream, though, everything seems clear. Stranger than that, it will remain clear after she awakens. She can remember small details that she wouldn't have latched on to if she had been conscious.

She is a little girl again, and the adults are all talking around her. Jenny and Harold and her parents are in some moribund conversation about the weather or the crops.

Her father looks over every minute or so to tell her to be careful.

Strangest of all, little Wallace is there. Georgia was only 10 when that Campbell and Cool Spring engine ended his life. He was in the second grade. She hasn't given Wallace McLaurin more than the most passing thought in many years.

Now, though, Wallace is before her, fully realized. She knows he soon will be dead. She knows everything, about Jenny and Harold and her parents, even as she is in the body of a little girl.

She begins crying, wanting everything to stay as it is, not wanting the losses about which only she knows. Her mother tells her she is acting silly, and the other adults try to console her, but even her father doesn't seem to take her discomfort very seriously. Wallace asks her if she will go and play catch with him—he did beg her to do that, she will remember when she awakens. He had few playmates around and was always eager for attention from her, an older child.

She goes outside. It is a sunny day; its brightness hurts her eyes. She can't see the rubber ball Wallace throws to her. After it hits her in the chest several times, she runs back inside, crying again.

When she re-enters the dark living room, only her father is there. She notices for the first time that he doesn't look as he would have when she was a child. He seems very old, the way she last remembers him. The other adults have vanished, as has Wallace.

She follows her father around the room. It is dominated by an old Curtis Mathes television set. Harold had bought one of the first TVs in the area. It has a frilly piece of embroidery on it, with the antenna box on top of that. There is a cheap, yellowish-brown plastic couch facing the TV, with two other unadorned straight chairs to the side. The room and most of the rest of the house are served by an oil heater. It sits in front of a fireplace that has been abandoned but never covered over.

Littlejohn McCain touches various object as he circles the room. Georgia continues to follow, expecting something, knowing it's coming.

Finally, he stops at the heater. He turns to her and smiles. It will remind her, when she wakes up, of how seldom he really smiled in life, choosing to stay deadpan even when he was saying something truly funny, his twinkling eyes the only giveaway that your leg was being pulled. Later, she thinks it might have been the bad teeth that were almost guaranteed in the pre-fluoride days she can

168

barely remember. He was ashamed of his teeth. Of course. That's why he would hold his hand in front of his mouth sometimes, shyly, when something made him laugh. She never thought of that before now.

He bends a little to duck under the stovepipe as he steps behind the heater.

He stoops and reaches into the fireplace, touching the painted-over bricks. She can remember, when she awakens, exactly where he touched them. He motions for her to come closer, but she shakes her head. He looks disappointed.

And then, she is distracted by the sound of birds, millions of them, crashing into the windows, and she is dragged harshly and unwillingly back into consciousness by the Hitchcock movie she had started watching.

The dream's vividness will haunt her for the next 10 days. She can even remember the sounds of her mother's and father's voices as they talked, the smell of her mother's perfume.

She does not believe dreams carry any kind of mystic power. At best, she sees them, like any good academic, as a manifestation of the subconscious.

Lately, though, she has been running across her late father in some unusual places, and it is hard not to lump this dream into the same category as her conscious sightings, filed under Nervous Breakdown.

She has gone back to Montclair once since she left, to take care of a few business matters regarding Phil Macomb's estate and pick up all the things she didn't think to pack for her original flight. She had lunch with Cathy Rayner, assuring her old friend that she would be coming back, sometime soon. She went to see Hubert Lefall and had a short, uneasy conversation with him about her sabbatical and the chances that she would be back, "fit as a fiddle," next September.

She wonders, lying on the couch and wrapped in a blanket, replaying the odd little dream, whether she is moving forward or backward, fitness-wise.

She hears a noise outside and thinks Justin and Leeza might be returning. It's Kenny, though, slamming the car door as he comes back from some errand or other. He seems to stay busy even in these dark days when the mere possibility of something growing from the cold, dead dirt seems out of the question.

She wants to see him, she realizes. She needs to talk to him.

He answers the doorbell on the second ring and ushers her in out of the rain. He still has his jacket on, over a work shirt and jeans. He's in his stocking feet. She's wet despite the umbrella, which turned inside-out on her in the brief run between their houses.

"I had this dream . . ." she begins.

He pulls her to him as she drops the sodden umbrella on his carpet.

"I've been having one myself," he says, low and urgent. "It starts like this."

For 20 minutes, they get no farther than the rug.

He kisses her long and deep, and she responds in kind, the two of them trying to devour each other. Georgia has always worried about things like her breath and her underwear in situations such as this, but nothing seems to matter now. They fall into a rhythm in which they are breathing only each other's breaths, as if they are giving each other artificial respiration. He runs his tongue into her ear and then—luck? skill?—discovers the place on her neck that has always driven her wild.

She doesn't even bother saying any of the obvious things she is thinking, has thought lately when she let her mind wander to this scenario. *This is so wrong. We shouldn't be doing this. What if someone sees us?*

He begins removing her blouse, a button at a time, then unhooks her bra from behind with one hand while she fumbles with his shirt.

"We'd better go somewhere," she gasps as her naked back slides across the floor, "before I get rug burns."

"Yeah," Kenny says, helping her with the shirt. "We ought to get a room. I think I know where one is."

She knew, somehow, that he would be this good, if she let him. She wonders, as he slides slowly in and out, making it last, giving her three orgasms before he's even had one, if it isn't the forbidden fruit aspect that so turns her on. She knows that she will feel terrible about this, later, when she regains her sanity.

For now, though, she is along for the ride. It has occurred to her before that sex keeps getting better, the older she gets. She wonders when that corner will be turned, too. The few men who have been open enough to talk about it indicate that it is the opposite with them. Another of God's cruel little tricks, she thinks. When they would have chewed through a chain-link fence to fuck us, we weren't really in the mood. Now, when we're more than ready, they'd rather watch a ball game half the time.

She wonders if this is the worst thing she has ever done, of a carnal nature. She never cheated on Jeff Bowman except to make a point. She did have a one-nighter during her second marriage, but Mark was so cold and self-contained that she didn't even think of it as being unfaithful, wondered if he would even have minded, except for the impropriety.

They lie there, after she has come as close to passing out as she ever has during sex. They've been in his bed for two hours, and he has spent almost all of that time stimulating her with his cock, his mouth and his fingers, usually a combination of the three. She has tried to reply in kind, and has made him come twice, which, although she has lost count, is at least a four-for-one bargain for her.

It is her experience that men, in this post-coital situation, do not stare back when you look deeply into their eyes. The remote control becomes a valued item.

Kenny, though, is different. Even as they exchange a very long, wet kiss, tasting themselves in each other, he keeps his eyes open, as if he is trying to memorize everything he sees.

"Do you know," she says, when she comes up for air, "that I don't believe I have ever come that many times in a week? What planet do you come from? How in the world did your wife tear herself away from you?"

171

She has his face in her hands, and she leans back a few inches. "I'm sorry. I'm getting way too personal."

"Nah. No, you're not. I will tell you, though, it wasn't this good. Nothing's ever been this good."

Georgia feels her face reddening, and laughs at the thought. "What?"

"Oh, it's nothing," she says. "I'm just thinking, I'm lying here in bed, buck naked in the middle of the afternoon with a likely blood relative who has just screwed me unconscious, and I'm blushing over a compliment."

"It's true, though. Really."

She resists the urge to tell him she bets he tells that to all the girls.

"Thank you. Thank you for—for all that—and thank you for telling me that."

They talked, once before, about the likelihood of Kenny's late father being the son of Littlejohn McCain and Rose Lockamy Locklear. It was an awkward conversation, one Georgia wished she hadn't started.

Littlejohn's belief in this unpaid debt to Rose' family has made Kenny's homestead possible. That one time, Kenny told Georgia that there had always been rumors in his family concerning his fair-skinned father's provenance, the occasional slip of the tongue by some maiden aunt entrusted with all the secrets. The rumors only multiplied after John Kennedy Locklear inherited 160 acres from a deceased white farmer. He'd hear them second- and third-hand.

"Some things, though," he told her, avoiding her eyes, "are best left alone. Littlejohn McCain was a good man, and he gave me what I had always wanted. Whether he's blood or not, doesn't make a bit of difference to me."

"What now?" Kenny asks as they lie sideways facing each other on the big bed.

"Nobody, I mean nobody, can know about this. You've got to swear it, Kenny."

He frowns and tells her she doesn't have to worry.

Shit, she thinks.

"Kenny," she says, trying to say it just right, "you know it's just because we might be, you know, related, right? And how disgusting it must look for an old broad like me to be screwing around with a hunk like you. Nothing else. I swear to God. You don't think there's something else, do you?"

It can't be that, Georgia thinks. Not race, the thing she was so proud to have blotted from her world view. She believes she is able to look at a person as a person, period. When she lies awake nights weighing her virtues against her many faults, she always gives herself a couple of points for that one. Surely she can't be worried about the disapproval of a bunch of old ladies at a church she might never see again after the farm is sold. For all she knows, they might not care. Everyone, as Forsythia has surely taught her, has secrets.

Times change, although there is not one person of color at Geddie Presbyterian, almost certainly never has been. When she and Forsythia were taking meals around on Thanksgiving, she asked who took food to the black shut-ins and needy, and Forsythia looked at her oddly and said she supposed the AME Zion church took care of them.

"It works well like that," she said, a little defensively, Georgia thought. "If we thought someone wasn't getting fed, we'd feed 'em, but I think they'd like to take care of their own."

Maybe that's so, Georgia thought. Maybe.

"You make everything too complicated," Kenny tells her now. "You had a great time. I had a great time. Maybe we'll have a great time again. Believe me, I don't want everybody knowing my business, either."

"Well," Georgia says, "I surely don't want it to stop. I mean, I can live with a little guilt for that many orgasms. A lot of guilt, actually.

"And, you know what they say about old ladies like me."

Kenny starts to tell her not to call herself old.

"They don't tell," she says, "they don't swell, and they're grateful as hell."

173

He is not a man to laugh long or loud, but he almost falls out of bed over this.

"I've got to remember that one."

"Just don't tell anyone who told you."

"Or where."

She is stroking him while they talk, and soon they are at it again. Georgia can't imagine what the Almighty was thinking, making her love sex so much at an age when she surely shouldn't be bouncing all over some younger man's bed, pushing her diminished flexibility to the limit. Why wasn't it this good when she was young and athletic?

When she makes him come a third time and looks up from where her head rests against his hard stomach, he looks as wasted, as drained and satisfied, as she feels.

"I don't know," she murmurs. "I don't know if I can keep from telling somebody about this."

"Give it your best shot," he tells her, pulling her up to lie on his chest.

She does remember to tell him about the dream, finally.

"Well," he says, lying there, still looking at her, not even glancing at his watch, although she has sneaked a couple of peeks at hers, "people do have dreams. I mean, you've been thinking about Jenny and that house and your daddy, too. It's probably just the power of suggestion."

"Maybe. OK, probably. But it seemed so real . . ."

"Georgia, I don't have a real strong leg to stand on here, with that rock out there drawing folks looking for a sign from their ancestors. But you're starting to worry me a little."

Join the club, she thinks.

They are silent for a couple of minutes when she turns and looks up, resting her chin on his chest.

"Tell me something."

"Tell you what?"

"If Pooh hadn't gone back to his truck like a good boy that time after the yard sale, what would you have done?"

He stares up at the ceiling, saying nothing.

"You'd have had to kill him, wouldn't you? Christ. I mean, could you have done that? Really?"

He makes eye contact again. He sighs.

"I probably shouldn't do this. You know, when you asked me if I had ever shot anyone?"

And so he tells her the story he'd planned to take to his grave, the one he knew he really, really never should tell anyone.

* * *

His sister's name was Rose, same as her grandmother. She was four years younger than Kenny. He had always tried to protect her when they were growing up, the two youngest kids in a big family.

The night he wasn't there, he was 21 and she was 17. He was in Raleigh, a senior, four months from being the first in his family to graduate from college. She would have started in the fall. Rose was worrying her parents and older siblings, though. She had gotten wild, more so since Kenny left for college. Her grades didn't really suffer that much, but she stayed out late, skipped school sometimes, hung out with what was generally considered to be a bad crowd.

He got the call at the off-campus apartment he shared with three other men. Rose was missing, had been since the night before. They found her car at the Quality Inn near the interstate. Kenny was back home in less than two hours.

They never found her body, never found any evidence of anything resembling foul play. The police hinted strongly that she might have run away.

But he knew Rose would not have done that. None of her friends confessed to any inkling that Rose Locklear might have been contemplating such a thing.

She was dating Cam Jacobs. Rose was a risk-taker, and Cam was a risk, everyone agreed, a rough-talking mill foreman with orange-hued skin and a scar across his cheek. He was 10 years older than Rose. He was, the rumor had it, rough with the ladies.

How many times has Kenny blamed himself for not telling her just how big a mistake he thought she was making? But she was not of an age to have listened even to him, probably, might have just run that much faster into Cam Jacobs' arms. Everyone knew Rose was a little wild.

Cam had a good alibi that night. He and Rose had met at the Quality Inn, had spent a couple of hours there, but then he had to go and help two friends move. He had said goodbye to her in the parking lot by 9:30. He thought she was going out to one of the fast-food places on the boulevard to meet some friends, but he said she told him more than once that she was thinking about running away, maybe going out to California.

His two friends told the same story, over and over: Cam Jacobs and they worked putting furniture into a U-Haul until after midnight, and then they had a couple of beers before closing time. Lots of people saw Cam at the Rendez-vous.

Kenny could hardly look at his parents as they were told about the room at the Quality Inn. The clerk had recognized them both as they checked in, but didn't recall seeing them leave.

There was no physical evidence. They found samples of Rose's hair in Cam's car, but as he said, they had spent a lot of time in his car.

Cam Jacobs was never indicted. Kenny would see him around town occasionally, before Cam moved to Lumberton. They never spoke about Rose.

His parents didn't want to believe that their daughter wasn't coming back. His father put up posters until the day he died of a heart attack, five years later.

Kenny was more pragmatic. He did his grieving, and then he put his plan in place. He knew it wouldn't happen quickly, knew he'd have to be patient if there was to be any chance of it happening at all.

Kenny was 28, a teacher for six years, when the first leak finally sprang.

He was in a bar one night, and he struck up a conversation with a Jacobs who, it turned out, was Cam Jacobs' second cousin. Kenny mentioned what a tough guy he'd heard Cam was, and the cousin started telling stories.

After relating a couple of bar brawls that ended with hospitalization, the cousin leaned a little closer.

"They say he killed a girl," the man said, his voice barely audible.

"I'd heard something about that, but didn't they clear him?"

"He's got some good friends," the cousin said. "Good friends will cover your ass when it needs coverin'.

"One of 'em, though, old Pete Oxendine, he had too much to drink one night, just me and him, I don't even know if he knew me and Cam was related, and he told me."

"Told you what?" Kenny's hand was shaking. He tried keep the shake out of his voice.

The cousin was quiet for 30 seconds, but Kenny knew he was just milking the drama.

"Told me Cam didn't come by 'til almost midnight. That they were real pissed with him, leaving them with most of the work. And he was all messed up. Him and that girl had got into some meth, and I don't know what all happened, but he burned his clothes in a trash can outside the house, got some new clothes, and he made 'em swear that he'd been there since 10.

"At least, that's what Pete Oxendine told me."

He'd lied for them before, and they lied for him, and didn't ask any more questions about it. By the time they had kept quiet for half a year, Cam made it clear that, whatever he had or hadn't done, anybody that waited that long to tell the police about it after lying for six months was in for some jail time.

"But Pete, he drinks a bit, as the song goes, and I suppose he said something he shouldn't of."

"Why did he kill the girl?"

The cousin said he never heard.

Kenny never found out all the details. He didn't care to know any more, didn't even want to find out where the body might have been dumped or buried or God knows what.

All he wanted to do was slip away from Cam Jacobs' cousin as seamlessly as he could, leaving such a mild impression that the cousin would barely remember him in the morning and might never recall telling him that story.

None of it would ever hold up in court, if it ever got to court. There was even that scintilla of a chance that Cam Jacobs had nothing to with Rose's disappearance. Kenny considered this, but he knew. He'd always known.

Maybe she wanted to leave him and he got crazy. Maybe it had something to do with drugs, taken or sold. Maybe she was pregnant and he didn't want to deal with that. It had occurred to Kenny, as he sifted through all the possibilities over the years, that she probably had been with Cam Jacobs since she was 15 and could send him to jail if she wanted to. Maybe she threatened to do that, or turn him in for dealing. There were a million possibilities. There always was the chance some fisherman would hook her remains in some remote stretch of the Campbell River some day.

Kenny Locklear thought it to death, trying to find some other answer to the mystery of Rose. All any sensible person could come up with, he concluded one last time, was Cam Jacobs.

It wasn't that hard to find Cam. He was still in Lumberton and lived in a trailer park. He'd led an exemplary enough life the last six years that he had never been arrested.

Kenny made the 70-mile round trip to Lumberton three times before he figured out how he would do it.

Cam worked the 3-11 shift at a textile mill. His habit seemed to be to come home to change, then go out again for a quick beer or two. He was living with a woman; they didn't seem to have any kids.

The rut road leading to the trailer park was so narrow that two cars meeting would naturally slow and move as close to the trees as possible to avoid colliding.

The fourth time Kenny Locklear went to Lumberton, he had a shotgun with him.

The night was overcast. Kenny drove down the rut road to the trailer park at 11, then turned around and headed back out. In his two previous trips, no one had come down the road except Cam Jacobs between 11 and 11:30. There were only a dozen trailers there, and half of those looked unoccupied.

It was not risk-free, he knew, but it would be worth it. Even if he got caught, it would be worth it.

He was on the stretch between the trailer park and the paved road with only his parking lights on, waiting. When he heard the car slow and then saw the headlights swing toward him, he started edging forward.

He managed to reach a particularly tight bend just as Cam Jacobs got there from the other direction. They were almost stopped when Kenny, with his window rolled down, motioned for Cam to roll his down as well.

"He might have recognized me. I think maybe he did. I'd kind of like to think he did."

The blast more or less blew Cam Jacobs' head off. It was impossible to mask such a sound. Kenny didn't think anyone at the trailer park had seen him, though, and when he pulled out on the highway, no one was coming. He could only hope Cam Jacobs was as dead as he appeared in the second he'd had to observe him.

"I threw the gun in the river, down by the old bridge. I got back home 40 minutes later, and there was nobody to see me. You weren't renting your daddy's place yet, Teresa and I hadn't moved in together. I was living in a trailer myself, while this house was being built."

It was, he said, about the last possible time he could have done such a thing. A year later, he was married and would have had to bring his wife into it.

Georgia is sitting up now.

"And did anybody ever suspect you?"

"Oh, one time a detective from Lumberton came by and asked me some questions. But Cam Jacobs had a lot of enemies, and was dealing drugs. If push had come to shove, they couldn't have proved I did it, and I couldn't have proved that I didn't."

"Did anyone suspect?"

"It's funny. When my family gets together, we'll talk about Rose sometimes, but nobody ever mentions Cam Jacobs, how he might have done it, how he got what he deserved. And I have this spooky feeling they do that for my benefit, and maybe they have a little more to say when I'm not around."

It's been 10 years since Kenny Locklear killed Cam Jacobs. When he tells Georgia he has never, ever told anyone about it until now, she believes him. She puts her head on top of his bare chest and can hear his heart pounding as she hugs him. She feels a shudder but doesn't look up to see if he's crying.

She doesn't go back home until after 4. She has showered and tries not to look quite so much as if she is in shock. She doesn't know if she has been affected more by the indecently wonderful sex or Kenny's revelation.

Justin and Leeza seem not to notice.

"I was worried about you," he says. "You ought to let us know when you're gone like that, even if it is next door. I mean, with that nut Pooh out there somewhere."

"So," Georgia tells him, already starting to make dinner, her face averted, "you going to ground me?"

Sometime after 8, the phone rings. Georgia picks up. She can hear heavy breathing on the other end, but no one speaks. She stays like that for a good 10 seconds before hanging up.

Justin looks over at her.

"Again?"

She nods.

"I didn't want to mention it, but I'm pretty sure I saw that big red truck, the one that Pooh drove, parked on the side of the road when we were coming back from town this afternoon. I didn't see him, but where he parked wasn't a quarter mile from the back property line."

Georgia doesn't respond. If he has put two and two together concerning the dead cat, he isn't admitting it, and she sees no reason to enlighten him, especially with Leeza in the room.

"Georgia," Leeza says, "do you think we should go see the sheriff or something?"

She shakes her head.

"No, probably not. They'd just want some evidence of some kind of wrongdoing, and I can't seem to give them any."

All I've got, she thinks, is ghosts and theories, a shoe, a missing ring and a dream that's stuck in my head like a bad song.

CHAPTER SEVENTEEN

December 7

W hat a week, Georgia tells her journal.

In the last seven days, she has taken a secret lover, given a baby shower, celebrated a birthday and fired a real-estate agent.

Peace has been declared. Blue, Kenny and Justin have come to an agreement. With, she writes, no small assist from me. It was her idea, pitched to Kenny on Friday, when he was somewhat vulnerable after a second session of love-making had proved at least as satisfying as the first.

"What about the right-of-way?" she asked him as she teased the almost non-existent hair on his right leg. "What if we give Annabelle and Blue the right-of-way? You know, the egress."

The way the will worked out, she owns the easement containing the clay road that is their only access to a paved highway. The old rut path that used to provide a back way in, connecting with the Ammon Road, has been cut off by the new interstate.

Kenny's land touches the paved road that goes into East Geddie, as does Georgia's, so access is no problem, but Blue and Annabelle's part is essentially land-locked. The other two parties made it clear that the road always would be shared, but the Geddies have a genetic distrust of promises.

Georgia became aware that this was still a worry when Annabelle mentioned it at the baby shower.

She and Sharita did come, and Leeza seemed so thrilled that they were there. She took great pains to introduce them both to everyone else, especially her friends from Virginia. The older women from Geddie Presbyterian knew Annabelle, having lived side-by-side in sometimes-separate, sometimes-shared worlds for their entire lives.

Georgia found herself in the kitchen, talking to Annabelle, who seemed to finally have accepted the fact that she was not ever going to try to take back the McCain land. She loosened up as much as she ever had in Georgia's presence.

They talked about Justin's idea, and what a shame it was that the three parties couldn't seem to make it work.

"It's just bothered Blue," Annabelle said, after Georgia had rebuffed her efforts to help her cut and serve cake. "I know he ought to of been just grateful for that land, but then that interstate cut off the best part of it, down by the branch, and he felt like he was cheated somehow."

She sighed, standing straight and tall while Georgia leaned against the kitchen counter.

"That and the easement thing, he seems like he worries about that all the time."

And so Georgia found out, at last, how worried the Geddies were that they would wake up one day and have a farm no one could get into.

* * *

"Why didn't you tell me that was still a problem?" Georgia asked Kenny as they lay on his bed. "I didn't know they were still worried about it."

"It's such a silly-ass thing to fret about," Kenny said. "Almost as silly as the mess with the interstate land. I guess I didn't think it was worth mentioning."

"But it could solve everything," Georgia said.

Later, she, Justin and Kenny discussed her plan, and then they all went to see Blue.

He appeared unwilling to believe that such a solution was possible, and it occurred to Georgia that perhaps Blue was looking for some reason not to make this commitment.

"This is going to work, Blue," Justin told him. "If you'll give it a chance, I know it'll work."

Kenny nodded his head.

"I want to meet you halfway," he said.

Blue was silent for a few seconds, staring at the ceiling. He looked over at Annabelle, who had come into the small den where they were talking. She nodded her head almost imperceptibly.

"OK," Blue said. "Let's all go broke together."

"All for one," Georgia said, smiling, "and one for all."

And so it was agreed that the other two partners would give over the two-lane clay track known as Littlejohn McCain Road to Blue and Annabelle, forever, to help make up for the ruined bottom land. There was always something to worry about, Blue would say later to his wife, but now there's a little bit less. Well-meaning promises were one thing, but a deed was something else entirely.

"You can even change the name of the road if you want to," Georgia said.

"Miss . . . Georgia, why in the world would I want to do that?"

She called the real-estate woman that same afternoon. The woman showed more enthusiasm for selling the farm than Georgia could remember since she first let her put it on the market, but Georgia told her it was too late, that her son was going to take over the place and try his hand at farming.

The "Good luck" on the other end of the line sounded more snide than sincere.

* * *

She looks out her bedroom window, facing west, and sees a burst of red. The temperature is supposed to reach the high 50s today, and Kenny Locklear is out at his homemade golf course, whose grass is now the color of wheat.

She has been in a fog the past week. She replays their two afternoons together in her head, over and over, and she hasn't yet gotten her mind around the fact that Kenny is truly capable of executing a man. Twice, Justin has had to repeat questions to her and ask her where her mind is. Sunday after church, she almost had an accident, backing the van out into the road beside the church without looking. Screeching brakes, a loud, angry horn and scowls informed her of her mistake.

Yesterday, she forgot it was her birthday until Justin and Leeza came walking into the kitchen while she was still making breakfast. He was holding a flaming cake Leeza, the ever-improving cook, had baked the night before after Georgia went to bed.

The two of them are watching TV when she walks past. Justin looks up but doesn't ask her where she's going.

"Hi," she calls out when she is close to Kenny, fearful of interrupting his swing on whatever imaginary course he's playing. "I'll bet Tiger Woods would be quaking in his boots if he knew you were working so hard on your game."

He puts the nine-iron back into the bag and looks at her.

"I love golf. I wish it loved me back."

He motions for her to come with him. It's a bright, pleasant day, only chilly when the wind picks up.

She falls into step, and they head toward the Rock of Ages.

"Why?" she asks. She doesn't know all the whys she wants to ask, so she lumps them all together.

He seems to understand.

"I've wanted you for a long time," he says. "I remember the day I met you, more than 11 years ago now. I thought you were the prettiest, sexiest woman I'd ever seen. I thought if I could ever make love to that woman, my life would be complete. The way you smelled, your voice, everything turned me on."

And I never knew, she thought. How much of life do you miss just because nobody ever tells you anything, or the important things anyhow, and you're too dumb to pick up the signals?

"Have you noticed," she asks him, "that I'm 11 years older now?" She kicks herself for saying it. Why belabor the obvious, especially when the obvious is not a positive thing?

"I don't see it. You look the same to me. And I'm 11 years older, too."

She doesn't point out the extra pounds, the graying hair, the cellulite she can see when she turns the mirror just right. Not a bad 52, but 52 nonetheless.

Well, maybe it's true, what he says. She can remember meeting old flames, decades later, and finding that, visual evidence notwithstanding, she could still "see" the boy she used to lust for. Maybe, imprinted in John Kennedy Locklear's mind, is Georgia McCain the way she was when he first took that mental picture, when she was a mere child of 40, two years older than he is right now.

They reach the rock and step around to the west side, facing the sun and out of the wind.

He puts her hand in his. Georgia, who inherited her mother's complexion, has noticed, when they are lying in bed together, that she is, top to bottom, the darker one. Only his hands and face, a farmer's, are more deeply tanned.

"Do you think," she asks, looking down at those hands and smiling, "that you might be too light-skinned for me? I never knew how pale you were, until . . ."

"I hope you weren't disappointed."

"I can't think of anything that's disappointed me when I'm with you."

He tells her again how good she is, how wonderful, and she basks in it. Indian summer, she thinks, and laughs to herself. When they kiss, they don't separate for five minutes.

"Can anyone see us here?" she asks Kenny, reaching for his zipper.

"Probably not," he says, "unless Pooh Blackwell is hiding in those woods over there, watching us."

"Let him watch," Georgia says. "He might learn something."

They make love standing up against the old Indian rock, her bottom pressed against the cold stone, one leg bent, as he thrusts against her with an urgency they never experienced inside. She has always been turned on by the prospect of danger, the chance of getting caught or being seen, and she hopes she hasn't offended any Lumbee spirits with her conspicuous climax.

On the way back to the house, he asks her to come inside for a minute.

"OK, but just a minute. I've got to get back. People will talk."

When they get inside, he hands her a box with a Talbots label on it.

Inside is a long wool scarf, bright red.

"Happy birthday. I didn't know all your sizes, so I figured . . ."

185

"Oh, I think you know my sizes pretty well," she says, grinning, delighted to see that he is blushing. "I think you've taken all my measurements. How did you know it was my birthday?"

"Justin told me."

"So I guess you know how old I am now, too?"

"Georgia," he says, "I've always known how old you were. I don't give a shit."

She goes out for groceries that night. Walking the aisles of the Food Lion, trying in vain to find some tahini because Leeza is suddenly craving hummus and she wouldn't mind some herself, she literally runs into William Blackwell, their carts sideswiping at the end of an aisle.

"Sorry," she mumbles, then looks up and sees who it is. "William. How're you doing?"

His glare softens. He looks so out of place, pushing the grocery cart, so . . . domestic. He appears lost, peering over his glasses at her, as if he hasn't done this very often.

"Well, hey, Georgia. Doin' fine. And you?"

Georgia confirms that she's doing fine, too. The way they're shopping, though, they meet again on the next aisle, coming in opposite directions, and then they're beside each other in the checkout lines.

"William," she says, trying to seize the moment, "can I talk to you?"

He says he's in kind of a hurry. His wife is sick with the flu, and he's got to get home with some groceries. He's worried about the ice cream melting.

"It won't take long, I promise. Five minutes, tops."

Her van and his car, a big Buick that makes the holy terror of her high school days seem sadly old, are parked near each other. Georgia loads her groceries into the trunk, parks the cart and walks over to where William Blackwell is waiting, leaning against the car.

Georgia knows she doesn't have much time.

She doesn't mention any of her suspicions about his son, just tells him that she was curious about Jenny's drowning and wanted to figure out how it happened.

"I didn't ever mean to imply that Pooh . . ."

186

Liar, the voice in her head whispers.

William holds his hands up, palms facing her.

"Georgia, if it wasn't you, it'd be something else. Pooh's always pissed off about something. I thought it might do him some good to get away from us a little ways, have to make do without his momma fixing half his meals, although she'll do it now if I don't stop her, and drive it over there."

Looking past her own first perception of William Blackwell, she realizes she might be seeing a man who is tired of fighting but doesn't really have another strategy.

"He's twenty-nine years old," he says. "Twenty-nine. My God, at twenty-nine, my fourth child had just been born. I was living in my own house, farming two hundred acres. I wasn't exactly a model citizen, didn't want to be, but I knew I had to be a man by a certain time, and that time sure as hell was well before I turned twenty-nine years old."

"They grow up slower," Georgia says, thinking of hers. "Every generation seems to."

He gives her a sharp look, a glimpse of the boy who used to bully football and basketball players.

"Some of us don't have the luxury," he says. "I mean, Pooh ain't got what you'd call a lot of options."

He crosses his arms.

"I got to admit, I was a little upset with you, Georgia, when I was told you thought foul play might have been involved in Miss Jenny's death. Not as upset as Pooh, but it did seem like you was pointing fingers."

Georgia starts to protest, but she doesn't feel like lying to appease William Blackwell.

"OK. When I realized the ring was gone, and later when I found that shoe . . ."

"Which you never should of been out there looking for in the first place. God knows what that boy would have done if he'd of caught you trespassing."

". . . I didn't know what to think."

"He's been in some trouble," William says. "I can't deny that. But the idea that he might have had something to with Jenny falling in that pond, that really hurt."

"I was making too much of it," Georgia says. "I have trouble letting stuff go when I sink my teeth in."

"Yeah," William says, grinning, "you always was a stubborn little girl. I still remember you arguing with that ninth-grade science teacher, the one that didn't want to hear about us coming from apes and such."

"Well," Georgia says, "I'm here to tell you I'm wrong. Jenny fell in the pond and drowned, period. I've been a little crazy lately, probably haven't been thinking everything out like I should. Would you tell Pooh that? It's to the point now where I don't even feel safe going to see him."

She knows that mentioning the hanged cat, the anonymous call, will only make him more sure she's persecuting her son.

William promises that he will talk to Pooh.

"You know," he says, as he pushes himself off the fender, "I didn't want those boys of mine to grow up the way I did, feeling like I had to fight all the time just to get some respect. It wasn't any fun."

For any of us, Georgia thinks.

"But, I don't know, it's just in the blood with some people. I think if we hadn't found a place . . . if Miss Jenny hadn't died and we hadn't inherited the house, one of his brothers might of shot him by now. He was always stirring something up.

"Georgia," he says, as she turns to go, "Jenny fell into that pond. Maybe you don't like the way she left us the house and all, but that was her doing. Didn't nobody twist her arm. And didn't nobody push her into that pond."

He doesn't say it angrily, but like someone who really wants to be believed, and who wants to believe himself.

"Good enough," Georgia says.

She reaches out to shake his hand, not knowing what else to do. It takes him a couple of seconds to understand. His grip is surprisingly gentle, as if he is afraid he might hurt her.

"Just, you know, give him a little distance," he says. "He'll simmer down."

Back at the house, though, the dream teases her again.

Let it go, she tells herself. Let it go.

CHAPTER EIGHTEEN

December 10

Suddenly, I remember.

When we would visit Jenny and Harold, Jenny would always have some kind of sweets for us. She loved to bake.

I said once, when I was all of 6, that I really loved Miss Jenny's tea cakes, and Mom or Daddy repeated it to her, of course. One of the things about living around East Geddie was that you could say something, not even something in the least memorable or witty, and it would be remembered for the rest of your life.

From then on, we always had tea cakes when we visited the McLaurins. I mean, from then until I left for college. Hell, Jenny mentioned my saying that the last time I visited her. People around here either really care what you're saying, or they don't have enough to occupy their minds. Either way, I'd have to say I've had a couple of husbands who didn't try as hard to please me as Jenny did with those tea cakes.

So, on this particular day, the one I've just remembered, Jenny had escorted me and Wallace into the kitchen, where there were enough tea cakes to induce diabetes. She made Kool-Aid to go with them. I can remember it was the orange kind, almost bitter compared to the tea cakes.

She went back into the den. Mom wasn't there. She was sick or something and didn't come that day.

They had a little dachshund, Pete, and Pete wanted a cookie. Wallace said his momma didn't allow them to give cookies to Pete, and I said, shoot, I'll feed him a cookie if I want to, and Wallace said he was going to tell his momma.

So I got up from the table to go and ask Jenny myself, a tea cake in my hand. I was sure she wouldn't deny me.

When I walked into the room where the adults were, they were all standing around that fireplace. I guess they didn't see me. Harold was holding a brick that I could see he'd taken out of the back of the fireplace, and Jenny was showing some papers to Daddy.

Jenny saw me first, and it was just about the only time I ever saw her look even briefly irritated with me.

"You go on back in the kitchen," she said, frowning. "We're talking grown-up stuff here."

I was so stunned that I turned and left the room, went back and sat down at the table and didn't lobby any more to feed the dachshund. I was not usually a child to take orders without demanding a reason. It was the source of much friction with my mother. So Jenny obviously made an impression.

On the way home, in the truck, I didn't ask Daddy about the brick and the papers. It seemed to me that they must have been doing something shameful, the way Jenny acted, and I guess I just didn't want to know about the kind of thing that made adults ashamed.

We were turning off the paved road when Daddy spoke.

"You're wondering how come Jenny acted like she did back there."

He spoke softly, the way he always did to me, but it wasn't a question.

I nodded my head.

"Well, I'm going to see how good you can keep a secret. You can't tell anybody this, and if I ever find out you did, I won't ever tell you another one. We can't even talk about it again. So promise."

I didn't even really want to know, but I was intrigued, and I loved that Daddy thought me a candidate to keep such an obviously important secret.

"I promise."

So he told me about the hidey-hole.

Jenny and especially Harold, like a lot of people who were children of the Depression, didn't trust banks. They had therefore taken to hiding their most important possessions. One brick in the fireplace was loose, and there was a hollow spot behind it, a little nook where you could keep a small box safe from burglars. Harold had had the fireplace built that way, for that purpose. His first cousin in Clinton had kept a safe in his bedroom, and one night thieves broke in and carried it, and all his money, off.

"You can't steal what you can't find," is what Daddy said Harold told him.

I don't know what they kept in there—probably Jenny's ring on the rare occasions like a trip to the beach when she didn't wear it. Maybe some government bonds, probably a lot of hard, cold cash, their will, a bunch of old letters. I don't even know what Daddy and they were looking at that day.

Well, they couldn't have pried information about that safe from me with bamboo splints under my nails. Daddy had entrusted me, and I wasn't going to let him down. He didn't say don't tell your momma, but I didn't, because he said no one.

It was at least three years later when Daddy mentioned the hidey-hole casually to Mom at dinner, and I realized that, of course, she had known about it, too. It wasn't just me and Daddy, which was vaguely disappointing. But I was proud that he would know I hadn't told her.

And now, lying in bed in the dark, my eyes so tired from reading that I can't hold them open but my body twitching and my brain running a hundred miles an hour, I know what Daddy was pointing to, in the dream.

I don't know where the information came from. I wasn't even thinking about the dream. Suddenly, though, there it was, in plain view of my addled brain.

Kenny and I talked about Jenny again, yesterday, although I'm sure he'd rather never hear any more about her or my runaway imagination.

He did indulge me, though, perhaps because we were both naked at the time.

We are going to the well too often, I'm afraid. My "visits" next door are starting to make Justin and Leeza suspicious, I think, even though most of their combined thoughts must be on the fast-approaching birth of their first child. They don't really have time to obsess over whether I'm engaging in inappropriate behavior. They probably can't even believe someone my age is capable of inappropriate behavior. Kids, I want to tell them, returning from a couple of stolen hours, you don't even know what inappropriate is, or how damn good it feels.

I remember being 27, and I remember how old I thought 52 was at the time. The very idea of someone that age having good, dirty sex might have, to use Phil's phrase, put me off my game.

It is difficult, though, to hide the aftereffects of something this good.

"Georgia," Kenny groaned, "you said you were over this. You're way too smart to believe you're being led around by some dream, some vision. What next, a Ouija board?"

He talked me through it again, especially the part about no evidence worth mentioning, and the part about trying not to give Pooh further reason to believe I was his mortal enemy.

I ran my fingernail lightly along his thigh and tried to explain how I'd never had a dream quite like this one, never had a dream that left me with anything except fuzzy images and unsupportable feelings afterward.

"Well," he said, "sometimes you just have to make yourself forget. Let it go."

"Should I do as you do," I asked, flushing with sudden anger, "or do as you say?"

He got my drift just as I began apologizing, telling him again that I would never, ever mention Cam Jacobs to another person.

"I'd just as soon you didn't mention him to me," he said.

I am used to talking things out, not letting go until an issue is resolved. No one knows better than I that if Kenny believed Jenny really met with some kind of foul play, he would go a long way toward exacting some version of justice. He seems, though, to be willing to accept the most likely scenario.

I told him I would forget the dream when he was able to look me in the eye and swear to me he had never seen anything he couldn't explain out by the Rock of Ages.

He chose instead to draw me to him again, in a highly successful attempt at distraction.

* * *

Now, though, I sit up in bed, remembering the dream, remembering the way my father was looking at me, and at the brick fireplace, and I know.

I know.

CHAPTER NINETEEN

December 18

One minute, Georgia knows that she must act, no matter what the consequences. The next, she steps outside herself and sees what the rest of the world must see—a woman who has suffered great loss and has already had one breakdown in the last few months, a woman acting on "information" she dreamed.

Write it out, an advisor told her once, when she came to him with an idea for a master's thesis. If it makes sense when you write it out, it's probably a good idea.

Well, when she writes this one out, it doesn't seem too persuasive.

My cousin drowned. Unsavory people somehow managed to get the deed to her house and land. Her valuable wedding ring is missing. I found an old shoe in the weeds beside the pond that matched the one on her foot. My dead father came to me in a dream and told me to look for the answer in a secret hiding place that probably was forgotten or sealed long ago.

And, of course, the secret hiding place is in the middle of a house owned and occupied by Pooh Blackwell.

The evidence is, indeed, tenuous. The risk seems great, the task beyond any skills a liberal arts major might have acquired from three decades of learning and teaching English literature.

And yet, sitting here on a cold, clear Saturday night beside the state highway leading out of Geddie, alone and more than a little afraid, she knows she has to act.

The red truck has been gone half an hour.

Forsythia Crumpler's new neighbor always leaves on Saturday night, and always comes home, loud and drunk, often with a few equally loud and drunken acquaintances, sometime in the early morning.

"I'd call the sheriff, if I thought they'd do anything," Forsythia told Georgia. "But they'll just come out and talk to him, and then he'll be mad at me."

Georgia didn't feel comfortable telling her to stand up for her rights. Who would protect her if Pooh did anything? Kenny, maybe, but she didn't want him to either kill again or be killed. The loaded gun she carries and the new information about Kenny's capabilities make her feel as if the raw and unthinkable, the thing from which she has always tried to shelter herself, is lurking just beyond her vision.

It hurt her to see her old teacher, one of the most fearless people she's ever known, cowed by old age and the inaction of others. Forsythia Crumpler was just one more reason to forget caution, if not sanity.

She is sitting in her van like something out of a bad detective story, wearing a sweater and, over that, an overcoat with pockets big enough to hold a flashlight and the Ladysmith that she hasn't fired since the day Kenny gave it to her.

She has decided she doesn't want Kenny involved. If she had pressured him to help her, and he had obliged, and then things had gone badly, that would be one more thing for the monkey to chatter about.

If I'm wrong, I'll be wrong in private.

Plus, as fearless as Kenny is, she doesn't believe he would ever break into someone else's house, even Pooh Blackwell's.

If Pooh should come back early tonight and catch her breaking in, she wouldn't even be within her rights to shoot him. He'd be entitled (and glad) to shoot her.

On a moral level, Georgia doesn't exactly see this as a break-in. Not really. After all, she does have the key.

That might have made the difference, in the end. She was getting out of the truck on Tuesday, and she dropped her key ring on the ground. Picking it up, she was struck with how many keys she had, some from houses in which she hadn't lived for many years.

195

And then she saw the one on the end, really looked at it for the first time in nearly a decade.

She holds it in her barely shaking hand now. It is a dull brown and has not been inside the lock for which it was cut since the day Jenny McLaurin gave it to her.

"It's just in case," she'd said that Sunday almost 10 years ago. "You know, in case something happens to me." She had given another copy to Forsythia.

Georgia didn't have the heart to tell her she wouldn't be in East Geddie often enough to matter. Better she should give the second copy to some other old friend at church. But Jenny wanted her to have the key, and Georgia sensed that refusing it would hurt Jenny's feelings.

Well, Georgia thought to herself, standing there looking at the key, something did happen to you, Jenny. So maybe it's time to see if that old key still fits.

The hardest part about tonight was getting away from Justin and Leeza. They seemed offended when she told them she was going up to Greensboro to spend the night with an old college girlfriend. It was the only way she could slip away without arousing suspicion. She'd done it once before, so that she and Kenny could have an entire night together in one of the motels out by the interstate.

She almost gave up on the whole idea this afternoon when she saw how lost Justin looked. The baby could come at any time. All that kept her from staying was the calm, fearless way Leeza told her everything was going to be fine, no problem.

So Georgia went to a movie she never really saw, then ate a fast-food hamburger she didn't really taste, sitting in the van, and now, here she is.

She is parked well beyond the driveway separating Jenny McLaurin's old house from Forsythia's. A path runs alongside the railroad tracks, overgrown from years of disuse, but it serves her purpose. She can sit beneath the pines, the van half-hidden in the bushes, and wait.

When Pooh came tearing out, rumbling down the drive as if he were fleeing a nuclear attack, she was afraid for a split second that his lights might have picked up the van as he careered from one side of the dirt drive to the other for no apparent reason other than to raise hell.

But the truck never slowed. Pooh couldn't have even looked for traffic as he spun out on to Route 47, headed for Port Campbell, or wherever psychopaths go on Saturday night.

Fifteen minutes later, she finally convinces herself that he is indeed gone for the night.

She gets out of the van, closing the door softly, pushing on it until it clicks and then locking it.

To her chagrin, her running shoes start squeaking in the dew-turning-to-frost along the side of the front yard. She stops twice to listen for a watchdog, or even a neighbor's mutt. Forsythia has told her that the only dog Pooh keeps is some kind of pit bull mix that she's never seen leave the pen back by the pond.

The key, she thinks, probably doesn't even work. I'm probably on a fool's errand, and if I can't open this door, then it's a sign, and I'll go back to being sane and logical.

She jiggles and works it for a long two minutes. Then, expecting nothing, she turns the doorknob, and almost stumbles into the living room. Of course, she thinks. Pooh doesn't bother to lock the front door.

The stench overwhelms her at first. She wonders if someone hasn't died in here. Maybe Pooh is keeping decomposing bodies under his bed. But then she realizes it's just an aversion to washing dishes or throwing out leftover food. She steps on something that crunches and gives, identifying it finally as a pizza box.

Georgia doesn't want to use the flashlight until she has to. She stands in the dark until her night vision lets her identify vague outlines and then specific items. She does bang her shin once on an unseen coffee table, but five minutes after she has entered the house, she is standing in front of the fireplace, separated from it by the oil heater. She works her way around the heater, being careful to duck and miss the stovepipe, burning herself once with a misplaced hand.

She kneels in the space between the heater and the hearth and duckwalks forward until she's so close she can smell the bricks.

197

Only then does she switch on the flashlight, trying to shield it with her hands and point it directly into the wall she's facing.

She thinks she knows which brick it was, from the dream, the one she saw that day as a 10-year-old. When she starts working with her hands, though, she can't discern any give, anything to indicate that one of the bricks is loose.

It takes her 10 more minutes. She has to switch legs often, finally moving out of her crouch and kneeling on the hard bricks. Her arms grow tired from holding the light and feeling for the opening.

Then, as she is entertaining the thought that Jenny McLaurin's hidey-hole was mortared over long ago, she feels something. It's just a small wiggle in one of the bricks, probably the first one she tried, but now her fingers are more attuned.

She sets the flashlight down so she can use both hands and works the brick a few seconds in the dark. It definitely is loose. She can feel a slight gap now between this particular brick and the next one up. She breaks one of her nails trying to get a grip on it. Finally, she is able to drag the brick out a quarter-inch, then a half-inch, then a whole inch. She puts one hand at each side and carefully removes it, setting it on the hearth beside her. She picks up the flashlight and shines it into a pitch-black rectangle that smells of dampness and clay.

She can make out something pale at the other end of the light beam, but she can't identify it.

Georgia has always been afraid of spiders, and it occurs to her that there is no place she could think of that would seem more hospitable to the black widows she remembers from her youth than this dark, bricked-in emptiness.

She needs as much courage as she's needed all night to reach in that hole with her right wrist.

She brings the notebooks out one at a time, five of them in all, each the same brand, each five inches by seven. She reaches in again, wishing that she had remembered gloves, tempted to go in the kitchen to look for something to put over her hands, but the idea of Pooh's kitchen scares her more than black-widow spiders.

In the end, she can feel nothing else in the hole she has uncovered. She makes herself touch every reachable inch of the hiding
place. There is no ring, no stash of 20-dollar bills hidden away in
1963, nothing but cardboard and paper.

Georgia sits cross-legged now in the hearth. She picks up one
of the tablets. There is no writing on the cover, nothing to indicate
what it is, but when she opens it, she recognizes the precise,
schoolgirl cursive script she remembers from Christmas and
birthday cards.

The one she has chosen was the last one she retrieved, and it
seems to be the oldest. Jenny has not written the year anywhere
Georgia can find, but she realizes that this first notebook must be
from the year she became a widow, 1991. Harold died in March,
and the first entry is April 6:

*It faired off today. The dogwoods are right pretty outside. Ilene and
me went to the Bi-Lo, and then ate at the K&W.*

And that was it.

Georgia wonders if someone urged Jenny to start a journal
after her husband died. Maybe whoever was minister of Geddie
Presbyterian told her it might help her get through her sorrow.

Whatever its genesis, the journal is slow going as Georgia sits
there in the hearth and flips through it with her free hand. It is
mostly concerned with weather and shopping and church and the
world outside her window.

Toward the end of the first year, though, Georgia sees something else, a sign that Jenny is starting to share more than the
weather report and the church bulletin. Growth, a grief counselor
or English composition teacher might call it.

*December 22. I got a Christmas card from Georgia today. Poor
thing. She's had it hard, with two divorces and Sarah and Littlejohn
dieing too. It doesn't look like she's going to be here for Christmas. I don't
blame her. Nothing but sad memories for her down here, I reckon.*

*It must be terrible to love somebody enough to marry them and then
have it fall apart like that. Harold and me had our moments, to be sure,
but at least I know he's gone. A clean brake, I reckon you would call it.*

Georgia remembers how she felt that Christmas, two husbands, a mother and a father gone in rapid succession. She had

taken one of those tests that are supposed to tell a person how stressed out she should be, and she didn't share the score with her friends, for fear they would put her on suicide watch.

She looks at her watch. 10:15. She doesn't know what Forsythia Crumpler defines as early-morning hours, but she knows she should pack these notebooks, put the brick back and tiptoe out the same door she entered an hour and a half ago. She isn't sure she wants to read them, even when she gets back to safety, for fear of seeing her own self-absorbed life exposed. But she knows she will.

She can't resist looking at the first journal she took out, though. It is the most recent, still half-empty.

Georgia finds the last page on which there is writing. Jenny's script has gotten a little more shaky over the years.

She works backward, stopping when she sees a familiar name:

July 29. William Blackwell come by again today. I reckon I am going to do it. He says I can stay here just a long as I want to, that him and his boys will take care of me. I hate not to leave anything behind, but there isn't much I can do. I thought 50 thousand dollars would be enough to last me forever, that and the Social Security.

I told him to go on and set it up with the lawyer.

Georgia turns another couple of pages, speed-reading through circle meetings, a heat wave and Jenny's fascination with a prime-time quiz show that offers to make millionaires out of morons.

Another entry makes her stop:

August 20. Pooh has started coming by without William. They are my kin, or at least Harold was their kin, and I reckon Pooh can do for me same as his Daddy. But he seems like he resents it more, and sometimes I think I might just as well do it myself. When I asked him to help me get them curtins down from the window, you'd of thought I asked him to brake rocks or something. And that grass hasn't been mowed in two weeks. But I reckon I've got to put up with it. I've got to make what Forsythia calls adjustments.

Georgia knows she should go, but it's as if she's watching the prelude to a train wreck. The entries fill her with anger and self-loathing. At one point, Jenny considers calling Georgia, but she doesn't want to disturb her "in the time of her loss." She feels guilty for not going to Phil's funeral. As if Georgia had made it down to North Carolina when Harold died.

She promises herself she'll go in five minutes. Just one more.

She turns to the last page on which Jenny's script appears, now coming at a disturbing slant and much less legible than it was a few years before. She reads the last entry.

Oct. 14. Georgia's in town. I'll give her a couple more days to get herself settled, then I'll call her, might even drive over and see her, if I'm up to it. I don't drive that old car anywhere but to church. It needs a change of pace.

I might ask her advise. She'd know what to do. I sure apreciate William and them helping me, but I don't think it's working out. That boy Pooh is just too busy, or lazy. It took him three days to get me my grocerys, and when he come yesterday, he was so mean.

About the only time he shows me any attention is when he wants me to go walking with him outside. He likes to go down by the pond, which I'd just as soon have draned, before some youngun drowns in it. Says I need to get some exercise. I think to myself I get all the exercise I need, trying to get the ones I give my house to to keep me from starving to death and mow my yard once in a while.

William's paying the bills now. At least I don't have to worry about that no more. But I need to get out of this, even if I have to get my house back, sell it and go into the rest home, go on Medicaid. That boy of his scares me. I can't hardly sleep worrying about it. I would ask Forsythia, but she'd just think I was a fool for doing it to start with.

Besides, she's not family.

Georgia closes the notebook. The goose bumps have run all the way down her arms from her neck. She gives an involuntary shiver. She wants to leave this house so much that she has to force herself to go slow, replace the brick carefully and put the five notebooks in the same pocket where the Ladysmith lies, remembered again when she touches it. She backtracks out from the hearth and across the room, trying to erase any evidence that she was ever in this place.

Too little, she is thinking to herself. Too late for Jenny. Still, she knows. Even if no one else knows, she does.

She cracks the front door and peeks out. She is grateful that Pooh didn't bother to turn on his porch light before he left.

She tries to step as lightly as a spirit as she goes back across the yard toward the highway, stopping and stooping low whenever she hears a car coming, for fear someone will somehow see her in the darkness. She is shaking. She remembers how, when she was small, her father's and uncle's beagles would run up on her in the night when she was walking between their houses, scaring her so badly she would almost wet her pants. She is, after all these years, still afraid of the dark. Ghosts, a voice whispers in her ear, are possible. You know they are.

She wonders if, in the morning, there won't be two sets of telltale footsteps in the frost, one coming and one going across Pooh Blackwell's yard. She wonders what clues she has left in the living room waiting to be exposed by daylight. Her uneasiness is assuaged only by the near certainty that no living soul knows the thing she has stolen ever existed.

Finally, she is back on the weed-covered dirt road. She wants to run the last few feet to the van, but she makes herself walk, out of a child's belief that, if you panic, they'll run after you and catch you. You can't let them know you're afraid.

She unlocks the van and hops up into it, the keys already in her hand. She drops them on the floor as she reaches out for the ignition switch and curses as she feels around for them, finally retrieving them.

Only when she rises does she notice that the condensation is on the inside of the windows.

CHAPTER TWENTY

He stepped over the pizza box as he negotiated the space between the couch and the little table he was always tripping over. His balance was impaired by the beer in his right hand and the six he had already consumed.

He knew he needed to get things cleaned up. Maybe his mother would come over again, when his father was out. Old William made it sound like such a goddamn gift that he had this piece-of-crap house, with all the work it entailed.

This is *my* house, he's going to tell the old man one of these days. I took it, and I can do what I damn well please with it. Don't ever have to clean it again if I don't want to.

He was supposed to meet some buddies at the Rack 'Em, drink and shoot some pool, maybe go over to Sally's after, if they had any money. He slammed the front door and then almost fell on the steps, catching himself on the railing.

Good thing, he thought, you don't have to drive standing up. He laughed and took another swig. He wished he'd had the foresight to bring another Bud for the road; this one was half-empty. But it was too much trouble to go back inside. Screw it. He'd stop at the Get 'n' Go and buy another one.

Pooh wedged himself behind the wheel, put the beer can in the cup holder and started his truck, his big red machine, in preparation for roaring down the driveway. His goal each time he left his new home was to see if he could clear the railroad tracks going at least 25 miles an hour, then make the almost-instant right turn onto Route 47 without hitting the brakes.

Brakes, like seat belts, were for pussies.

He almost didn't see the van.

There was just a quick flash, maybe light off a mirror or a windshield, as he was wrestling the big truck over the tracks and on to the state highway. It didn't really occur to him until he was a quarter-mile up the road that perhaps he ought to investigate.

His father always told him, if something doesn't seem right, it probably ain't right. Daddy, he concedes, was probably on the money on that one.

It was easy enough, after he left the Get 'n' Go, to turn on to the Ammon Road in Geddie and then double back on the old road that came out half a mile east of his driveway. When he completed his circle, he saw it, sitting there on the dirt trail on the other side of the tracks, where no car really ought to be.

It could be kids parking, he thought as he slowed down and eased off the pavement, but it was a little too early in the evening for that, and it didn't look like something a teenager would be driving on a date.

Either way, he thought, it might be good for entertainment value. If it was just some kids, he'd at least scare the shit out of them.

He turned around and backtracked to the next place where he could cross the rail right-of-way, then bounced along the old parallel trail in the dark until he was no more than a hundred yards behind the partially hidden van.

He closed the door softly and walked as quietly as his weight and blood-alcohol level would allow, half-expecting the van to go tearing out on to the highway at any second.

But when he got there, there was no one inside. And then he noticed the Virginia plates, and suddenly he knew.

He went back to the truck, pondering how best to maximize this opportunity. One of the toolboxes behind the front seat yielded some duct tape. There was a workable length of clothesline back there, too, among the clutter on the floor. It was easy enough to break into the van. Pooh was not without his skills.

He thought about calling Eddie on the cellular phone to tell him he wasn't coming tonight, but then he said to hell with it.

He wondered, hiding as best he could in the back seat, behind the driver, how long he'd have to wait, and whether she would be alone. He didn't really care, he told himself. Maybe that little Indian asshole would be with her, too, and he'd just take them both out right here, with the snub-nose .38, or maybe shoot him in the balls and make him watch what happened after that.

His father had tried to convince him that she didn't mean him any harm, that she just wanted to be left alone. Well, the old bastard couldn't be right all the time, could he?

* * *

Georgia thinks later that she said something, at least part of a word, in that terrible second of recognition before the pain came. She thought her head must have been split open like a ripe watermelon, the first blow was so hard and unforgiving.

She is actually surprised that she still seems to be breathing, her heart still beating, although she feels as if she is drowning in blood. She gradually comes to understand that her mouth is taped shut, so that what air she gets is through her broken, blood-clogged nose. She can feel hard pieces of what she knows must be some of her teeth, loose in the sticky, metallic-tasting mess she tries to keep from sliding down her throat.

She can't move her arms and legs; she is prone across the back seats, and the van is moving, bumping across something that is definitely not paved.

She knows who is driving, as much by his sweat-and-stale-beer smell, which she didn't even know she recognized until now, as by the back of his obscenely wide head silhouetted in front of her as she looks up.

She knows she isn't dead but wonders if she soon will be, or wish to be.

He hasn't bothered to blindfold her. Even through the pain and terror, she knows how bad this is.

Each jolt of the truck's suspension seems designed to add to her pain. She is distracted from this by the fear that she will suffocate.

By force of will, she makes herself breathe in and out as slowly and regularly as she can through her ruined nose. She remembers taking lifeguard lessons, when she was 19. She had to beat back the panic and learn to live with a certain rhythm which would not fail her as long as she didn't abandon it. Head to the side. Breathe in. Head into the water. Up again and breathe out. She gets into such rhythm as she can and tells herself that she isn't dead yet, she can still survive this. She is still able to appreciate the irony: As her life seems to be passing before her eyes, the thing she first remembers is life-saving lessons.

Other things seem to be broken, too. Ropes that are tied too tight bind her awkwardly, but most of the damage feels as if it is on various parts of her head and her left shoulder.

The truck stops suddenly, throwing her against the front seat face-first and ratcheting the pain up to another level. Her muffled scream makes Pooh look back.

"You think that hurts, bitch?" he asks, his voice floating somewhere above her. "You don't know what pain is. But you will."

She thinks she hears him laugh.

The van door slides open, then, and she is yanked out. It feels as if her shoulder is being ripped from its socket. She staggers and is half-dragged away from the truck.

Ahead of her is an open darkness. She thinks at first it must be a large field, cleared for winter. But then she feels and smells the breeze off it and knows it is water.

He grabs the duct tape and rips it from her mouth, causing her to scream in pain before he puts his large, meaty hand over her face, covering her mouth and nose at the same time. When he takes it off, he replaces it with a gag of some sort so she can breathe.

"Don't want you to suffocate, ma'am," he says, grinning. "I don't want nothin' to happen to you, not yet. You and me are gonna have some fun."

To her amazement, he unties her arms from behind her, but it is only meant to be a temporary reprieve. He pushes her face-down on what appears to be a rotted-out picnic table and is reaching for her left wrist, set on retying her to metal rods that seem to be part of a shelter, when she remembers the Ladysmith.

She is somehow able to reach into the coat with her free right hand. It is still there. She fumbles it, then knows she has it in her grip. She makes herself wait until Pooh moves in front of her, working on tying her other hand.

She will never know how she was able to pull the little gun out of her coat and point it at the large mass in front of her. Her shoulder, as mangled as her nose and cheekbone, should have made her pass out from the pain. Somehow, though, she does it. She tries to do just what Kenny told her. Don't hesitate. If you have to use it, use it.

The noise startles them both, and then she hears Pooh howling in pain. Her heart sinks as she realizes the animal she has shot sounds very much alive, more angry than mortally injured.

She aimed at his considerable gut, but somehow the shot managed to hit him in his right forearm, which he is now rubbing, looking for blood. She fires a second time, amazed as she does at how fast a man that large can duck and scramble. Before she can fire again, he has her wrist and has taken the Ladysmith, her last hope, away from her.

There is a large red stain through his work shirt and jacket, but she hasn't done what she meant to do. She has not killed him.

He curses as he flings the little gun away with his left hand and slaps her. It sounds so inconsequential as it lands almost soundlessly in the sandy soil beside the water. How could she have thought such a tiny thing could save her?

Before Georgia can get her partially tied left wrist free, Pooh has secured it again and bound her other one as well. He then ties her ankles to something behind and beneath her. Despite the gag, she can make noises, although not loud enough to draw anyone's attention to this lonely, God-forsaken place. She has the sense that he wants to hear the noises she will make.

She looks to the side, wanting to get some image of the last terrain she will ever see, trying to focus on something other than the terror. Her eyes are adjusted to the dark, and she realizes she knows this place.

People used to come here to fish or to pick huckleberries, although she was forbidden to go anywhere near it by her father, who said it was a place for bootleggers and other ne'er-do-wells. The tea-colored water wasn't really fit for swimming, he said, only drowning. When she was a teenager, it was a popular place to go parking, if you had a vehicle that could get back here without getting stuck.

Maxwell's Millpond. He has taken her into the swamp that borders the Geddies to the east, on the edge of Kinlaw's Hell, the place Scots County residents have always gone to do business that will not stand the light of day.

She can't beg him, and she hardly knows what she would say if she were allowed that luxury. Certainly nothing that would change his mind.

She is shivering from fear and from the cold. The temperature has dropped below freezing, and when she feels him cut her dress and panties off her from behind, she feels burned as the air hits her naked skin.

Pooh is on top of her now, half-leaning into her. He whispers obscenities as he applies more and more of his weight. He has already entered her when he presses down on the broken left shoulder. She blacks out from the pain, relieved at last.

At some point, either dreaming or dead, she's sure, she sees a face looming above her, hard and cold but somehow, she senses, meaning her no harm.

When she comes to, she is aware of footsteps fading in the distance. She is not able to determine for some time whether she is alive.

Only the pain, increasing as she regains consciousness, makes her think she might not yet be dead.

Weighed against that, though, is the surreal world to which she awakens.

Her wrists have been cut free, but the suffocating weight on top of her makes it impossible to move at first. She is finally, an inch at a time, able to extract herself from underneath it enough to understand that the weight is Pooh Blackwell, and that he is dead.

His pants are still unzipped, she sees after she is able to roll him sideways enough for gravity to carry his 350 pounds off the edge of the table and on to the bench and then the ground. She has an urge to cover him up, but then she is distracted by what used to be his face.

She had thought at first that she was bleeding too profusely for any hope of survival, but now she realizes that the stickiness in her hair, and the sickly, soft pieces she touched when she was able to reach it with her one good arm, are part of the late Pooh Black-well's brains.

She is finally able to reach back and free her legs, one at a time. As she rolls herself to a sitting position atop the picnic table, she almost passes out again from the pain. Then her head clears and she sees the gun, much larger than the one she carried. It is lying on the ground, next to Pooh's body. Beside that is a cellular phone. She is struck with the incongruity of Pooh Blackwell carrying a cell phone.

It takes her at least five minutes to get to it, and then she finds she can't remember the phone number at the farm. Somehow, though, she recalls Kenny's. Even then, it takes her five minutes more to dial it correctly, she is shaking so badly. She alternates between thinking she might freeze to death, bleed to death or just die from the sheer outrageousness that has overtaken her world.

Kenny answers.

"Hello," she says, surprised at how strangled and strange her voice sounds, but taking it as proof that she is still somehow among the living. "Kenny? I'm sorry to call you. Could you come get me?"

CHAPTER TWENTY-ONE

December 21

Whatever they're giving me, I hope they don't run out.

The drugs seem to be my main topic of conversation when the occasional visitor catches me awake. They just tell me to get some sleep, that everything's going to be OK.

Well, that could be. Anything's possible.

The doctor told me I have a fractured skull, a broken nose and cheekbone, a somewhat dysfunctional shoulder, and a couple fewer teeth than I had last week.

Everybody's tiptoeing around mentioning the r-a-p-e, as if that was the worst of it. Maybe that would have been so when I was younger and a little more precious and fragile. Maybe if it had lasted longer or I hadn't passed out. Maybe if what the police detective called "the perpetrator" hadn't been missing a large part of his head the last time I saw him.

The worst was just thinking I was going to die there, being almost sure of it at times, some goddamn victim violated and butchered on the shore of Maxwell's Millpond.

The terror hasn't completely receded. I don't want to be alone, and I haven't been for the most part. Kenny and Justin, even Leeza, have taken turns, and the women from the church—organized by Forsythia, of course—have filled in when those three had to be elsewhere. I look over now—turning my head is no mean feat, believe me—and there's Alberta Horne, snoring away in the chaise longue the hospital provides for those willing to spend the night in them so someone won't have to die alone, or even be alone.

I didn't really think I was going to die, once the rescue squad and Kenny found me. I didn't know until later that he hadn't called them until he was almost there, to the only part of the pond to which you can drive. But he told me, to my puzzlement, that they were already on their way when he called, that they got there at the same time as he did.

These drugs are supposed to make you sleep like the dead, but I have been having the damnedest dreams.

I've been carrying on the most delightful interchange with my late father. I can't say that we are actually talking, but somehow, we get our messages across to each other.

In the dream, he's always out there at that rock. The Rock of Ages. I stand close enough to touch him, and he makes me know that it's OK, that I am absolved—at least by him—of everything for which I've been beating myself up these past 11 years. Maybe that's just one part of my brain conspiring to give the rest of me a free pass I don't deserve. Maybe it's the fractured skull, or the trauma.

Whatever it is, I've had this dream three times now, and it seems to go pretty much the same.

Daddy is slouched against that rock, his eyes twinkling, trying to suppress a smile, the way he did. I want to know so much, about what happened that last day, about Rose and him, about the Big Questions.

The first time, I awakened just as he was starting to wave his hand in some kind of expansive gesture that encompassed the three parts of what used to be his farm.

The second time, the reel went a little farther, to where he leaned toward me and kissed my forehead. I swear I could smell him, not just the Pinaud aftershave and Old Spice, but *him*, the way I had forgotten he smelled. Can you smell in dreams?

The last time, just a few minutes ago, he gave me a little hug and then turned and walked away. I didn't try to follow him; I knew not to. He looked back one last time and waved, and then he was gone, fading into the near woods.

And when I woke up, I knew he really was gone, and that everything was all right, although there are so many ways in which the casual observer would dispute that assessment.

211

I mean, what you have here is a woman who, some might say, is a little too finely tuned, a bit too high-maintenance, someone who is trying to recover, without benefit of professional help, from a breakdown, who has lost three husbands and a couple of parents in less than 12 years.

Then, pile on this fall, the fall of my free fall. (Today, the Weather Channel's happy moron tells me, is the first day of winter, the shortest day of the year.) Add the stress of trying to sell the farm, plus dealing with an imminent first grandchild whose father is not married. Then throw in Pooh Blackwell.

Everything definitely should not be all right. Everything should be more in the general neighborhood of all wrong.

Somehow, though, it is all right.

I don't know if this was nature's own little shock therapy or just the peace that passeth understanding like it's standing still, the kind you get from knowing that you have taken life's best Sunday punch and you're still standing, figuratively.

Phil liked to watch the fights on TV. He even got me to watch, in horrified fascination, and this flashes through my addled brain now: I feel like I'm not going to be knocked out, carried off feet first in the sixth round. I think I can go the distance, in hopes of at least a split decision.

A policeman came by this afternoon, a detective I think.

They let him ask me questions for about five minutes. He was an earnest-seeming young man with short black hair and, incongruously, an earring. He seemed to be confused about some of the details, and I told him I was, too.

He asked me about how Pooh got shot, and I told him about the Ladysmith.

"But I don't think I killed him," I said. "It just seemed to piss him off." I giggled and apologized for my language.

"Ma'am," the detective said, "it wasn't the Ladysmith I was wondering about. It was the .38. I don't reckon you know what a mess . . . what a hole . . . how much damage that .38 did.

"I need to know. It's OK, either way. Hell, we want to give you a medal. But did you kill Pooh Blackwell?"

I told him I certainly didn't think so, that the last thing I remembered was lying across that picnic table, tied down, waiting to die. And being raped by a madman, I wanted to say but didn't for fear of bruising the young detective's tender sensibilities.

And then, talking about it, I remembered the other thing.

"I heard a really loud noise, like a cannon going off. I think that might have been what revived me."

"A loud noise," he repeated, tugging slightly on the earring and frowning. "Yes, ma'am, that .38 would make a right loud noise, I expect."

The thing was, he explained, it was hard to see how Pooh had managed to do that to himself.

I allowed that it was hard for me to imagine that, too. Pooh seemed like the type who would rather inflict pain on other people than himself.

The detective said the way he figured it, I would have had to reach behind Pooh and shoot him in the back of the head, while my own head was turned away from him, "on account of the blood and . . . and all."

He also wanted to know, of course, why they found Pooh's truck parked a hundred yards or so from his empty driveway. They wanted to know how and where I got abducted.

I had enough of my wits about me at this point to tell him I had gone over to talk to Pooh about what really happened to Jenny McLaurin, that I still had my doubts. I had gone up to the front door and knocked, and that was the last I remembered. He must have hit me from behind about then.

"So you went out there by yourself, at night?"

I didn't try to defend it, couldn't think of a good answer, just nodded my head.

"Well," the detective said, "maybe he sneaked up on you or something."

He didn't look convinced. Who would have been? I had the feeling, though, that nobody was too surprised it had turned out this way. They just couldn't fathom what role I played in Pooh Blackwell's demise. It was supposed to happen in some barroom brawl, something with knives, or a horrific wreck, probably involving an innocent victim.

"Well," he told me, "if you think of anything, let me know. I might be back later."

I'm pretty sure he will be. It wouldn't take Columbo to find some holes in my story. At some point, I know, it will be necessary to tell Wade Hairr or one of his worthless minions that I did indeed walk uninvited into Pooh Blackwell's house and take something that didn't belong to me.

Today, though, is not that day.

When Kenny came by a little later, I asked him if he had retrieved my belongings.

He said he had.

"Including the purse?"

"Including the purse."

"Were there some, ah, notebooks in there?"

There were. I don't suppose either Pooh or the police had any interest in going through my possessions.

I told him to hang on to them, maybe keep them at his place for a while.

Kenny has been so sweet, so considerate, so wracked with guilt.

I'm the all-time league leader in guilt, I told him. I know guilt. If somebody sneaks out in the middle of the night, lies about where they're going, and if that person is well into middle age and allegedly of sound mind, you've done about all you can for that person.

"And," I added, beckoning him to move closer, "that person is absolutely crazy about you."

He said he knew, that he felt the same way, and I said I was glad.

H turned his face from me and squeezed my arm until the pain forced me to stop him.

"You did your best," I told him. "You gave me a gun and taught me how to shoot it. It isn't your fault that I couldn't hit that sack of garbage at point-blank range."

214

CHAPTER TWENTY-TWO

December 24

The nurses finally convince Kenny and the women of Geddie Presbyterian Church that Georgia is able to stay unattended in her private room.

"You'd better take good care of her," Forsythia Crumpler told the head nurse, a woman whose force of character was nearly equal to her own. "You all had better not let anything happen to that lady."

She said this outside the door, at a time when the patient was supposed to be napping. Georgia could think of nothing she had done to deserve such care.

The flowers have almost taken over the room, several poinsettias among them to remind her that she is missing Christmas. The doctor has told her she may be able to go home early next week and start physical therapy, but she will definitely be opening her presents in Room 202 of the Campbell Valley Medical Center.

Justin has not been by today. Kenny told her that he was staying close to Leeza. The baby could come at any time.

Kenny left just half an hour ago to get something to eat. Georgia wonders how he can bear to look at her. The one fleeting glimpse she got in the mirror when they were helping her to the bathroom was horrifying. She wonders how much she can ever recover of her already-fading looks.

She knows this shouldn't be a priority, that she should be worrying about getting to the point that all her body parts function, and all her memory returns. She still has blank spots. There are old friends whose names she tries but fails to remember.

Kenny, though, seems not to see this new, damaged Georgia at all. Or, he does a good job of hiding it. He looks after her, even helps her to the bathroom. She thinks of how much she hated having to do that with her own mother, when she was dying of pancreatic cancer. She can only draw one conclusion: He's a better person than she is.

Maybe, she thinks, it's part of opposites attracting. Nurturing, giving people are naturally drawn to the self-absorbed.

He has assured her that he will help her get through this, whatever it takes.

When he leaned over and kissed her cheek—just about the only part of her head that didn't hurt—she was inclined to believe him.

Now, the night creeps past. She can't sleep but is trying not to ask for more painkillers. The same drugs she was so fond of three days ago, she now sees as the enemy. If intelligence is her strong card, she thinks, she doesn't want to intentionally reduce her IQ 20 points if she can bear the pain at all.

Still, she is about to buzz for a nurse, anticipating the usual half-hour wait, when she hears footsteps out in the hall. Someone is wearing shoes too heavy and stepping too loudly on the terrazzo floor to be staff.

Her door is cracked open just enough to let a thin sword of light in; she has never been fond of total darkness. Whoever is outside has interrupted the beam, and then she sees the door open a couple of feet.

At first, she sees only a bulky shadow, and she wonders what visitor might be coming at this time of night, after the nurses have banished everyone else.

And then she knows. Some combination of the work shoes, the smell, the gleam of pomaded hair.

"William."

She has allowed for the possibility that the Blackwells might get it in their heads that she is responsible for their son's death, but until this moment, she hasn't really given it serious consideration. Kenny has told her that, from what he hears and knows,

216

Pooh's siblings—while being "mean as blacksnakes"—do not share their late brother's untreated insanity.

But now, William Blackwell is hovering over her bed, looking as if he hasn't slept in the nearly six days since a deputy knocked on his door at 2 a.m. and informed him of his oldest son's death.

Georgia thinks about buzzing for a nurse, but the movement required to do so would be hard to disguise and easy to intercept by a healthy person. Besides, William could hack her up and haul her away in little plastic bags before one of the nurses answered her call.

"I'm sorry." It's all she can think to say. She is not in the least sorry that Pooh Blackwell is dead and buried in the family cemetery. Looking at his father, though, she is sincere in her condolences. Nobody, she thinks, ought to have to bury their children, no matter what kind of monsters they grow up to be.

William is silent for half a minute. Then, he eases himself into the chair beside her and sighs.

"I'm sorry, too."

He doesn't say anything else for what seems like a very long time. Georgia, who can't turn her head well enough to see him straight on, wonders if he has fallen asleep.

Finally, he leans forward. He is speaking almost in a whisper.

"I'm kind of surprised they let me in here," he says, and he almost laughs. "I figured somebody'd stop me, but I had to try. Nurse out there looked like she was sleeping.

"I had to get this out, tell somebody."

He sighs again, and if Georgia didn't know better, she would have sworn that the meanest boy in Geddie High School, who grew into one of the meanest men in eastern Scots County by all accounts, was silently crying.

He speaks again after a couple of minutes.

"I should have done it a long time ago," he says. "There wasn't no other solution for it.

"They sent him to that therapy, that anger-management shit and all the classes about treating women right and all, but it didn't take. I knew that. It was up to me. You clean up your own mess.

"Hell, I don't know," he says, after a pause, "maybe it's just who he is—was. Who he was. Just another damn mean-ass Blackwell."

William seems to be talking to himself more than her, and then he appears to suddenly remember she's there, who she is and why he made this late-night Christmas Eve visit.

"Georgia," he says, "do you want to hear a real sad story?"

When William Blackwell was a boy, his father, Bartholemew Bullard Blackwell, owned 22 acres of land alongside Route 47. The big farm they were working then was north of town. The land outside Geddie was for corn mostly, which they used to feed themselves and their livestock.

But then the Averitts, who owned just about everything, overextended themselves, and the Blackwells came into possession of some of the best black dirt in the area at a price so agreeable that they were rumored to have stolen it, flat-out. No one ever proved that, although many a local farmer bemoaned the fact that the land was sold before he had a chance to match the Blackwells' offer.

Their land, formerly a strip along the highway, now extended almost to the edge of the swamp itself.

Tol Blackwell moved his family to this new acreage, which was far better than what they were working before (although he kept the old spread and employed a black tenant farmer). He built a house far off the highway, because he had gotten so sick of people throwing trash in his yard as they drove by the old place. The road leading to it remained a rut path until it was paved five years ago. Even now, it is no more than a rude, sandy trail after it passes the last modular home and goes on into the swamp. There, it picks up the route of the old tram rail line that was used to haul pines out of Kinlaw's Hell long ago.

It runs out on the north shore of Maxwell's Millpond.

The night of the 18th, William Blackwell had been walking around his back yard, checking things. He liked to check things, liked to be on top of the situation. He wanted to inspect the pump house, make sure the pipes were wrapped snugly enough to avoid freezing. He wondered if his feckless daughter and son-in-law had put antifreeze in their car yet, or if they were going to have a repeat of what happened last winter.

He liked to be outdoors anyhow, even on a cold night like that. You learned things being outdoors, and you stayed tough. The last time he took two of his grandchildren camping, they whined about being too hot when they went to bed, then whined about being too cold when they awakened at 2 a.m. Indoor living made you soft, and he took pride that, no matter what else people might say, they would never say the Blackwells were soft.

If he had stayed indoors, he wouldn't have seen the red truck come past. You couldn't have heard it inside, in the back room with the TV on.

He thought at first Pooh was coming to visit one of his siblings, which would have been a good sign, as relations had been somewhat strained lately. It was one reason William was so glad things worked out as they had with the old McLaurin house. Pooh, he realized, needed some space. And they needed some between him and them.

But the truck bounced along past the last dwelling, until the final glimmer of light disappeared into the swamp.

Even then, he could have just let it pass, could have told himself that whatever his oldest son was up to, let him be up to it and leave the rest of them the hell alone.

William Blackwell wasn't like that, though. Whatever he had gotten in life had been attained by always having an ear to the ground, always being willing to deal head-on with life's little surprises. It gave you an edge. If something troubled you, you didn't turn your back and hope it would just go away, because it wouldn't, not in William Blackwell's experience.

And so, he walked over and eased into his wife's little Toyota, because it was the one farthest away from the house and least likely to be heard. There was no sense in letting everybody know your business if you didn't have to.

He didn't turn on the headlights. He didn't need them, after all these years. He could negotiate the old trail blindfolded.

Half a mile back, still a few hundred yards short of the pond, he cut the ignition and coasted a few more feet before coming to a stop in the sand and pine straw. It was a one-way road. What came in had to come back out, as he told more than one teenage couple returning from unwisely using his land for amorous purposes.

219

He closed the door softly. Outside, he could see his breath in the damp swamp air. He hadn't walked 100 feet when he was able to make out the red truck up ahead, and then he saw movement off to the side.

What might have made the difference was that Pooh's hearing was not first-rate. His father figured it was the result of sitting too close to too many head-banging redneck rock bands for too many years.

When William saw what his son was doing and knew immediately what he intended to do, he allowed his mind only a very few seconds to consider the general horror. Then, he did what he had always done, whether he was strong-arming a weaker high school kid or working his way through the porous net of local law enforcement: He came up with a plan.

He could have shot them both. He had the little pistol he always carried. He could've done it with that. Throw the weapon in the millpond and let the cops figure it out.

He could have just confronted his son, told him to stop, then tried to make things right somehow.

He can admit to himself that he considered a third alternative: Help Pooh dispose of the body and get rid of the evidence. He was sure Pooh had not even begun to consider what came after he had raped and murdered a woman to whom he was known to bear much animosity. Thinking ahead was not Pooh's strong suit.

In less than a minute, William knew none of those would work, because he didn't think they could get away with it, and because he just didn't want to. Lately, on those watchful nights outside, he sometimes had the feeling that he was not alone, just a little shiver now and then, a rabbit scurrying across your tombstone. He would have beaten anyone who suggested he was growing afraid of the dark in his old age, but he was starting to feel as if Something was watching him, keeping score.

And he knew Georgia. She had never meant him any ill will, that he knew of. He had done terrible things to people, all his life, but he always could convince himself that he had been wronged, that he was the aggrieved party.

She had been snooping around, asking questions about Jenny McLaurin's death, and that had irritated him, but he supposed he would have done the same thing, if it had been him.

It had occurred to him, more than once, that she might be right in her suspicions. Standing there in the darkness, watching his son brutalize a woman old enough to be his mother, William Blackwell knew he had slipped. He had done the thing he tried to never do—ignore trouble and hope it would just go away.

He knew, standing there, that his son probably had done the thing Georgia suspected him of doing.

And he knew what came next.

If he had allowed himself the luxury of contemplation, he might not have been able to do it.

"I was going to use my own pistol," he whispers to Georgia, who is wide awake and turned as much as she can to face him. She has the feeling he is whispering not to keep others from hearing but because he can barely get the words out.

"But then, I kept coming closer and closer, 'til I was right there, right behind him, and he had that .38 hanging out of his pants pocket, easy to slip out.

"He heard the click, because I saw him start to turn his head, but I'm pretty sure he didn't know it was me."

He stops and sits there, staring into the empty darkness across the room.

Georgia puts her right hand on top of his left one.

"I heard footsteps," she says, "going back across the woods. And then I thought I heard a car start, off in the distance."

She shifts, trying to get comfortable. She is wide awake and wishes she had called for the pain medication already.

"And the 911 call," she says. "I wondered why they got there the same time as Kenny did. I thought I must have called them before I passed out. I can't remember everything.

"But it was you."

He pulls his chair closer to the bed.

"You know this never happened," he says, a glimpse of the school bully in his face. "I never told you this."

Georgia nods and swallows.

"But I just wanted you to know. Some things, you just have to do something about, you know? No matter what."

His voice catches, and he pauses. He adds that he hopes she won't be put off from living in her old hometown. If this didn't do it, Georgia thinks, nothing will. She says she doesn't know what she is going to do, but that her son is probably going to stay and work the farm.

"A farmer?" William Blackwell seems amused by this. "Well, you never know how things are going to turn out, do you, Georgia?"

There is nothing else either of them can think to say.

Georgia turns to lie on her back and closes her eyes for a few seconds, less stunned by all this than she would have been if she had been less distracted by the pain.

When she opens her eyes, William Blackwell is gone. Only a small impression in the bedside chair is left to prove it wasn't all another drug-addled dream.

She has been medicated and is sleeping like the dead when a hand on her wrist awakens her.

"What?" she says, irritated that the nurses won't ever leave her alone, except when she needs them.

But she sees that it is Justin.

"Mom? I'm sorry to wake you up. But I just wanted you to know. Leeza is here."

"What? Why?" She's still coming out of her sleep.

"She's gone into labor," Justin says. "She woke me up at 1, and we've been here since before 2. The doctor says today's the day."

"That's great, honey," Georgia says, trying to smile and to wake up. "That's really nice. I'm sorry I can't be there to help, to be with you."

"Don't worry about that. Kenny's here, too. I guess I ruined his night, too. He said he'd come see you later, that you'd probably rather sleep, but I wanted you to know."

He gets up to leave, then turns at the door.

"Oh, and Merry Christmas."

"Couldn't be merrier," Georgia says. Justin is already headed down the hall.

222

CHAPTER TWENTY-THREE

December 25

Georgia has had her share of quiet Christmases in recent years. Having lived half the last dozen holiday seasons as an unmarried woman and lapsed churchgoer with almost no family, she has often spent the day itself in the homes of friends and colleagues, like a charity case. Usually, the hosts have been people with whom she did have a real bond, but most of the others there would be the host's family, while she was the sad refugee from the English department. When Justin was younger, she would bring him, and he felt just as lost as she did. One year, they spent the day with two Jewish couples and a man who claimed to be a Zoroastrian and tried to hit on her.

She would always be sure to bring two bottles of wine and at least token gifts for any children who might be around, and usually she would get one or two presents from the more thoughtful adults. But Georgia has come to dread the season. For her, it is a temptation to wallow in loss, a hard slap to remind her that her interesting and stimulating life somehow has led her to the doors of strangers on Christmas day.

Today, though, is not turning out to be one of the quiet ones.

She thought it might be. The hospital would be short-staffed. Kenny would want to spend the day with his mother's family, surely. She could expect Justin and Leeza to be otherwise occupied, to say the least.

She had prepared herself to be a little depressed, lying here neglected by one and all while her broken parts mend. She was determined not to show it.

What has happened, though, has left her no time for the blues, or introspection of any kind.

For one thing, Kenny has been by her side most of the past seven hours, since just after dawn, leaving every so often to check on Leeza's progress and report back. When she woke, he was there, in the same chair where William Blackwell had told his story a few hours earlier. She wondered how long he had been staring at her, and she yearned for some makeup, or at least a paper bag to put over her head. The last time she looked, her eyes still had greenish-yellow circles around them, giving her the appearance of a large, festive raccoon.

Then, at 10, Forsythia Crumpler walks in, carrying a fruit basket for which there is no room until they take some of the older flowers out. Alberta Horne and Minnie McCauley are with her, and they all have small gifts for her to open—a bottle of perfume, a scarf and a fruitcake.

And then there are Justin and Leeza. Kenny has brought their gifts to Georgia's room, along with Justin's apology and promise to be there as soon as the baby comes.

Kenny leaves at 12:30. The visitation arrangement allows him to keep Tommy from 1 p.m. on, after the boy has opened his gifts from his mother and her family in the morning. But Kenny tells her that Tommy has agreed to open his gifts from his father at the hospital. He's visited Georgia twice already and seems more fascinated than repelled by her appearance.

"Wow," he said the first time. "Did you get in a fight?"

"You should see the other guy."

The boy laughed for the first time in her presence.

Two other groups of church members come by in the early afternoon, and Georgia has begun to suspect something other than spontaneity.

Blue, Sherita and Annabelle Geddie and two of Blue and Sherita's children arrive around 2. They add more food to the growing bounty. They and one of the groups from Geddie Presbyterian get there at about the same time, two sets of neighbors who might never have shared a hospital visit before. They are cordial and wish each other a merry Christmas.

Everyone wants to know about the baby.

"Gonna be a grandma," Annabelle says, shaking her head. "You're gonna love spoilin' that grandbaby."

One of Blue and Sherita's children allows that Annabelle hasn't been spoiling him with anything except a switch.

And then, with the room holding exactly twice its allowed occupancy, Justin seems to appear out of nowhere, looking dazed.

"Well," he says, "it's a girl. Seven pounds, six ounces. She has all her fingers and toes. Bald as a coot. Leeza's fine."

He goes to his mother, and the two of them embrace, both of them in tears.

"Love you," he says, then gives the rest of the room perhaps more information than they even wanted about the birthing of his first child.

"What you gonna name her?" Blue asks his new partner.

Georgia can hardly hear him through the din, exacerbated by a nurse who is telling them that somebody has to leave.

"What?" she calls to her son. "I didn't hear you."

"We're going to name her Georgia," he repeats. "Georgia Noel."

Lying in this hospital bed, her head and upper body a mass of stitches and breaks, with a long stretch of surgery and rehabilitation ahead of her, she wonders if there has ever been a more perfect Christmas.

Kenny and Tommy get there in mid-afternoon. Tommy has brought her a present, one Kenny says he picked out himself. Georgia opens it and sees that it is a Swiss army knife.

"So if somebody tries to hurt you again, you can run 'em off," he explains.

Georgia gives him a hug. The boy doesn't respond well to hugs, she knows, but he makes allowances on this occasion, another gift.

The crowd drifts in and out of Georgia's room all afternoon and into the evening, some of them coming to congratulate Justin on the baby, some probably at Forsythia's urging, but their sentiments seem genuine. Most of the ones from the church tell her they hope she'll stay in East Geddie "anyhow." All of them are thrilled about Justin and Leeza and the baby. They all remark on

225

how wonderful it is to have a "little one" in the community, by which Georgia assumes she means the church.

The young couple has started attending Littlejohn McCain's old church on a more or less regular basis. Leeza likes it because she doesn't sense she is being judged. Justin seems pleased to have some link to his family, even if most of the McCains whose names he sees on the bronze plaque outside are almost wholly unknown to him. Georgia supposes that she and Jeff did little to give him any sense of belonging to a family beyond the three of them, and then when Jeff left, it was just Georgia and Justin, a family of two. She wishes now that she could remember all the old stories. She hopes he remembers at least some of the ones from his grandfather.

There is something else, too, driving the well-wishers. It is mentioned only obliquely by a few of the church members.

"We want to thank you," Murphy Lee Roslin says, looking down at the floor and speaking so low she can hardly hear him, "for what you did and all."

Others praise her, calling her a "brave woman," or just saying, "Jenny knows what you did. She knows." Or, best yet, "Littlejohn McCain would be right proud of you."

Nothing beyond the bare essentials of the story made the *Port Campbell Post*. The rape was not even mentioned. It was just a story about an abduction that ended with the perpetrator dying from what must have been a self-inflicted gunshot wound. Police were still investigating.

Kenny and Tommy leave at 7, just after one more well-wisher has thanked Georgia "for everything."

"How does everybody know?" she whispers to Kenny.

"They just do," he winks at her. "You can't keep anything from these people."

He tells her, as he's leaving, that he will be back tomorrow, then Monday to take her home.

"And every day after that," he adds.

At 8 o'clock, when everyone has gone and Georgia has dimmed the lights and is just about to beg for one more dose of pain medication so she can get more than two hours' consecutive sleep, she hears a sound and sees a familiar silhouette in the hallway, short and solid.

"Forsythia."

The older woman eases herself into the chair. She looks tired.

"I've just been to see Leeza and the baby," she says. "She's a beautiful child, but then, I never did see a baby I didn't want to eat up with a spoon."

She seems almost as happy as Georgia herself over the baby's name.

"And that little Leeza," she adds, "I just think she is going to be the best mother. She just seems so easy with the baby, even now."

Georgia admits that Leeza probably will handle her first child a hell of a lot better than she handled Justin. It occurs to her that Leeza has the gift of being able to put someone else's life before hers, without even resenting it. Georgia knows that her son's girlfriend could go on to college, could make a career for herself, but if she doesn't, she probably will be content with what she has right now.

It is not a talent, she thinks, to be taken lightly.

The two of them sit there, both of them resting, for a few minutes, saying little.

"That was really something you did," Forsythia says at last.

"That's what I hear. All I did was get myself half killed."

Forsythia waves her off.

"You did what nobody ever does. Or almost nobody. You risked your life to do what you thought was right. I wouldn't have wanted you to take the chance you did, and I don't know what possessed you to go to that . . . that maniac's house like that in the middle of the night. Somebody surely was watching over you."

You'd never guess who, Georgia thinks.

It turns out that the same sheriff's department that couldn't keep from telling Pooh Blackwell about Georgia's suspicions also couldn't stifle itself when it came to the details of her abduction, withholding information only from the *Port Campbell Post*. And almost no one on the east side of Scots County was more than one degree of separation from somebody wearing a badge.

"You know how it is in a little place like this," Forsythia says. "Or, maybe you don't, or you've forgotten. But everybody here thought, without saying it, that Pooh and maybe William had something to do with what happened to Jenny. But you have to live, you have to get along. That's what we all tell ourselves. Don't make any enemies.

"We were cowards."

Georgia tells her that isn't so, but Forsythia talks over her.

"I went over there to talk to Kenny, to see what in the world happened. He was so torn up about it, Georgia. He blames himself for, you know, the rape and all." She struggles with the word, as if it is the worst profanity. "I told him that everybody knew he would have gone with you, or stopped you, if he had known what you had in mind.

"But he did show me the notebooks."

"He what?!"

Georgia tries to sit up in bed and pays a price in pain, falling back with a groan.

"Godalmighty, can't anybody keep anything to himself around here?"

"It's all right," Forsythia tells her, patting her wrist, still bruised from the IV needles. "He knows I can keep a secret. He read them, and I guess he felt like he had to show someone else what you had done.

"It made me cry, seeing how lonely and afraid she was, what she was living with, and I'll always blame myself for not doing something."

"Me too," Georgia says.

"We talked just about every day, and she never once mentioned that she was keeping a journal. I knew the Blackwells made her uneasy, but I guess I just didn't want to know how bad things had gotten."

Forsythia pauses, then presses on.

"Kenny and I both have a pretty good idea, reading those diaries, that you didn't just find them in the front yard. You went inside that house, didn't you?"

"Maybe I'd better take the fifth on that one, Forsythia."

"Well," she says, "maybe someday you'll tell me where you found them, and how you knew where to look."

"Maybe," Georgia says. "Maybe someday."

The older woman doesn't appear to have the energy to stand up, let alone drive the seven miles to her home.

"Forsythia," Georgia tells her, "you look worn out. You shouldn't be on the highway tonight. Why don't you just put your feet up and stay right here? You've already spent two nights in that big recliner, so I know you can sleep in it. I'm worn out, but you look like you need a rest worse than I do. And I could use the company, to tell you the truth."

To Georgia's amazement, Forsythia offers only a feeble demurrer, one that is easily overridden.

"Well," she says, "maybe I will close my eyes for a few minutes here, if you think the nurses won't throw me out."

"They'd better not try."

"Yes," Forsythia says, laughing a little. "I doubt they would want to tangle with you."

Forsythia avails herself of Georgia's bathroom, then helps Georgia get to the toilet and back.

Then the two of them lie there, Georgia in her hospital bed, her old teacher propped up in the recliner. A nurse finally comes and delivers the pain pill. She objects to Forsythia, but Georgia tells her that her friend is staying, "period."

"Well," Forsythia says, "goodnight, Georgia. Merry Christmas."

Yes, Georgia thinks, drifting away. It is.

CHAPTER TWENTY-FOUR

January 2, 2000

Georgia has yielded to consensus and allowed that they all have passed into a new century. She is tired of pointing out the illogic of it, of insisting that it won't really be the 21st century for another year, maybe even longer if you make allowances for the vagaries of the Julian calendar.

"Mom," Justin told her, "we're going to form a new society, Leeza and I. It's called 'We know better, but we don't care.'"

The world was not brought to its knees by computers or terrorists yesterday. They all watched on New Year's Eve as it seamlessly became 2000 in Australia and China and Egypt, then Europe.

Georgia spends most of her non-sleeping day sitting up now, and a physical therapist comes by to torture her for a couple of hours each morning. Her memory seems to be returning, she has an appointment with an oral surgeon on Tuesday, and she'll have to have the nose re-broken and set next week. Somewhere down the road: plastic surgery. It hurts her to move about much, and she hasn't yet trusted herself to hold Georgia Noel, as much as she wants to.

On Monday, two days after Christmas, they all came home. Leeza left the hospital carrying her two-day-old baby, with Justin walking alongside as if he could protect his new daughter from anything life might send her way. Kenny pushed Georgia's wheelchair to the pickup area, then all but carried her into the van. He and Justin were in the front seats, three generations of women in the back, all looking a little worse for the wear.

Justin and Leeza, who never did get around to fully preparing the baby's room, had to further deal with a disabled 52-year-old who, instead of an asset, had become a liability.

Kenny saved them, cooking meals, going out on errands three times that day as the others remembered things they absolutely had to have and helping deal with the crowds of well-wishers. It seemed half of East Geddie dropped by at one time or another. At the end of the day, he told Justin he thought it might be easier all around if he just moved into a spare room at the McCain house for a while, and nobody tried to stop him.

Georgia had never truly bonded with her bed at the farmhouse. It wasn't as firm as the one she left in Montclair, and it was smaller. After two weeks in a hospital room, though, she thought it was the best one she had ever slept on.

She didn't wake up until almost 9 on Tuesday morning. She was still trying to get dressed, dreading the ordeal of giving herself a bath later, and the first visit from the therapist, when Justin knocked and told her she had a call.

It was David Sheets.

He wondered if he might come out to the farm. He had something rather serious to discuss with her.

"Can you make it after noon?" she asked. "I think it'll take me that long to get dressed."

He said he could be there at 2.

Kenny and Justin sat in on the meeting, too. David Sheets used a language understood best by lawyers, but finally the three of them figured out what he was saying: William Blackwell did not want Jenny McLaurin's house. He wanted to give it to her next of kin.

"Which," Georgia said, "would be me?"

The lawyer nodded.

Georgia shook her head.

"Is there anything that I, ah, need to sign or anything?"

"Not right now. Probably later. But my client wanted me to tell you that you are welcome to take over the property whenever you want. He is prepared to turn it over to you, fee simple."

He never mentioned William's or Pooh's name, and when he left, even the former Dwayne Sheets expressed his sorrow and dismay over what had happened to her, and told her she was a strong woman in such a way that she was sure he must know the story, too.

When Kenny and Justin drove over to the house later, they found that everything of Pooh Blackwell's had been removed, leaving it on the bare side but at least more or less clean. It smelled of ammonia and Comet. Georgia wondered if the quiet, put-upon woman she had met that afternoon at William's had been dispatched to obliterate her dead son's scent.

Georgia thought she might have to re-employ her erstwhile real-estate agent. But then she had a better idea.

When Forsythia stopped by two days later, Georgia told her what she had in mind.

One of the many problems facing Geddie Presbyterian Church was the manse. It had been built on the cheap shortly after World War II, and it was only a small exaggeration when one of the deacons told Georgia, back in November, that it was falling down.

Hardly a month went by that The Rev. Weeks or his wife didn't complain, mildly but firmly, about some aspect of the house. The roof leaked. The oil furnace was in its dotage and had once covered all the Weekses' belongings in a fine patina of soot. It needed painting, although it had last been painted just three years ago. It was too small; the belief among the older churchgoers was that, once Mrs. Weeks got pregnant again, they would be looking for another church, one with a manse that could hold a growing family.

It had been given to the congregation by an old and relatively well-off widower more than 30 years ago. The more mean-spirited members said he gave it away when it couldn't be rented any more. It also was located well out of town, halfway to Port Campbell.

"So," Georgia said, "I was thinking, if William Blackwell really is serious about giving the house back, what better way to use it? I mean, the church did a whole lot more for Jenny than I ever did."

Forsythia shook her head.

"You ought to hang on to what you've got, Georgia," she said. "Everybody around here thought it was very civil of you not to fight it when your daddy gave most of his land away to Kenny and the Geddies in his will. This time, you ought to do something for you. If you don't want to rent it, sell it. Keep the money. There'll be a time when you'll need it. Believe me."

"So," Georgia said, smiling as much as her face would allow, "you don't think I'm being selfish enough? I can't seem to hit a happy medium."

Forsythia frowned and spoke slowly, the way she might have explained something to one of her more challenged students.

"I'm just saying, only rich people can afford to give away houses. And you are not rich."

But Georgia had already thought it through. She knew she should be at some kind of ebb, a mental wreck to match her physical state. Somehow, though, it hadn't worked that way. She could see, once the pain-killers wore off and she considered what was before her, that she could do whatever came next, that she could teach college English standing on her head until she was 80 if she had to, that she could go back to Montclair, get her own house in order literally and figuratively, that she could go on.

She didn't think it was as simple as the old joke about paying someone to beat you because it felt so good when they stopped, but she did feel, without any evidence to back it up, that the storm had passed, that she had a good and long life in front of her, one she was surprisingly eager to encounter.

And she knew, as surely as if her late father had come and whispered it in her ear, that she would never need Jenny McLaurin's spacious, well-kept house.

"My mind is made up," she told Forsythia. "This is what I want to do. Jenny would love it, too."

Her old teacher patted her on the knee and told her to sleep on it, that William Blackwell might change his mind anyhow. It wasn't like any Blackwell she had ever known to give rather than take.

"I'll mention it to some folks," she said as she was turning to walk down the steep back porch steps.

Friday, New Year's Eve, was the day she found out about the ring.

Wade Hairr himself came by, accompanied by a deputy. They, Georgia and Kenny sat in the living room where, after inquiring about her health and expressing his sympathy, her old classmate reached into his pocket and produced a small, dark-blue box. He leaned forward and handed it to Georgia.

"It showed up in one of the pawn shops west of town," he explained. "We got to looking around, and one of the deputies, Eldridge here, came across it."

"I saw the initials," Eldridge said proudly, then looked down as if he had overstepped his boundaries.

Georgia took the ring out and examined it.

"Yes," she said, after a pause. "This is the one. I remember. I'm sure of it."

"It was sold on," he checks his notes, "October 23rd. The man who sold it gave what apparently was a false name. When I showed the clerk Pooh Blackwell's picture, he said it was him."

He said it in a self-satisfied tone, as if he had thought of looking for the missing ring himself.

"Well," Wade Hairr said, "I think you ought to just go on and take it, don't you?"

It turned out that the pawn shop owner wasn't making any claim for a ring that had no receipt to go with it. He was more than happy to exchange a two-carat ring for what the sheriff called his "stay-out-of-jail card."

"I don't reckon we'll ever know exactly what happened out there," he went on, "although we can surely guess. To tell you the truth, Georgia, I just don't want to go into it, if you don't. If you could dig the bas . . . if you could dig Pooh Blackwell up, I expect you could probably get him executed by about any jury you wanted in Scots County."

The sheriff got up and paced around the room.

"But he's dead. And then I've got all these other loose ends. I've got some woman's shoe prints inside Pooh's house that night that I don't have any stomach for trying to match, plus Lord knows what kind of fingerprints."

He came back and sat down.

"So," he said, "I'm thinking that Pooh Blackwell took you out there to Maxwell's Millpond, and he, he did what he did, and then he saw how worthless and hopeless his life was, and he shot himself."

Georgia restrained herself from asking, "In the back of the head?"

She nodded and said that seemed reasonable to her. She could feel Kenny squeezing her hand, trying to keep her on course.

Wade Hairr looked straight ahead, then at Georgia. He nodded.

"Sometimes," he said, "things will just take care of themselves, without any intervention at all from trained law enforcement experts."

It was the closest thing to humor she had ever seen from the adult Wade Hairr.

"Yes," Georgia said. "Sometimes they do."

As she and Kenny waved at the departing lawmen, he whispered to her, "And sometimes, they need a little goosing from some nosey broad."

Kenny and she talked about the notebooks.

"You shouldn't beat yourself up," he told Georgia when she was moved to tears by the accumulated evidence of Jenny's loneliness and fear. "You can't be everywhere all the time."

"You can be somewhere, some of the time," she had responded, clearing her throat and wiping her eyes.

He was a fine one, she'd told him, to be preaching about self-flagellation. For the last 13 days, he had barely been able to meet her eyes. They had talked, without resolution, of what they might do about each other.

Finally, after Wade Hairr and his deputy left, they had "the talk." Georgia tried to explain how much she had thought about it and how conflicted she was.

"I never thought," she told Kenny, holding his hand and forcing him to make eye contact, "that I would have, you know, these kind of times again. You know, the sex and all."

She felt like some teenager, struggling to make the words right.

"But I've got to go home. I don't even know if I have a home, to tell you the truth, but I think I do. And I do have what they call meaningful work, if I can ever get my ass back to it again."

"You've got a home here," Kenny told her, squeezing and then releasing her hand as she winced.

She said it was too much. It wasn't just what was called—when it was called anything—"the attack." She had come to the conclusion, she said, that she should not be living under the same roof with Justin and Leeza and the baby, at least not after she healed and then stayed long enough to give them a little help. It would suffocate everyone, she told Kenny. Justin needed some room, without a second-guessing, judgmental mother around.

"You don't have to live here, in this house," he said, his eyes fixed on hers now, forcing her to look away.

"I know. I know. I want to. But I can't. Won't. Whatever. What. . . ?"

"What would people say?" he finished the question.

Justin and Leeza knew already. Justin had uncomfortably broached the subject while she was still in the hospital. When she asked him why he hadn't said anything before, he told her it wasn't any of his business, and the way he said it was like another gift.

Still, she knew there was something there that she couldn't seem to escape. She had always prided herself in her ability to endure censure and guilt, but now she didn't know if she could.

She and Kenny didn't even mention Littlejohn McCain, or Kenny's father, although Georgia alluded to it.

"It's funny, the thing that brought you here, that secured you this farm, is one of the things that's keeping me from staying. Staying with you, I mean."

"My great-grandparents were first cousins," he told her. "They lived a long and happy life together, and almost none of their kids had six fingers or were congenital idiots."

The part she could never tell even Kenny or Justin about was William Blackwell and Christmas Eve. She still couldn't believe he had told her, or that he had done what he did. Sometimes, she thought she must have dreamed it.

And so she told Kenny she would be leaving as soon as she was able, perhaps as early as the middle of February.

She promised to return for several weeks every summer, and he promised to visit her when cold weather gave him a chance to get away.

"I haven't given up," he told her as he was leaving.

"I'm only going to get more wrinkles," she told him. "The cellulite in my butt will just get worse."

"I haven't given up," he repeated.

She knew she didn't want him to.

And then, topping all that, there's the wedding today.

It was Leeza's idea. She told Justin, when they brought the baby home from the hospital, that she wanted to do it, that she was ready.

She told Georgia, when they talked about it, that she wasn't really sure Justin wouldn't run screaming in the other direction at some point in the pregnancy. She'd seen enough of that in her family. She said she thought, if he wants to leave, I'll be better off raising the baby by myself than with some of the male role models I've experienced.

"But I know he's here now," Leeza told her. "He's going to be here for me and Georgia Noel. I couldn't trust my good luck, I guess."

Georgia can't get used to the fact that the baby has her name. She is startled every time she hears it. She is inclined to believe Justin when he tells her that the name was Leeza's idea.

"She really does look up to you," he told her. "God knows why."

They go to church together, the five of them. It takes them half an hour to get everyone from the house to the car and then the mile to church. The older congregation acts as if they had descended straight from heaven. The old women make such a fuss over the baby that they finally succeed in waking her up. Everyone who isn't surrounding the infant is trying to talk to Georgia, all at the same time. She is still a little shaky and finally has to ask for a chair so that she can reluctantly hold court outside the sanctuary.

The Rev. Weeks gives a forgettable sermon but does take time to praise the generosity of Georgia McCain, in such a way that there is no doubt the church already has accepted her offer.

And then, before he goes into the sermon itself, he tells everyone they are invited to the wedding afterward.

It isn't a large event, befitting a bride and groom whose first-born is being held by the groom's mother, sitting in the front pew. When Forsythia heard about it, she organized the same women who had fed the shut-ins on Thanksgiving to handle the reception in the fellowship hall. Someone came up with flowers.

"All I wanted," Leeza whispers to Georgia between the services and the wedding, "was just to get married. I didn't want anybody to make a big deal about it."

"It's their gift to you," Georgia whispers back. "It's the gift of acceptance."

"I know."

Justin is going to buy her a ring, but for now, he has the one that was on Jenny McLaurin's finger three months ago. No one seems to think it's bad luck, and it appears to fit.

Georgia sits holding her granddaughter, praying that the baby won't wake up again until the wedding is over, looking down into her perfect face and thinking about how she has never in her whole life seen anything coming, never been able to figure out what was next.

It used to drive her crazy, when she labored under the illusion that she was in control.

Today, she finds that the unknown leaves her with an odd combination of peace and excitement, an unsubstantiated faith that everything will turn out well.

She looks at the little band gathered around the Rev. Weeks. There are four of them—the bride and groom, a friend of Leeza's who came down to be maid of honor, and Kenny, the best man.

Georgia and Kenny make eye contact.

Solemn as a judge, he winks.

She smiles and wonders what comes next.